A
BODY
TO
DYE
FOR

Stonewall Inn Editions

Stonewall Inn Mysteries

A
BODY
TO
DYE
FOR

Grant
Michaels

ST. MARTIN'S PRESS NEW YORK

Library of Congress Cataloging-in-Publication Data

Michaels, Grant.
    A body to dye for / Grant Michaels.
       p.   cm. — (Stonewall Inn editions)
    ISBN 0-312-05825-X (paperbk.)
    I. Title. II. Series.
    [PS3563.I3317B64   1991]
    813'.54—dc20   90-28597
                                               CIP

10 9 8 7 6 5

for Sharkie

Thanks to good friends
for help and encouragement.

And thanks to Michael Denneny
for opening the door
when Stani knocked.

CONTENTS

A
BODY
TO
DYE
FOR

1
A BOY FROM
THE GOLDEN WEST

Soggy noodles.

That's what I thought as I gazed down at the head I was rinsing in the shampoo sink. Here was a male Medusa with overcooked pasta instead of serpents.

Suddenly he spoke sharply. "Hurry up, Vannos! He'll be here any minute, and I can't be seen like this, in the middle of a dye job!" His voice resonated harshly in the porcelain basin.

I placidly continued rinsing the muddy-colored fluid from the strands of hair dangling through a perforated rubber cap. "Take a Stresstab, baby," I murmured. "Art cannot be hurried."

It was a gorgeous Indian summer afternoon in Boston, rare for late October, the perfect Wednesday for some smart shopping, followed by high tea at the Copley Plaza or an ultradry martini at the Ritz bar. But instead I was at work—at Snips Salon—enduring verbal abuse from one of my regular clients, Calvin Redding. Calvin's snit today was about the time, though he'd arrived late for his appointment. He was expecting a friend, a new friend, last night's trick, to meet him at the salon, and I secretly hoped the guy might show up early and witness him in the ugly rubber cap, looking as bedraggled as Gertrude Ederle after swimming the English Channel. That would fluster Calvin, who was always perfectly groomed.

I studied his face under the spray of warm water. Through the mist his skin shone coppery and smooth, revealing the American Indian genes from his mother's side, something Calvin often bragged about, as though he'd worked hard and earned his natural good looks. The cheekbones were high, eyebrows and eyelashes black. He opened his eyes suddenly. They were amber and intense. It was no wonder that people desired Calvin as soon as they met him. Except people like me, who got to know him first.

Calvin raised his wrist, and the silky kimono sleeve of his protective robe slid down to reveal a wafer-thin gold watch on a gold mesh band. He glanced at it nervously. "Can't you hurry!"

"Cool out, Calvin. You'll be in the chair in a minute."

Though I can remove a skull-tight frosting cap so that my clients won't lose a single hair shaft, for Calvin I yanked brusquely at the taut stretchy rubber. He winced but didn't complain. That was Calvin's impersonation of a man.

"Vannos, are you sure it won't show?"

The solemn words "Trust me" slipped from my lips. I applied shampoo and worked up a creamy mousse. "Calvin, the honey-blond highlights will look completely natural in your straight black hair."

Because some of my clients are theater celebs and top models, people imagine my job is all glamour. Frankly, I'd love the kind of life they imagine I have, but in the real world, many of my customers, whether stars or mere mortals, regularly exercise their inalienable human right to behave like asses. Maybe they think they're getting their money's worth, or maybe their "nice" defenses are down. Whatever the reason, Calvin Redding was the champ ass in my book.

I rinsed the shampoo out and wrapped a towel around his head. Then I clapped my hands once loudly and jerked my thumb toward my styling station. "Okay," I barked like a football coach. "Hit the chair!" (That was *my* impersonation of a man.) On the way Calvin picked up the latest issue of *QT*, a men's fashion magazine that would occupy him while I faced the challenge of creating yet another masterpiece.

I seated him, and with a flourish worthy of a toreador, swirled a nylon drop over him. I glanced in the mirror and saw Calvin's reflection, all angular and dark and handsome. Behind him was me, red-haired, pink-skinned, and hazel-eyed. I'd inherited my Czechoslovakian mother's tendency toward roundness, and keeping weight off was a constant battle, especially after thirty, after expulsion from the "boy" club.

"Shake your head," I commanded, and Calvin obeyed. I combed and sectioned his wet hair, and I was pleased to see that the random strands of gold color had taken perfectly. While I worked, Calvin flicked magazine pages, which relieved me of talking with him. At one point he stayed on the same page for a long while, and I peeked over his shoulder to see what was so interesting. In a two-page panorama of sullen attitude and divine musculature, a blond male lay across the open magazine. He wore a swatch of gleaming Mylar to satisfy the censors, yet his smooth thighs were spread wide, and his eyes said, Wanna taste? The ad was for diamond cuff links, but the only jewels on that guy lurked under the Mylar hankie covering his crotch. I knew that Calvin Redding got dates with men who looked like that, while I just wondered about it. Not that I have a thing for blond models. Give me a good old-fashioned Homo sapiens who prefers a man to a mirror.

Calvin caught me glancing, so he flipped the page over. "He's late!" he snapped.

"Who?"

"Roger! The one who's supposed to meet me here!"

"Calvin, you were worried he'd be early."

He clicked his tongue. "Probably got lost."

Or maybe he got smart and changed his mind, I thought. I worked on a particularly stubborn cowlick over Calvin's right ear and asked him casually, "Where'd you meet this one, Calvin? The Crankshaft?"

Calvin huffed. "I don't go to places like that! I met him at Caffè Gianni."

How silly of me! Where else would Calvin meet a man worthy of himself but in a temple of designer cologne and fashion awareness?

Calvin continued, "We went to his hotel."

"Hotel?"

"Yes, he's here on vacation or something."

"Insertion with discretion?" I asked.

"Of course! I know who I penetrate."

Whom, I thought. The abused, neglected objective case. Yes, even a hairdresser can appreciate the rules of grammar.

Calvin boasted, "He *loved* it. Real hot, but safe."

If such a thing were possible. To me, safe sex was like decaffeinated espresso. But given the times, one had the choices of foolhardiness, caution, or abstinence. I sighed as I recalled the last time I'd had hot sex. It seemed long ago.

I switched to the left side of Calvin's head, cutting and blending the shorter hair there with the longer, newly frosted stuff on top. My fingers and my eyes could already tell he was going to look great when I finished. Calvin spoke from within the pages of his magazine. "I showed him around my office before we had lunch today."

Calvin worked across the Charles River in Cambridge with a bunch of hoity-toity architects. They've won a lot of awards, so I guess they're good. Maybe I'm a little jealous, too, since Calvin and I are about the same age, but he has a respectable career—a Profession—and all the outward signs of success. And me? I just make people beautiful, but I also happen to love it.

"Was he impressed?" I asked.

"Of course," Calvin said vacantly.

I finger-fussed his hair to see how it would lie. That's when Nicole Albright, the shop's manicurist, sauntered by my station. Today she wore a loose-fitting dress of mushroom-colored silk, set off with bright red pumps and matching red bead necklace and earrings. I noticed a drastic change in her makeup. Except for the obligatory false eyelashes, it was much subdued from its usual uproar. Then it clicked: We'd been to a cabaret last night, a pre-Halloween drag show where men did lip-synch imitations of female celebrities past and present, portraying them far beyond any woman's imagination. After the first act, two of the cast had joined us at our table. (I'd styled their wigs and they looked—in a word—*fabulous*.) One of the drag queens had admired Nicole's makeup as "total glamour." The compliment must have vexed her, because on the way home she mentioned that perhaps it was time to try another look. My silence only encouraged her.

Nicole eyed my client and said to me in her smoky voice, "I see you've got another of your cover boys here today." She placed her hand on his shoulder in approval. "And such cheekbones!" She pinched the firm skin that covered his perfectly formed face.

Calvin said, "It's me, Nicole."

His familiar voice confused her. "Who's that?" she asked.

"Calvin," he said flatly, as though bored with himself.

Nicole faltered. "Calvin? Calvin Redding?"

"The same."

"I didn't recognize you. What's changed?"

"His hair color," I interjected.

"No, dear. I see your hallmark. It's something else."

Calvin said, "I shaved my beard and mustache."

"That's it!" Nicole giggled boisterously as though she'd just won a round on a television game show. "But why? It was so handsome on you."

Calvin shrugged under the nylon cape. "I was through with it. Facial hair is useful if you have to compensate for something, like thin lips or a weak chin or a big nose. Otherwise, it intrudes on the features."

I pulled offhandedly at my own red mustache and sighed loudly. "I wonder what I'm compensating for."

Calvin answered quickly. "You should shave it. You might look good."

"As opposed to how I look now?"

Nicole patted my head like an affectionate aunt. "You'll always be my little dumpling." I caught the allusion to the twelve or so extra pounds I always seem to be gaining or losing—the "love handles" that, alas, are not used very often.

Calvin resumed flicking magazine pages noisily. Nicole said, "I'd better get back to my table. I imagine Baroness Kreutzlager's enamel is dry by now."

As she turned to leave us, Calvin moaned plaintively from within his magazine. "Byyye."

I echoed his lifeless voice. "Yeah, byyye, Nikki. Why don't you go play in the acetone?" She responded by blowing me a kiss. I watched her maneuver back through the busy shop on her three-inch heels. Nicole carried her 130 pounds on a five-foot-four-inch frame like a big lithe cat. Her modeling days for Revlon in Paris had ended over twenty years ago, and after that she freely gave in to her love of food and drink. The years of pleasure showed in her thickened waistline, but she'd maintained that runway strut.

I turned the hair dryer on high and pulled and poked at Calvin's hair under the blast of heat. I softly whistled an old jingle about loving from the oven while Calvin squirmed in discomfort, but he took it all without a whimper, just like the man he always tried to be.

Within moments Nicole was coming toward us again, but this time she was escorting someone I'd never seen before, except perhaps in a boyhood dream about cowboy buddies. He was tall, at least six three, with broad shoulders, sandy brown hair, a rugged face lined from too much sun, bright blue eyes, and a smile right off the magazine photo taped inside the lid of my hope chest. But he was *real*, and I was dazzled. He carried a single leather bag slung over a strong muscular shoulder. Nicole led him through the shop like a prized borzoi.

Calvin looked up from his magazine. "Here comes my stud now."

The word seemed inadequate and crude for the heroic figure who approached my station. "I thought you said he played bottom." Was that a tremble in my voice?

"He likes to switch," said Calvin.

My kind of man, I thought.

Nicole arrived in bliss, hanging on to biceps, triceps, and deltoids that challenged the shoulder seams of the young man's blue and red plaid flannel shirt. He smiled at me and I wanted to touch him.

He introduced himself as Roger Fayerbrock, but the blow-dryer was noisy, and I thought he said Faircock.

I took Roger's big warm hand and voiced a breathy "Hi" as my heart thumped.

He spoke in a rich baritone. "Pleased to meet you." But over the buzz of the dryer, I thought he said, "I love you, too." His blue eyes looked me over for a long moment. I felt pudgy as a piglet and wished I'd signed up for that two-for-one special at the aerobics studio. Suddenly my hair was wrong and my mouth tasted like the chicken burrito I'd had for lunch. I was a mess. But his smile told me that he liked me anyway. It was time to turn the blow-dryer off.

Nicole must have sensed our mutual attraction, and to counter it, she affected her "high Brit" accent and introduced me as Vannos. The odd name seemed to puzzle Roger, so I explained that my real name was Stan but I went by Vannos in the shop. Roger said, "Like a stage name?"

I nodded. "Exactly." My mind was already busy with visions of me serving Roger breakfast in bed.

Calvin glanced at Roger's leather bag and remarked, "Is that all you've got?"

Roger said simply, "Everything I need is in here."

Nicole said, "Everything?"

"Everything I need for travelin', M'am."

Nicole gasped. "Please call me Nikki!"

"My mother told me always to be polite to ladies."

"Well, Roger, I'm not your mother."

"And she ain't no lady," I added.

Nicole glowered at me, then smiled warmly back at Roger. "You don't have to be polite with me, Roger. In fact, you can say whatever you like, whenever you like."

"Brazen hussy!" I hissed. "He could be your youngest son."

"Or your oldest nephew!"

"My sister's not married."

"Neither am I!"

Roger's face showed concern as Nicole and I bantered. Calvin looked bored with life, as usual. I said to Roger, "It's just a friendly little joust. Nicole and I really like each other."

Nicole retorted, "Says whom?"

"Who, dear. Nominative case."

"Darling, don't gloat over the only grammatical nugget you retained from sixth grade."

Calvin's voice whined drearily from within his magazine, inter-rupting our repartee. "Roger works at Yosemite National Park."

Nicole went, "Ooooooh!" Then she cooed, "That's in Wyo-ming, isn't it?"

Roger spoke warmly to her. "No, M'am." Nicole wagged a finger at him. He blushed and said, "Oh, sorry, M'am. I mean, Nicole." (That face! I could almost smell rashers of bacon sizzling over a campfire at dawn.)

Nicole smiled and winked at Roger. He smiled back and said, "Yosemite's in California."

Nicole shrugged. "California . . . Wyoming. What's the dif-ference when you're here right now?" She nestled up to Roger. Meanwhile I imagined him crawling out of our pup tent for two near a secluded mountain lake. Nicole asked him, "How about a little stroll outside while Vannos finishes with your host?"

"Host?" I said, as the tent collapsed and the campfire went out.

Calvin piped in, "Didn't I tell you? It's the only reason Roger is here now, to pick up the keys. He's staying with me for the rest of the time he's in Boston. Aren't you, Roger?" Roger nodded, but I thought I perceived annoyance in his bright eyes. Calvin continued, "Why should he spend his hard-earned money on a hotel when he can stay in my comfortable downtown condo?"

"He'll probably spend something else to stay with you, Calvin."

Calvin bristled. "There are no strings attached!"

Right, Calvin, I thought. Knowing you, *ropes* is more like it.

"Roger agreed to stay with me of his own free will. Didn't you, Roger?"

Again Roger nodded, almost troubled. Nicole murmured to him, "Honey, if you need a place to park yourself, I got plenty of room."

Roger shifted uneasily on his long legs. I got the feeling there was more going on than the "pure spirit in a god's body" that met the eye, although there was plenty of that, too. His thigh muscles wrestled against the denim of his jeans as he moved his legs. He sounded reluctant when he said, "I'll get going now. I want to rest a while. I'm still tired from the time change."

And probably from the lack of sleep last night, I thought. I had a strong urge to rescue him from Calvin, to take him home and make him feel welcome in my own way. Draw a bath and massage his back and nestle in his big arms. Then in the morning . . .

Suddenly he was making motions to leave. He put his hand out to me again and said, "Nice to meet you, Stan."

"Same here," I answered. The guy was Gene Autry, Roy Rogers, and Hopalong Cassidy all rolled into one living, breathing creature. He held my hand longer than was necessary, or polite even, but I didn't mind. I was enjoying his strong, warm grip. Then I felt the floor shake with a tremor and heard a heavy metallic crash in the alley behind the shop.

"What was *that!*" said Nicole.

"Felt like an earthquake," said Roger.

I ran out the back door to see what had happened. The supply-service van, which usually arrived once a week, was lying on its side in the alley. It looked like a fake setup for a television movie. I went to check on the driver just as he emerged from the passenger-side window, using it like a ship's hatch.

"I'm all right!" he said.

"You sure?"

"Just shook up."

"Practicing acrobatics with the truck?" I asked.

"I'm new on the job. Didn't see the curb," he answered sharply. "Must've cut my wheels too hard."

I saw the tire marks where he'd gone up onto the curb and plowed through the small patch of soil that separated the salon's back door from the paved alley. Since I tended the grass there, and planted the flowers, and put in a small wrought-iron table and two chairs, I considered the tiny plot my personal domain. Stanley Kraychik, landed gentry with thirty square feet of Boston turf. Now it was ruined.

He asked, "You got a phone inside I can use?"

I pointed the way into the shop, and he hurried through the door. I was about to follow him when I smelled two familiar scents: honey-petal shampoo and berry-blossom conditioner. Then I noticed a golden creamy fluid with streaks of red and pink dribbling out through the back door of the capsized van. When I looked through the back window, I saw that the entire cargo of five-gallon plastic barrels of shampoos and conditioners had overturned and was voiding itself into the van and from there, out into the alley. My Boy Scout's conscience said, Do something! So I slid open the van's side door, which was facing skyward, and climbed in.

Once inside, I began turning the heavy containers upright and resealing their lids, but the van was loaded full of the things, and I couldn't work fast enough to stop the steady flow of viscous hair-care products. Slippery liquids were filling the cargo area like bilge in a leaky boat. Then I sensed someone above me, and I turned and saw Roger's face looking down through the open cargo door above my head.

"Need a hand?" he asked.

"Two would be even better, but you'd better take off those cowboy boots first." My own spongy-soled canvas shoes were already squishy wet.

Roger pulled off his boots, then squeezed himself into the tiny space alongside me in the van. By now the plastic barrels were slippery with shampoo, and grabbing them securely was almost impossible. Finally, the weight of the containers coupled with all the slipperiness won out—I lost my footing and fell into the pool of sweet, fragrant slime. The stuff soaked in immediately, which didn't surprise me, since hair chemicals are mostly wetting agents and emulsifiers.

Down on the floor I continued sealing the partially open containers, while Roger somehow maintained his footing. I was breathing hard. "It should reach equilibrium soon . . . or else we'll drown in it."

Roger laughed. "Don't worry, we can just climb out."

I smirked. "Try it," I said, pushing another plastic lid tightly back onto its half-empty tub.

Just to prove himself, he did try, and in a second was down in the pool of shampoo and conditioner with me. He laughed. "I needed a shower anyway," he said, and pretended to lather himself up with the creamy concoction. With Roger's strong energetic body moving so vigorously next to mine—well, let's just say the problem

at hand didn't seem so serious. We sat there like tw
a bathtub. All we needed were toy boats and rub

After more slipping and sliding and falling
finally stopped the flow of liquids. We stood i
moment, relieved. Roger grinned at me and asked,   ᴛ ᴛᴛᴛᴛɢs always
get this exciting around here?"

"This is just the scrub room. You ought to see me in surgery."

To get out of the van I gave Roger ten slippery fingers. Once he
was out, he pulled me up through the open cargo door. Outside, a
few of the shop's staff members applauded the conclusion of our little
drama, then Nicole sent them back into the shop.

"Are you two all right?" she asked.

"We're fine, Nikki. But the patio garden is ruined."

Nicole shook her head. "I've heard the back alley called a lot of
things, but 'patio garden' takes the prize."

I said, "We'd better rinse this stuff off before we go back in."

"I'll get some towels," she said, and went inside.

Roger and I used the hose near my "property" to rinse the soapy
goop from each other's clothes, but quickly discovered it wouldn't
work. We'd have to remove our clothing to rinse off completely, but
since we were outside, and it *was* Boston, we stopped at our skivvies.
Roger's were plain white briefs. And mine? Wouldn't you know that
was the day I wore my zebra-stripe boxer shorts? We caught each
other's gaze, and there was that awkward moment when two people
are attracted to each other, yet are still surprised by sudden intimacy.

Roger's body was, simply, a strong healthy male body with
classically laid planes, curves, and fullnesses. His wet Jockey shorts
immodestly revealed all. He was definitely spousal stock, maybe
even a contender for Olympus. He spoke first. "You acted fast with
those chemicals. Someone else might have let them run out and
pollute the environment."

I hosed him down without answering. I didn't want to disillu-
sion him by telling him that all styling chemicals eventually end up
in the same place, whether they're wasted on the street or used in a
salon—down the drain.

He looked me over as I rinsed him off. "You've got a nice
build."

I'm sure my skin blushed even pinker than usual. A body is a gay man's stock-in-trade. Mine's okay but far from perfect. "Thanks," I said, studying his strong shoulders.

Then he took the hose and aimed it at me. "You work out?" he asked as I rinsed off.

"I tried once."

"What happened?"

"When MetroPhysis opened—that's the hottest gym in town—I went for a free introductory workout. But somehow, even with the hunky trainer showing me how to use the machines, I broke the chains on two of them."

Roger laughed. "King Kong!"

I struck a "mighty gorilla" pose for him, then shook my head. "Not quite," I said. "They invited me not to join and suggested I take up yoga."

"That what you do now?"

I nodded. "And dance. I prefer timing and balance and motion to anatomical measurements."

Roger looked at me warmly and said, "I agree."

Nicole arrived with an armful of towels. Our state of near nakedness didn't seem to phase her at all. In fact, when she handed Roger his towels, she paused and surveyed the muscular terrain of his body with obvious approval. "Don't catch cold, boys," she sang as she returned to the shop.

We dried ourselves in what had once been my peaceful little garden. Roger was certainly at home outdoors. His face glowed in the autumn sunlight streaking down diagonally between the buildings. As he toweled himself, he studied what was left of my miniature horticultural efforts, now ruined by the van's wreckless tire tracks before it had tipped onto its side.

Roger asked, "Did you do all this?" He indicated a small patch of undestroyed flower bed and the ground cover.

I nodded sadly and said, "It once bore the distinctive mark of an urban fairy."

"I like it."

"You ought to see what I can do for a home and a husband."

Roger smiled. "Maybe I should."

During the quiet seconds that followed, I heard only the faint hum of city traffic muffled by buildings, then the soft flutter of sparrows' wings as the small birds anticipated their daily portion of brioche crumbs from Saint Stanley of the alleys. "Sorry, kids," I said. "Not today."

Nicole stuck her head out the back door and said, "You boys coming in, or are you taking tea out here?"

"We're coming, Nikki." I quickly fashioned some smaller towels into "bunny booties" for Roger and me. Then we wrapped ourselves in larger towels, gathered our wet clothes, and scuffled back into the shop.

I heard Calvin yell, "What about my hair?"

"No problem, Calvin." I dumped the pile of wet clothes near his chair. Then I set up the infrared lamps around him and turned them on high. "You're still too damp for me to finish. I'll be back after I change."

Roger got his bag, I got some dry clothes and sneakers out of my locker, then I took him to the changing stalls, which are for customers who prefer to remove their shirts or blouses before putting on a robe. For us, they would be dressing rooms. We spoke over the shoulder-high partition as we put on dry clothes.

"Roger," I said, "I don't understand why you're with Calvin. If it's just for a place to stay—"

"I have my reasons," he interrupted. His smile had vanished, but his bright eyes looked into mine as he continued. "It's not what you might think. I'm not attracted to him or anything like that."

"You don't have to explain. I didn't mean to pry." (Of course I did!)

His eyes looked away. "Calvin's not my type anyway. If I were looking, it would be for someone like you."

"Me?" I said stupidly.

Roger nodded. "I have a good sense of what's real and what's an act. Nature does that. And your flighty stuff is just an act. I can tell what's real underneath it."

And I thought I was the psychologist manqué! No one had ever come on to me psychologically before. Usually it was with active verbs, like "I'd like to exfoliate you." Now here was this guy going beneath the surface immediately. He already appreciated my inner-most beautiful self, whoever the hell that was. Me, simple soul that I am, I just wanted Roger's magnificent body in my arms.

"I've got to finish Calvin," I said suddenly, breaking the spell. I led us back into the bustling activity of the salon. Calvin was still sitting at my station, but the lamps had been turned off. He looked annoyed. I felt his hair. "Perfect moisture content for finishing," I said like a knowing master.

Within seconds Nicole was back with us. "Did you boys finally warm up back there?"

"Nip it, Nikki."

Calvin said dryly, "I hope I'm not in the way, or anything."

Roger ignored him and asked me, "Where are my wet clothes?"

Nicole answered, "I put them in the laundry for a rinse and dry."

"I can bring them by later, if you want," I added hopefully.

That seemed to please Roger. "Thanks," he said. "Maybe we can have a drink together then, too."

I blurted, "I'd like that!"

Calvin rustled his magazine pages loudly.

Nicole caught my eye, then shifted her gaze to Calvin. Meanwhile, Calvin looked up at the three of us, scowled, then stuck his face back into his magazine. Roger asked, "Is that okay with you, Calvin?"

"I suppose so, if you don't think you'll be too tired."

I thought it strange for Calvin to give a hoot about anyone else's comfort. Roger said, "No problem. I just need a nap, a couple of hours."

Calvin replied harshly, "Then I suppose it's fine. I'm going back to Cambridge now. Don't forget your keys, Roger." He nodded toward his sport coat, a hand-tailored garment in creamy shantung, which hung near my station, within eye's view. Calvin believed that people were always about to steal his precious clothes. "They're in the left pocket of my jacket there," he said to Roger.

Roger went to Calvin's jacket, pulled out a flat snakeskin-bound case, and held it up. "This?" he asked.

Calvin nodded. "It keeps the keys from ruining the lines of my clothing."

Roger waved the key case angrily at Calvin. "Don't you know where this stuff comes from?" he asked.

"I don't care!" answered Calvin. "Just take the extra set on the copper ring."

Roger got the keys, then put his hand out to me again. "See you later, Stan." My heart hopped a few times. Then he took Nicole's hand. "Nice to meet you, Miss Nicole."

Nicole gave a resigned sigh and said, "I'll walk you out, Roger." As she went by, she poked my shoulder. "You get back to work!" She led Roger back through the shop like a docile bull back from pasture. Nicole was not a creature found in Roger's version of Nature, and he was clearly smitten with the patina of her glamour. I was smitten with his smile, among other things.

As I put the finishing touches on Calvin's hair, I carelessly released a large cloud of hair spray around his face. Calvin squinted and turned his head away to avoid the mist. I said, "Oh, is that getting in your eyes, love? Sorry." But it was a moment of satisfaction for me.

I removed the nylon drape and Calvin stood up. He turned his body sideways and admired himself in the mirror. He wore pleated linen slacks the color of rich cappuccino, a pale mauve shirt of fine Egyptian cotton, and a raucous bow tie with abstract patterns in violet, blueberry, raspberry, and gold. As he gently tweaked the tie back into shape, he said, "What do you think?"

I said, "I'm thinking of animal husbandry."

"I meant my new outfit."

"Calvin, you're flawless as a fag-rag photo."

"Hmmmmm. Yes." He passed his fingers through his hair a few times, messing up my fine work. Then he got his jacket and took out his wallet. He thumbed carefully through the pile of money inside and handed me a single wrinkled dollar bill. "That's for you."

"Thanks, Calvin," I said, accepting the chintzy tip. "You're a sport."

He draped the silk jacket carefully over his shoulders like a cape. He cocked his head and raised his nose a bit. "Did I tell you

I'm in line for a promotion? The project I'm on now almost guarantees it. It's a junior partnership. That's pretty impressive for someone *our* age."

"I'm impressed, Calvin." I handed the dollar bill back to him. "But maybe you should keep this. You might need some breath mints later." He scowled at me, then grabbed the money and jammed it into his pants pocket. I clucked my tongue and said, "Don't wrinkle your pants." He turned abruptly and stormed out of the shop.

"And don't hurry back," I said in his wake.

Nicole came by as I prepared my station for the next client. I muttered, "I'd like to kill that bastard. He always stiffs me."

"Darling," she almost sang, "how can you think of tips after meeting someone like Roger?"

I sighed. "I wouldn't mind him stiffing me."

Later, with the shop closed and locked, Nicole and I unwound with a cocktail in the back room. Though Nicole owns Snips, she doesn't let the customers know. Instead, she maintains the guise of the manicurist. She claims people will open their hearts and wallets to a sympathetic working woman but not to a shrewd entrepreneuse. She must be right, because the shop is a gold mine, and she hears scandalous stories every day, which is the stuff of her life.

While Nicole poured us each a drink—cognac for her, gin for me—I pulled the gold cigarette case out of her purse. She caught me.

"If you insist on taking one, at least try to smoke it before you destroy it."

I chose a mint-green cigarette and put it to my lips. "If it's the last thing I do this year, I'm going to learn how to smoke."

"You're a fool!"

"I'm a thirty-year-old Newbury Street hair burner! I *have* to smoke!"

"Just don't waste it. You know I order those special from Perrini's Tobacco Shop."

I repeatedly snapped my thumb in vain at her lighter, a slender gold ingot adorned with red lacquer. She took it from me and gave it one delicate flick. It jumped to life and I lit my cigarette. I took a long drag and tried to relax, but my throat burned and my eyes stung. I croaked, "I'll never figure out how you people do this and enjoy it."

Nicole inhaled deeply on her own maize-colored cigarette and released the smoke in slow pleasure. "It's something you learn to enjoy."

"Just like most perversions," I said. "What I want to know is, how do people like Calvin get to meet people like Roger, while people like me are still looking?"

"Stani, there are no simple answers in love." Nicole and my Czech grandmother were the only two people who could ever use the diminutive of my true surname, Stanislav.

"I've given up on love," I said with a lie. "I'll settle for serial monogamy."

"That should be easy enough to find."

"Easy when you have a lot of money or a prestigious career like Calvin."

"Don't whine! You had all that when you worked in the psych clinic."

"Yeah. I had a studlet then, too."

Nicole shrugged. "Maybe you should go back."

"Never. I'll shrink 'em at the sink, thank you." I nervously tapped the ash from the end of my cigarette.

"Stanley!" Nicole used my full Anglicized name whenever she was serious. She frowned at me. "Stanley, I've told you before . . . *roll* the ash off, don't bang it." Then she calmly sipped her cognac and continued our previous topic. "Maybe it's the simple law of opposites. Roger is nice, Calvin isn't. Therefore, they're together."

I took what I thought was a graceful puff from my cigarette. "With that reasoning, Calvin and I should be having a torrid affair."

"Didn't you?"

I coughed on the smoke. "Never, ever, past, present, or future, would, could, or might such a thing happen!" I smashed the cigarette out violently.

Nicole grimaced at the cigarette's untimely demise. "I thought differently," she said sadly, but her remorse was for the crushed stub lying in the ashtray.

"You thought wrong."

"In any case, just behave yourself tonight." She poured herself some more cognac. "Calvin was extremely annoyed about the invitation."

"He's always annoyed."

"After that *tango d'amore* between you and Roger this afternoon, he won't appreciate losing Roger to you tonight."

"Nothing will happen, Nicole." But secretly I hoped Roger and I would greet the dawn together.

"Stani, have you already forgotten last summer?"

I paused, then remembered the sordid episode as though it had happened that afternoon. It was the moment of truth between Calvin Redding and myself. While drunk, Calvin had tried to have sex with me in the men's room at Caffè Gianni, and I refused him. But then, in a rage, he proceeded to slander me throughout the bar all night, saying I had made the move on him, and wasn't it disgusting the way some people had to have sex all the time? The memory of it always provoked me. Calvin, of course, didn't remember a thing.

"Maybe I *will* try to win Roger tonight."

"That neatly folded laundry ought to do the trick," Nicole said.

I kissed her on the lips. "Wish me luck."

"Just stay safe."

2

HOW THE
OTHER HALF KILLS

It was around 8 P.M. when I left Snips. The warm day had turned into a bleak, dank night, reminding me that mukluk season in Boston was approaching. I'd looked up Calvin's address and discovered that it was only a few blocks from the shop, in the ultrachic area near the Boston Public Garden, so I walked. As I stood in front of the six-story brownstone structure, I thought hopefully of Roger's smiling face and wondered if he really awaited me in there. It all seemed too good and too sudden to be true.

Like almost every decent old building in Boston, Calvin's place had been converted to luxury condominiums. At least with this one they'd retained the sense of the old architecture during the renovations. Even the windows were double-hung with sashes that slid up and down. No cranks. No louvers. No anodized aluminum. Just wood and glass. And class.

I opened the outer door, a slab of inch-thick plate glass. When I entered the foyer, I faced another door, this one of solid oak panels. The oiled wood glowed softly under the simulated gas fixture overhead. I pressed a small button near Calvin's name and waited. There was no response. I checked to make sure I was pressing the right one, then tried again. Nothing. I wondered, Was it over already? Had the plans changed? Had Roger become content with Calvin after all?

Frustrated, I turned to leave just as a stranger was entering the foyer from outside. He was about my height, five ten, but very slim, with dark hair and beard, probably in his late twenties. He was dressed completely in black leather: pants, jacket, and cap. The drag was severe, but the scent was appealing. Peering over a brown paper bag full of groceries, he acknowledged me with a wary smile and a silent nod. He unlocked the big oak door, then he turned to me and said in an unnaturally low voice, "Coming in?"

I nodded and followed him. "I'm here to see Calvin Redding, but he doesn't answer."

"Doorbell must be out again." He was diligent about keeping his voice in the bass register. "Follow me."

He led me into a small elevator and pressed one button for the fifth floor, and another for PH. I asked, "What's PH?"

"That's where Cal lives, the penthouse."

I thought, A penthouse in a six-story brownstone? If *my* building had an elevator, the button would say TF—for top floor.

The ride up was slow and bumpy, which made me wonder if the authentic restoration of the building had been carried a bit too far. We stood in silence but stole brief glances at each other. I reeled at the heady aroma of the guy's leather. Finally, the tiny chamber bounced to a halt and the door opened with a groan. As he ambled out he said, "If Cal's not home, I live right under him."

I wondered how literally he meant that, then realized it was an invitation of sorts. "Thanks," I said, but the gesture was wasted on me, who would soon be in Roger's presence.

One floor up, Calvin's apartment was easy to find. I'd figured correctly, that of the two suites on the top floor, his was the one with the view of the Charles River. Opposite his door was an alcove with a small garden of ficus trees, miniature rhododendrons (fashionably out of season) ranging in reds from claret to rose, and a ground cover of lamb's ear. The aroma of fresh mulch and the dark night visible through a large glass skylight over the garden gave a sense of being outdoors. Roger would like that, I thought.

I pressed on a discreetly concealed button in the woodwork around Calvin's door. I waited for him to answer. A minute later I pressed it again, then remembered the leather man's comment about the doorbell being out of order. As I raised my fist to knock, the door in front of me swung inward with such sudden force that I almost got sucked in. Calvin stood there, clad only in a flimsy silk robe. The way it clung to his body, I knew he was naked underneath. His hair was disheveled and he looked surprised and angry, but he said nothing. I waved a hello; he blanched. I'd never seen a live person's skin turn gray the way Calvin's did at that moment.

"Am I, er, interrupting something?" I asked, hoping I wasn't.

He didn't answer. We stood and looked at each other in silence. Seconds passed.

"Should I come in, Calvin?" I felt awkward.

He twitched his hand nervously and gestured me in, so I stepped through the doorway into his apartment. He closed the door soundlessly and whispered, "Did anyone see you?"

I said boldly, "Your downstairs neighbor sure showed a lot of interest."

"Ssh!"

"What's wrong with you, Calvin?"

"Nothing!"

"Where's Roger?"

Calvin's body jolted stiffly. "Roger? He's . . . he's not here."

The energy in that place sure was strange. I handed him the bag containing Roger's dry clothes and said, "Maybe I'd better come back another time for that drink." I was turning to leave when Calvin grabbed me.

"Help me!" he wheezed. "Something's happened."

Why did I have the feeling I wasn't in for much fun that night? He fell onto me and sobbed heavily. In spite of my dislike for Calvin, I tried to comfort him. Counseling experience comes in handy sometimes. I felt his body shaking in my arms. I hadn't held another man for what seemed like centuries, and *now* I was embracing the wrong one! What would Roger think if he found us waltzing together like that? I looked over Calvin's shoulder into the living room behind him. All was still. I asked him again where Roger was.

"He's gone," he said as he sobbed into my shoulder.

"Gone where?" I asked, still hoping Roger had got smart and walked out on Calvin.

He released his grip just enough so that he could look at me. His face was only inches from mine. "He's . . . oh, God!" His eyes were wet with tears and I found myself vaguely fascinated to see him crying so helplessly. Must be my perverse Slavic blood that appreciates people expressing pain.

Finally Calvin let go of me. "Come and see." He turned and led me into the living room. Then he pointed to a hallway leading out toward the river side of the apartment. "In there," he said. "Go. You'll see."

"Where?"

"The bedroom. At the end, on the left."

I went where he pointed and stepped into a long corridor whose left wall and entire ceiling were enormous glass panels. It was like walking into a European crystal palace at night. The parquet floor was lined with narrow Persian runners. The glass wall on one side faced out over the Charles River. The other wall was paneled with huge mirrors, which reflected the river view. The only light was from the outside, just stars and street lamps and automobile lights glittering and reflecting in the mirrors. Nice to see how some people lived.

The bedroom door at the other end of the walkway was open. It looked inviting, with a nice warm glow coming from within. The whole corridor smelled of wool carpeting and dried eucalyptus. The comforting aroma relaxed me somewhat and rekindled my lovey-dovey hopes as I approached the room. It certainly didn't prepare me for what was in there.

Roger was on the bed, lying on his left side, facing the door. Behind him, a continuation of the glass wall and the river view provided a romantic urban backdrop. The sheet was drawn up in front of him, with his right arm and shoulder exposed. He could have been sleeping, and it would have been my dream come true to find him like that, waiting for me after a hard day at the shop, eager to lie together and help each other forget the troubles of the working world. But there was an ugly stillness in that room: Roger wasn't breathing.

My stomach lurched. I could have run and screamed, but hysterics have never been my style. Instead, I deliberately switched myself into a detached state of mind. My heart's response was sealed off and frozen for now. It was a survival tactic I'd learned as a boy dealing with unpleasant situations. I would face this nightmare with objective, focused senses.

I went to Roger and touched his face. Cool and dry. I lifted the exposed wrist in search of a pulse. The arm was leaden. I felt along his neck for a signal from his heart, but all was still.

Next thing I knew, my legs were wobbling and my mouth was dry as French talc. The soft lights pulsed in waves of brightness. I bit my tongue to get the saliva running again, a trick I'd learned from a dancer friend. I steadied myself against the bed. When I was sure I wouldn't faint, I lifted the sheet away from Roger's body. The odor of recent muscular exertion wafted upward. His skin was pale except along the mattress, where it was darker, almost bluish. The stagnant blood had already begun to settle. Then I saw them.

"Calvin!" I yelled. "Get your ass in here!"

Calvin appeared at the door in seconds. He was still sniveling. I screamed, "What the hell are these bow ties doing on him?"

"I . . . I don't know." Sniff. "He was like that."

Roger's body had been tied with two expensive silk bows, one around his cold neck and one around his bluish genitals.

"What the hell were you guys doing?" I noticed a glassine envelope of white powder on the nightstand. "Damn, Calvin! Are you still messing with that shit?"

"No. Honest!" he wailed. "I came home and he was lying like that!"

"Then what are you doing dancing around in that robe?"

Calvin caught his breath, then he stammered, "I . . . I came in here . . . and saw him lying there like that . . . naked. And I figured it was an invitation."

"So you took drugs and got into one of your stupid scenes." My body wanted to punch and kick and hurt him—a typical male response. "You went too far this time, Calvin."

"I didn't do it! All I did was get my clothes off and jump in with him."

I noticed Calvin's clothes were neatly laid over a leather sling chair in the corner, not flung into a rumpled pile any old place. I snarled, "Just admit it, Calvin. You killed him!"

Calvin shuddered. "I didn't! I . . . I put my arms around

him." Sniff. "He felt cold, so I lay close to him. Then, he wasn't moving."

"And you rammed it into his dead body? Is that what you did?"

"No! I didn't do anything!"

"You're lying Calvin. You've been home all afternoon. You left the shop before three o'clock."

His voice wavered. "But I went back to work. And I was late getting home." He seemed on the verge of bawling again. "That's why I was in a hurry to have sex with him. I knew you'd be here any minute."

"So what? You didn't have to answer the door." I turned on him and spat the words into his face. *"Did you enjoy yourself?"*

Calvin moaned and fell onto me, limp and heavy. Great! He'd fainted. I eased him onto the floor, then got a glass of cold water from the adjoining bathroom. I hoped it would bring him around, since my only first-aid training is from the movies. And sure enough, when I splashed some of the water on his face, he regained consciousness. But then he grabbed me and pulled me down to him desperately. The stress that Calvin was going through was evident—his breath stank. "Don't leave me in here with him!" he said, shaking me. "Take me out! *Take me out of here!"*

I helped him back into the living room and laid him down on the leather sofa. When I picked up the phone, Calvin asked, "Who are you calling?"

"The police, who else?"

"Don't! They're going to think I did it." The look of terror on his face gave me a twinge of pleasure.

"You *did* do it, Calvin. You can't blame anyone else this time." I wondered how I'd got into a mess like this. Was it just because Roger had said things I'd wanted to hear? By the time I finished dialing, though, I was feeling kind of smug, as though I understood the whole situation and had it completely in my control. Someone finally answered, and I explained who I was and what had happened. I had to repeat myself many times. Finally, in exasperation I yelled, "There's a goddam body here, and the killer is here, too!" From where he sat, Calvin mouthed the F word at me.

I hung up and turned to him. "They're on the way," I said with conviction. I was really feeling powerful, especially over Calvin. Boy, was that a delusion!

Calvin stood up. He was shaking. "I need a drink."

"Don't drink! It looks bad when they take the report."

"Fuck off! I'm having a drink."

"On second thought, Calvin, have a double." I left him alone. He wouldn't be going anywhere in his bathrobe anyway. I went back to the bedroom. I wanted to find out exactly what had happened between him and Roger, and I thought maybe the residual energy in the room would give me some clue. As I stood in the doorway, I became aware of a spicy aroma I hadn't noticed before. I moved toward the bed, thinking the scent might be coming from Roger, but it wasn't. I saw a bottle of cologne on the dresser. I opened it, but it was nothing like the scent that lingered in the air. I sniffed around the bedroom until I discovered where the smell was coming from. It was strongest near the louvered closet doors. I slid one of them open and took a deep breath. There it was, that dark and spicy smell, something like frankincense, almost like patchouli, but not quite like either of them. I took another breath to fix the scent in my memory, then closed the door.

I turned around to look at Roger and felt a wave of sadness. Roger was beautiful and gentle-looking. The bow ties would have been a playful come-on if he hadn't been dead. But now they looked insidious. Then something strange caught my eye. I could have been mistaken, but the knots looked different from each other. The one around his neck was loose and fluffy, while the one down below was crisper and tighter.

Before I left Roger, there was something I felt compelled to do. It was a weird notion, and I knew the cops wouldn't approve, so I had to act before they arrived. I breathed deeply, then took Roger's hands into my own. I wanted to say good-bye, even though I didn't get the chance to know him well. Holding his lifeless hands, I discovered strange thick calluses roughening the tips of his fingers. Perhaps he used to play a guitar? I sighed heavily and put Roger's hands down. I turned to leave the bedroom and saw Calvin standing in the doorway. He'd been watching me.

"What the hell are you doing to him?" he asked with a sneer.

I blushed, embarrassed at being caught in a moment of maudlin sentimentality. "Just saying good-bye."

Calvin sneered, "You're sick!" He turned and strode angrily back down the hallway to the living room, his robe flying open behind him. I caught a glimpse of the back of his body and thought that somewhere there was justice: For all the hours he spent pumping and primping himself at his gym, Calvin still had lousy legs.

When I returned to the living room, he'd turned up the lights and propped himself among the pillows of the dove-gray leather sofa. Calvin's eyes had a soft glaze that told me he'd already belted down a few drinks. He was fidgeting and pouting like a child in a doctor's waiting room. He lit a cigarette. I envied him. It seemed perfect to be smoking at a time like this. He flung the heavy crystal lighter onto the rosewood coffee table. It nicked the tabletop but surprisingly didn't shatter.

"Damn!" he muttered. "What am I supposed to do now?"

"You're supposed to get your story straight for the cops. And you'd better be ready, because they are going to trip you up and knock you down." And I secretly couldn't wait to see him undone.

"How can they? I didn't do anything."

"Right, Calvin. There's a body on your bed, you're prancing around in a silk robe, and nothing happened."

"He was just a trick. I don't even know him."

"Calvin, those are *your* bow ties on him!"

He swooned and looked almost ready to faint again, but he recovered quickly. "Since you're so smart, Vannos, why don't *you* tell the cops what happened? You already got a head start on the goddamn phone."

"But I wasn't here, Calvin."

"That's right, Vannos, you weren't. So why don't you just shut up. They don't know who was here and who wasn't. In fact, it's my word against yours. Maybe I'll just tell them I came in, and you and Roger were having a fight, or even better, you were on the bed yourselves."

"You ass! You're going to look pretty stupid spouting that kind of garbage sitting around in a flimsy silk robe, naked underneath."

It was then that we both heard horrible sounds in the hallway outside Calvin's suite, the heavy tread of authority, loud voices, squawking radios, sudden banging on the front door.

"Police here! Open up!"

Calvin leaped up from the sofa and ran for the bedroom. He hollered from within, "Don't let them in! I'm not ready!"

"This isn't a fashion show, Calvin!"

I opened the door and he was there, all six feet of him. My senses switched to slow motion to take it all in. He stood with his weight shifted onto one of his long, muscular legs. His blue-gray eyes glittered. Though recently shaven, his beard cast a bluish shadow against his satin olive complexion. He didn't smile, but I knew when he did, it would be luminous. His curly dark hair was tousled. An aroma of balsam surrounded him. One second had passed.

"You got trouble here?" he asked, restraining the natural power in his resonant voice. A clean white cotton shirt was slightly wrinkled; a striped necktie lay loosened at the collar; sleeves were rolled to expose powerful, hirsute forearms; gray pleated slacks tried in vain to conceal the assertive strength in his loins; shiny black loafers enveloped broad feet with high insteps. When my gaze returned to his face, I saw his eyes looking straight into my own, and felt a Mediterranean zephyr caress my face. Two seconds.

"Who are you?" he asked curtly.

"Stan Kraychik," I answered.

He pushed his way by me, and three other cops followed him. I heard him say, "Lieutenant Branco," as he went by. Of the other three cops, one was a plainclothes officer in his late twenties. I sized up his compact body and styled blond hair. A fitting assistant, I thought, but maybe a little too cute and cool. The wedding band on his left hand relieved some of the mystique.

Another of the three cops was a uniformed officer, a hefty woman almost as tall as Branco. Her arms and shoulders dwarfed mine. Her features were dark and rough, but I sensed a warmth in her.

The last cop was the lab expert, a reedy black man slightly taller than me. His big bright teeth took up one-fourth of his face when he smiled, which he seemed to do easily. He seemed too gentle to be a cop.

Branco looked around the room quickly, but I could see him register every detail in a computerlike mind. He scribbled words into a small black notebook while he surveyed the room—and me. "There'll be more personnel arriving shortly. Now, what happened here?"

I tried to answer coolly. "Someone's not breathing in the bedroom. No pulse either." My stomach lurched again and a tremor ran up and down my spine. Branco nodded to his assistant and the lab man to go check out the body. Suddenly we heard the frenzy of banging drawers and slamming closet doors, even the flushing of a toilet. Branco whirled at me. "Someone else here?"

I rolled my eyes and nodded, as though letting him in on a secret. "You bet." I began to explain, but was interrupted by Calvin's arrival from the hallway. He'd put on a puffy salmon-colored cotton shirt and baggy white linen pants. The stuff was expensive, just the perfect togs for a Palm Beach reception, but it was out of season in Boston. I was surprised that Calvin could commit such a fashion blunder. He was under more stress than I thought.

Calvin looked Branco up and down. "Well!" he exclaimed, "I thought that blond you sent to the bedroom was a nice piece, but the prize bull is definitely out here."

Branco ignored the comment. (Was he used to it?) Instead he spoke brusquely to Calvin. "Who are you?"

"I live here. So the real question is, who are you?" His voice quivered with an artificially induced energy.

Branco said evenly, "Lieutenant Branco, homicide."

"No uniform? How do I know you're a cop?" Branco flashed his badge. Calvin looked at the badge, then at Branco. He said. "You seem quite real, Mr. Bronco." I was certain Calvin had mispronounced the name intentionally. He continued, "I'm Calvin Redding and I own this flat. And some rather unpleasant events seem to have occurred this evening. I hope your men will able to set everything straight." The female officer glared at Calvin and cleared her throat.

I said, "Something's weird, Lieutenant. He wasn't like this before." I sounded defensive.

Branco looked at me coldly. "Quiet, you!" Then to Calvin he said, "We'd appreciate your cooperation, Mr. Redding."

"You want *me* to cooperate? I'd be only too happy to help you, but I think Vannos here may be the one you want to talk to."

Branco turned on me. "Just what *is* your name?"

His sudden vehemence startled me. "I, uh . . . it's . . . Stan," I said. "I mean, *Stanley*. Well, actually, Stanislav is the most correct. But in the shop it's Vannos. But my grandmother used to call me Stani."

Branco shook his head and muttered, "Jesus!"

Meanwhile, the blond assistant returned from the bedroom. He looked at Branco seriously and said, "You'd better have a look, Lieutenant."

Branco said, "Okay," then left Calvin and me in the living room with the female officer while he and the blond cop went back to the bedroom.

Calvin whispered to me, "Some cop! No uniform, and he has hairy forearms." He frowned in distaste.

The female officer moved between us and grumbled to Calvin, "Anything you got to say mister, speak up!"

When Branco and his assistant came back out, he sent me to the kitchen with the blond one while he interrogated Calvin in the living room. I told the assistant everything that had happened since I first arrived. Talking to him was easier than with Branco, and my fumbling defensive tone went away for a while. Branco took longer with Calvin, so I watched them both from the kitchen doorway. Calvin sank lower into the leather sofa as Branco pressed him for answers. He began to resemble a dog left outside a restaurant while his master went in for a steak dinner. He was quite a different Calvin from a few minutes ago, or even earlier that day. Branco finished and came into the kitchen. He sent the blond cop back out to question Calvin again. Then he sat down, opened his black leather note pad, and took a deep breath. "Okay," he said. "Let's hear your side of it."

"Again?"

"Just talk."

I tried to tell him everything I'd told the other cop, but his physical presence unnerved me, and I lost track of exactly what had happened. To make things worse, Branco would jot things in his little black book, but it always seemed at the wrong time. When I'd say something I thought was important, he'd do nothing. Then, when I'd pause to remember a detail, he'd write like a demon, which made me wonder what kind of game he was playing. When I finally finished, he asked me without looking up, "You haven't touched anything, have you?"

"No, sir." I lied calmly, but I had to look away from his steely eyes. By examining Roger and touching him, I knew that I had technically tampered with evidence, but then, so had another hero of my youth, Perry Mason. When I glanced up, Branco's hard eyes were narrow and staring at me, full of doubt.

At that moment more cops arrived, along with a photographer, a doctor, and more lab people. The place was suddenly full of men on a mission. Branco said, "You can make your formal statement downtown."

"Doesn't this one count?"

"There's less distraction. You'll be able to think clearly."

"I'm thinking clearly now."

Branco arched an eyebrow. "Something else may come to mind."

"You don't think I did it?"

He didn't answer.

"You're not going to book me, are you?"

"That depends," he said coldly.

"Don't I get any points for calling you guys in?"

"The law's the law."

"That doesn't sound hopeful." Here I thought I was innocent! Then, amidst my growing fear, I remembered the most unlikely thing: Sugar Baby, my pet cat, a taupe-colored Burmese exactly the shade of her namesake candy. I suddenly remembered I hadn't fed her. "I've got to feed my cat!" I said urgently. "She'll destroy everything!"

"You can do that later." Branco slapped his book closed and stood up. "Let's go then!" And the four cops took Calvin and me downstairs where two cruisers were double-parked with their flashers going. It had begun to rain.

3

THE BOY NEXT DOOR

The cops took Calvin and me in separate cars, probably to prevent our talking on the way to the station. Funny thing is, I had only two words to say to him, and they weren't *love you*. Calvin got to ride with Branco and his blond assistant, who drove the cruiser. I was in the second car with the other two cops, and I felt horribly alone, almost like a criminal. I wondered, Would riding along with big Italian Branco have given me more confidence about the outcome of the night's events?

I struggled to see into his cruiser ahead of us. Through the rainy windshields I could barely make out three silhouettes. Branco and Calvin seemed to be chatting it up, and I wondered what was so damn interesting. When they ran a red light, we lost them in the wet snarl of traffic.

By the time we got to the station, Branco's crew and Calvin were already inside. I got out of the cruiser and the big female cop escorted me quickly into the station. She took me to a tiny dark room with a table and a gooseneck lamp on it and left me alone with the door slightly open. I looked around. The small chamber resembled a storage closet with painted cinder-block walls and no windows. Suddenly the door swung open and banged against the wall behind it. An big-bellied cop reeking of smoke and sweaty clothes tromped in and flung a dirty clipboard onto the table in front of me. A leaky ball-point pen rattled on the chain that attached it to the scarred old clipboard.

He belched loudly. "You here for that faggot killing?"

"I'm here to talk to Lieutenant Branco."

He scratched his scalp, then sniffed at his fingertips. "He's gonna be a while."

"I'll wait," I said.

He pointed to the blank form on the clipboard. "You can make your statement there." Then he left and slammed the door closed. A sour smell remained in his wake. I wondered if the door was locked. I didn't hear a ventilation fan. The walls felt closer every second. Drops of perspiration rolled down my back between my shoulder blades. Claustrophobic panic tickled the base of my throat and began to inhibit my breathing. I said my mantra, trying to calm myself and think about what I would write. (They give you a pen so you can't change anything once it's down, unless you cross it out. If you do that, they figure you're lying and they perk right up.) I tried to remember how much I'd said in my report at Calvin's place. All I remember is trying to act cool and not succeeding at it. I'm sure they noticed that. They're trained to notice everything you do and say, as well as the stuff you don't. The best cops can already do it before they go to police school.

I replayed the whole evening in my mind and pulled out the important moments, the ones that would help incriminate Calvin. Then I wrote it all onto the official form in front of me. It came out all short sentences written with simple words: *I said this*; *he did that*; *I saw this*; *he said that*. There was no confusion in the writing. When I finished, my thoughts wandered back to my own apartment. What were Sugar Baby's claws hooking into at that moment?

The door opened again and Branco entered, bringing with him the aroma of clean cotton and balsam. I wondered whether it was his after-shave or his laundry detergent. Maybe it was both.

"How're you doing in here?"

His voice seemed a little friendlier, but I didn't dare trust him.

"I'm finished," I said. "When can I go?"

"What's your hurry?"

"My cat—"

"Oh, right. Your cat. I thought you might have a big date."
Was he curious? Did he care? Was he laughing at me?

"It's more practical, Lieutenant. I'd like my apartment to be intact when I get home."

"Why don't you get the cat declawed?"

"Same reason you don't amputate your fingertips."

Branco frowned and pulled my written statement toward him. He leaned his chair backward and balanced it on two legs. He seemed to be taunting me. Was he doing it purposely? Was he enjoying it? I watched him read my statement while I sat mute and sullen. Even in that dim little closet of a room, Branco's face had a healthy glow. The curly dark hair showed no sign of gray, and his blue-gray eyes shone with a light of their own. I gazed at him and felt a warm tingle dissipate the tension in my chest. I resumed my silent mantra, but I couldn't blot out the effect of Branco's body in that small room.

When he finished, he straightened up in the chair and put the report back on the table. He spoke with his purrbox on extra soft. "This is written really well."

"They learned me English good at school."

"It almost sounds prepared."

"I had a goddamn half hour to write it!"

"You sound upset."

"Of course I'm upset! First some jerk kills a man, then you guys try to blame the murder on me."

Branco scribbled something on his note pad before he said, "Maybe you had a reason for killing Fayerbrock."

The words stunned me. It sounded like an accusation. I spoke with a slow, measured rhythm. "Lieutenant, I'll tell you one thing. If I were going to kill anybody, it wouldn't be Roger Fayerbrock. It would be Calvin Redding."

Scribble, scribble went Branco.

I continued, "That bastard's into weird sex. They were doing drugs and the scene got out of control."

"Mr. Kraychik, that's a very neat explanation, and I'd like to believe you, but I can't."

I felt a heavy pressure on my chest. "Why not?"

Branco just stared at me.

"Tell me!" I shouted.

Branco nodded calmly. "You prefer the bitter truth, eh?"

"More than sweet-sounding lies that dance around and tease you. What is it?"

Branco stood up and walked around behind me. He was so close I swear I could feel his own pulse on my neck and shoulders. I think the SOB was using his body to unnerve me, and damn it, it was working.

His voice was low when he asked, "What exactly did you say to Roger Fayerbrock when you were alone with him?"

"What!" I turned my head to face him, but he pushed me back around.

"Did you say 'I'm sorry for doing this'?"

· "What the hell are you talking about!"

"What *did* you say? Huh?" Branco shoved me, but not hard enough to hurt me.

I was speechless, but he kept on.

"When did you take off the ties? Before you held his hands? Or after?"

It took me but a second to realize that Calvin had told Branco about me being alone with Roger, and he'd embellished it all to incriminate me.

"Did you enjoy yourself?"

Those had been my words to Calvin! Could I have sounded that harsh? But I was angry and jealous when I said that to Calvin. My words were driven by emotion. What would drive Branco to say that to me?

I realized I'd stopped breathing. I tried to hear my breath, but there was just blood pounding against my eardrums. I concentrated for a few minutes and got the air moving in and out of my lungs again and the blood pressure lowered. Then in as calm a voice as I could produce, I said, "I didn't do anything wrong. I just held his hands to say good-bye. That's all I said, and that's all I did. If you want to arrest and book me for that, go ahead. I'll make one phone call, and you'll have a civil-liberties case on your head that'll make you sorry you ever bullied a gay person in your life."

Branco stood quietly behind me for a long time, and I felt his eyes on my back. Then he came around to face me again. "Redding's and your stories disagree widely."

I looked directly into his eyes. "Mine is true."

Branco gave a slight nod, as though agreeing with me. Then, almost apologetically, he said, "We've booked Redding."

Whew! I thought. I was off the hook!

"But not for murder," continued Branco.

"For what, then?"

"Possession of drugs. He'd taken cocaine just before we arrived."

Stupid Calvin, worried about wasting drugs. "How long will that hold him?" I asked.

"Until someone comes up with bail. Meanwhile I'll keep shaking both your stories until the loose pieces fall out."

"All that's going to fall out of Calvin are nickels and dimes."

"Then that leaves you, doesn't it?"

"What?"

"*Your* story will have to be the one we follow then."

"Lieutenant, that is the first hopeful thing you've said all night."

"Don't be so cocky."

"What should I be?" I wanted to ask him, How do you *want* me to be? Then he could tell me, and I could do it, and we could get along. But I knew it wasn't going to be that way with Lieutenant Branco.

He said, "I know you're involved in this somehow, but I don't have enough on you to make a charge."

"That's a big comfort, Lieutenant. You know, sometimes you guys are so nervous around people like me, it's almost unnatural."

He ignored my remark. "You can go home. Get back to your cat. Unwind. Have a drink."

"Only one?"

Branco almost smiled. "Just don't leave town." With those words he sent me out of the room.

It was ten-thirty when I left the station, but I had no intention of having a drink—not until after I paid a visit to Calvin Redding's downstairs neighbor. A purely social call, I assured myself. I thought about going home to feed Sugar Baby first, but at this point she'd probably exhausted herself in a destructive frenzy, so I figured it wouldn't make much difference. So much for the rose-colored grille cloth on my new stereo speakers.

I walked back to Calvin's place. The rain had slowed to a pleasant mist. The walk took about twenty minutes and gave me time to think. I wondered exactly how Calvin had tried to incriminate me. What had he said in his report? Then I wondered how he'd actually killed Roger, and why. I had to find out, not only to prove his guilt but, with the police suspecting me, to clear myself real fast. Perhaps I also wanted to establish a good scout image in Branco's eyes. But why should I have cared about that?

Calvin's building looked gloomy and uninviting now, and my envy at how well he lived had vanished. Two police vans with flashers going were still double-parked in front. I went inside and rang the buzzer for the suite just under Calvin's place. A controlled low voice projected from the intercom. "Who's calling?"

I marveled at how clearly the intercom transmitted his voice. I answered, "The guy you met in the elevator."

He buzzed me in. That was the easy part. Digging up the dirt in Calvin's life was going to be a bit trickier. That, and keeping the guy off my back, literally. I'll never understand why the serious leather types are attracted to me. I'm not exactly a model of machismo. Maybe my pheromones are out of kilter.

When I got out of the elevator on his floor, I found him standing halfway out the open doorway to his suite. A white T-shirt and white socks now complemented his black leather pants. His wiry body was well proportioned and attractive, without the standard health-club physique. His beard and mustache were trimmed to a uniform one-quarter-inch length. His brown eyes seemed opaque and impenetrable, yet showed a vestiage of warmth deep within.

"I was kind of hoping you'd come back," he said with a voice that sounded easy to get friendly with.

I flirted. "I thought you might be able to help me out."

"I hope I can," he said. He still smelled like leather heaven, as he had earlier that evening in the elevator.

"The cops just left my place. Maybe we can relax together."

I didn't answer him, but I put out my hand. "I'm Stan. Stan Kraychik." I pronounced my name clearly and simply. People often have a hard time with it.

"I'm Hal Steiner." His basso voice insinuated itself beyond the words he spoke, as though it had its own personality. We shook hands. His grip was warm and surprisingly strong for his trim build. He invited me in.

The living room was illuminated with soft light from numerous sources: candles mounted in wall sconces, oil lamps with stained-glass shades on the tables, and all the reflected white and rainbow-colored flames in the mirrors on the walls about the room. The gentle recorded music of a harpsichord and a wood flute filled the room's dark places where the light didn't penetrate.

The floor plan was exactly like Calvin's on the next floor up, and the similarity ended there. I'd expected the decor to include racks and slings and harnesses everywhere. But instead, this leather-oriented man had surrounded himself with old dark furniture and carpets, footstools, antimacassars, and gilt-framed pictures. Everything had a long past.

He murmured, "You like it?"

"I do, but I'm surprised."

"Why?"

"I expected something harder, given your wardrobe."

He drew his full lips back as though he would smile, but he didn't. "I've reserved one room for that side of my life. Would you like to see it?"

My pulse quickened. "Maybe later. I'd like to talk."

"Nothing wrong with getting to know each other first. You want something to drink?"

"Sure. Something light, like a tumbler of gin."

He tried to smile again. "Is that what you want?"

"Juice or water is fine." I wanted to keep my wits about me.

He went to get it. I watched the sheen of black leather caress the cheeks of his firm butt and recede into the dimness. I sat down in a dark velvet chair and let it envelop me. It was the first moment of peace I'd had all night. I rested my feet on an ottoman upholstered with bargello needlepoint. A jacquard tablecloth with a four-inch fringe covered a round table nearby, with a Tiffany lamp resting atop it all. The stained glass spattered gemlike colors on a tarnished silver frame containing an old sepia-tone photograph of a handsome military officer. I stared quietly into the soft glow of the lamps. When my host returned, it was his fully packed, leather-clad crotch that greeted me at eye level.

He placed a goblet of bubbly water on the table near me. Then he placed what looked like two plump and expertly rolled joints in the center of the table. "Help yourself," he said.

"Thanks," I said. "Maybe later." Later, later—that's all my life seemed to be about.

He sat in the other chair near the table and faced me. He held a delicate porcelain cup and saucer with gold filigree. The cup contained something hot. He took a sip and said, "You're here because of what happened upstairs, aren't you?"

I nodded.

After a quiet moment he said, "I was hoping you'd come for something else." He sighed, and when he spoke again, his voice was lighter. "All right, then, how can I help?"

Relieved that the sexual pressure was off, at least for the moment, I asked him, "Do you know what happened?"

"I assume, from seeing the covered gurney going down the stairs, that someone died."

I tasted my water. There was a fragrance of roses. "You're almost right," I said. "Someone was *killed*—a real fine man—and I want to find out who did it."

"Why?"

"Because he was here this afternoon, and now he's not. And because the police think I'm involved, which I am not. And because I think Calvin probably did it, and I need evidence against him to prove it."

"Sounds like you've got it in for him."

"Calvin's the kind of person who causes trouble and blames

others. He gets away with too much. This time he went too far, and I want to see him pay."

"Maybe he had cause for what he did."

"There is no cause for murder."

The leather man sipped again from his fragile cup. "Could've been passion."

"Passion! They tricked. They just met last night."

"Passion doesn't work on a timetable."

"And passion doesn't excuse murder."

"People live, sometimes they feel passion, then they die. Everything else is nonessential."

His words sounded like the kind of reasoning some people use to allay a guilty conscience.

"Do *you* feel passion?" I asked.

"I did, a few times. Hope to again."

I sipped some more rosewater. "That's a lovely philosophy," I said, "but I'm concerned with a killing."

"Sometimes people kill each other."

"How can you be so blasé about it?"

Hal shrugged. "I'm not blasé. I accept things as they are and try to fit in with them. Like, for example, my seeing you as a potential sex partner and then finding out that you're really here for information about Calvin. If that's why you're here, then that's what I'll deal with."

The guy was an enigma, a leather man who lived in the past yet had a handle on cosmic consciousness. I asked him, "How chummy are you and Calvin?"

He smiled like a sphinx, without parting his lips. "The only thing I know about Calvin is that he entertains a lot of good-looking men up there."

"Did you guys ever make it?"

He hesitated before saying, "Who?"

"You and Calvin."

Hal shook his head no.

I said, "Were you home this afternoon?"

"Suppose I was?"

"Did you see anyone coming into the building around three o'clock?"

"The only person I saw today was Aaron Harvey."

"Who's that?"

"Calvin's lover. He doesn't live here, but he's around a lot, usually stays a few days at a time."

"What time was it?"

He thought a moment, then said, "Around two o'clock."

"You saw him come in?"

He nodded. "I was in the lobby downstairs. Hey, are you a lawyer or something?"

"No. Why?"

"This is like a cross-examination."

"Sorry," I said. "It's *my* passion for facts. Sometimes it's rude."

"If you're not a lawyer, it's okay. You're certainly more interesting than the police who were just here." His eyes glanced below my belt.

If he thought the police weren't interesting, he'd obviously not met Branco yet. I was tempted to tell him about the lieutenant, to jabber like a cheerleader over a varsity dreamboat, but I decided to continue with the questions. "When did Aaron leave?"

"I don't know."

"You didn't see him go out?"

Hal scowled. "I'm not a concierge!"

"Sorry, didn't mean to press you. Was there anything unusual about him this time?"

"He arrived as he always does, carrying one of those leather bags embossed with gold initials and fleurs-de-lis."

"Louis Vuitton." I nodded. "But they're not leather." I spoke as though divulging one of life's great secrets. "They're made of vinyl-impregnated canvas. Only the trim is leather."

Hal shrugged. "They're not the kind of skins I'd own anyway."

"I wouldn't think so, but I hear they're good for gym bags." I sipped some rosewater. Lovely. "Hal," I continued, "what does Aaron look like?"

"Medium height. Slender. Light brown skin. Gorgeous pale blue eyes. Dresses flashy."

"Have you ever talked with him?"

"Just small talk, like with you earlier today."

"You ever have him up here?"

Hal's eyes narrowed. "Do you care?"

I smirked. "Just trying to get a sense of how well you know him. Do you know where he works?"

"Last I knew, he was at Neiman's."

"And you saw no one else? No tall, rugged cowboy type with sandy hair and blue eyes?" How could I talk so easily about Roger, now dead? Stanley the Heartless Inquisitor.

"I'd remember someone like that," Hal answered.

"Yeah, you would. Except he's dead now."

Hal sat back and closed his eyes. I sipped my rosewater; he sipped his tea; the soft lights and peaceful music sustained an intimate mood. I was tired and lonely. I found myself wondering about Hal's other room, the one reserved for pleasure, then quickly brought myself back to the business at hand. "From what you know, do you think Calvin could kill a man?"

"I think we're all capable of it, given the proper circumstances."

"What do you think those would be for someone like Calvin?"

Silent moments passed as Hal studied the gold filigree on the delicate teacup he held. "Well, the only thing I could say about Calvin is that he's completely self-absorbed. I'd guess anyone who could prevent him from getting something he really wanted might see his murderous energy, though I'm not sure he'd kill them."

"Could that include sex?"

"I'm not sure what you mean."

"Say he was expecting a certain performance level from a partner and he wasn't getting it . . ."

"You mean, would he kill for that?"

I nodded.

"I doubt it. Maybe as some accidental consequence of his own selfish behavior. He does a lot of drugs. Sometimes that obscures your perceptions. As I said, adequately provoked, I think every person is capable of murder."

"Including you?"

He carefully placed his cup on the table. "Every person."

I put my goblet down heavily and said, "I want to see Calvin burn for what he did."

"You really believe he killed that guy, don't you?"

I nodded, realizing that I *wanted* it to be Calvin.

He said, "Be careful your anger doesn't derail you onto the wrong track."

"Hal, Calvin tried to convince the cops that I was the killer, and I know I'm not. So it's tit for tat now. I'm going to convince them it's Calvin. Even if I'm wrong, I may find the real killer while trying to prove Calvin guilty." I shrugged. "Nothing lost." I got up to leave. I extended my hand for a shake, and he took it. Then he yanked me toward him and hugged me hard—too hard. He was trying to impress me with his strength.

He spoke low into my ear. "The offer is open," he said. "I'd like to show you that other room sometime. I think you might like it."

I laughed nervously. "I'm afraid I might."

"You know where to find me."

"Thanks," I said, and left his place more troubled than before.

It was after midnight when I finally got home. There was one consolation awaiting me: Sugar Baby had not destroyed the apartment or the stereo speakers as I had imagined. Instead, with microtome exactness, she had severed but one plump linen nub from the grille cloth of a speaker. I picked her up and hugged her. She purred vigorously, which I hoped was an expression of joy at seeing me home safe at last, but which I knew was simply the happy anticipation of her late supper. I danced around the kitchen holding on to her, singing to her as I prepared her meal. (Hers before mine, of course.) Then while she ate, I popped some frozen lasagna into the microwave oven, mixed myself a martini, and called Nicole.

She answered the phone with throaty brusqueness. "At this hour, it better be good."

My voice faltered. "N-N-Nikki?"

"Stani? Baby, what's the matter?"

"Oh, Nikki . . ." Then I broke down and sobbed and told her the whole night's story.

4

DIAMONDS, FURS, AND RUBY RINGS

Next morning I was in the shop working as usual, though the events of last night persisted in my mind. Had it all really happened? Had I really met my cowboy fantasy man, then found him dead a few hours later?

But the world turns, and no matter the horrors or sadness of my personal life, my clients expect technical perfection and emotional nurturance from me. So temporarily, I dismissed my own troubles while I tried to salvage what was left of a young woman's hair.

Someone—and I happened to recognize his work—had been abusing her hair shafts with careless perm technique. It was was the wrong approach for her wispy type of hair. Consequently, last time he'd literally dissolved and rinsed almost a fourth of her silky blond tresses down the drain, what we call in the trade a "chemical cut."

The twenty-year-old looked desperate. "Can you fix it?" she asked, close to tears.

I was standing behind her. I held both her shoulders firmly, put my face next to hers, and looked warmly at the reflection of her sad eyes in the mirror. "It's going to be all right," I murmured softly into her ear. "We'll do an asymmetric cut and you'll look divine." She couldn't see my physical and mental exhaustion from last night's turmoil, nor the restless, fitful sleep I'd endured. To my clients I am always lighthearted, concerned only with their beauty.

"Will my hair ever grow back?" she asked.

"It will. But until then, no color, no perms, no blow-drying, nothing in your hair except the shampoo and moisturizer I give you today." I didn't have the heart to tell her the whole truth: Her hair might never be the same as before. Like the name of the process that can cause it, chemical damage can be permanent.

Forty minutes later I finished the emergency work on the young woman. She looked pretty good, considering what I had to work with. I cleaned up my station and headed toward the front door. Nicole stopped me. "And just where the flying hell do you think you're going?"

"I'm off to Neiman's."

"How can you go shopping after what happened last night!"

"Doll, this is official police business."

"Stanley, please don't lie. If you must shop to get your mind off your problems, then go ahead. But don't lie."

"I'm not lying!" She wasn't convinced. "Nikki, I expect the cops to mistrust me, but not you."

"Oh, I trust you, Stanley. I just don't believe you. And what about your photo session this afternoon?" She was referring to my contract to style the models for a magazine shoot at a new hotel opening on the waterfront.

"It's only eleven now, and I don't have to be there until one. I've got plenty of time, Nikki."

She smirked in disapproval. "Then as payola for running out on me, you can bring back two truffles from Neiman's Epicure Shop."

"Sure, doll. You want the Perigord or the Belgian variety?"

"What?"

"The Perigord truffles are the ones the pigs sniff out from the ground. The ones from Belgium are chocolate."

Nicole's eyes glittered impatiently. "The chocolate kind, of course! What would I do with a pig's truffle?"

"For starters, braise it in cognac and chop some into an omelette."

Nicole winced. "I'll take my cognac in a snifter, thank you."

"Or a Styrofoam cup."

"Will you just leave and get me the damn chocolate!"

"I'm going, I'm going. One Grand Marnier and one Bitter Midnight, right?"

Nicole answered in her broadest, breathiest, fake Brit accent. *"Thank* you, *dearest* darling!"

I walked to Neiman-Marcus, known to some as Needless-Markup. The store was only a few blocks uptown from Snips, on the other side of Copley Square. The air was cooler than yesterday but still clean and breezy. It felt good on my face, like a moment in a country meadow. As I crossed Boylston Street, Boston's great east-to-west dividing line, I smelled rubrum lilies. I saw them swaying gently in cream and coral glory at an outdoor flower vendor on the corner. Their sweet bouquet, usually a cue for romance, only encouraged a heavy sadness now.

I began my little field trip in men's accessories, which is where my friend Eduardo works. Eduardo is from Costa Rica and a family of laborers. Here in the U.S., though, he portrays the deposed aristocracy. His skin is smooth and the color of hazelnuts. His face is set with a square jaw, hollowed cheeks, and dark brooding eyes that gaze from under a deep brow. He looks the model of Latin machismo, but he is, at heart, a *principessa.*

Eduardo strutted the floor as though he owned Neiman's, as though he were overseeing his private atelier. In truth, his wealthy older "patron" could probably have bought the store for him. But instead, he furnished Eduardo with a South End duplex condominium, a German convertible, and a robust portfolio of securities. "Is all in my name," Eduardo had told me one well-sodden night when I'd asked where Daddy was. (We'd just finished our second round under the sheets.) "But I can never live with him. We will kill each other." Nowadays I styled Eduardo's wavy black hair and he continued to flirt with me.

His burnished bronze face shone within the crowd of fashion-conscious men milling around the counters of ties, jewelry, cologne, and leather accessories. He saw me and called out, "Astan!"

"Querida!" I wailed.

Eduardo left his other customers and came to me.

"What you doing here?" he asked with a welcoming smile. He

wore an Italian suit of navy blue worsted wool, a white shirt, and a silk necktie of slate, purple, and silver stripes.

"I need your help, *bebe*."

Eduardo gave me a ladylike tap on the shoulder. "Oh you, Astan! You such a bad boy! Why I love you so much?"

"Because we think the same, always about sex."

"No! I never tink about asex!" But then we both broke up laughing.

"Eduardo, I'm looking for a certain cologne. I don't know the name. All I know is the smell."

"We have everyting you can buy in dis country. What it smell like?"

I winked back and said, "Like you. Mysterious and spicy."

He grinned, then fluttered his fingers over the display of bottles. A solid gold ring adorned one finger of each hand. One was set with a large marquis onyx and the other with an oval lapis lazuli. Finally his slender hands lighted on a bottle. "Maybe you like this? Is the most espensive one." He handed me the bottle, a triangular prism of frosted gray glass. The word *Orynx* had been etched into the glass in small Roman script. I whiffed it and felt its vapors go directly to the back of my neck.

"That would give me a hangover."

Eduardo wrinkled his nose and shook his head. "Smell like apoppers. How deese stupid people can buy dis ting?"

I could tell this technique for finding the cologne I'd smelled in Calvin's apartment would cause serious side effects on my sinuses. So instead of continuing, I leaned close to the counter and whispered, "Baby, I need some information."

"What you need, honey?" He rolled his shoulders and swayed his hips slightly. "You know *La Marquesa* can help."

"There's a guy named Aaron who works here."

Eduardo suddenly reared back and slapped me on the arm. "Oh, you bad boy! You cheating on me! That bitch is no good. You keep away!"

"Just tell me where he works."

"Why you want Aaron? He's mean."

"*Querida*, I just want to talk to him. It's about his lover. It's serious."

"Promise?"

"Eduardo, I don't even know him!"

His eyes shifted left and right as he decided whether to believe me. Then he said, "Hokay. I tell you. I tell you because I love you, Astan. He work upastairs in men furs." He pointed up to the mezzanine level, and as he lifted his right hand, a small gold watch with a lizard band peeked from under his monogrammed shirt cuff.

"Thanks, *bambino*," I said, and kissed him on the cheek.

"You such a nasty boy, Astan."

I headed toward the escalator. In my haste, I'd neglected to ask him what Aaron looked like. All I had to go on was Hal's description from last night. But it turned out real easy. I got up to men's furs and there were only two salespeople. One was a blond youth, eager to help me. He was pretty enough, but in my mind too young to be selling coats that started at five thousand dollars. And the other, the one assisting a customer into a full-length blue fox overcoat, was Aaron.

He was slender, around five-ten in height, but his long, lean legs made him appear taller. The hair on his small, finely sculpted head was cut close. He wore a dark gray pinstriped suit, hand-tailored and double-breasted, with a white shirt and bow tie. The bow tie was navy with bright red dots. It was knotted neat and tight. His eyes met mine, and even from fifteen feet away I could tell they were pale blue.

There was a knowing look, that moment when you recognize someone even though you've never met before. And then it happened. Aaron dropped the fur coat he was holding and bolted. I sprang to action on my Slavic locomotives and followed him, running and crashing through racks of furry jackets and coats. He ran through a door marked EMPLOYEES ONLY and I was right behind him. But once through, I faced a narrow hallway with four other doorways and no Aaron. He'd vanished.

I thought quickly. He'd have to have taken the nearest door to disappear that quickly. But that door opened onto a roomful of empty hangers and racks and office supplies, one desk, one chair, and no person. I tried the next door and it was locked. The third one was a stairway, which I took to so quickly that I almost tumbled down. I caught myself on the railing, then I smelled it, the familiar spicy scent from Calvin's bedroom closet. Immediately I recalled the image of Roger lying dead on Calvin's bed. That's the one, I thought.

The stairway led me back onto the main floor of the store, where Aaron could easily disappear, since he knew his way around. Eduardo saw me come out from the stairwell. He pointed frantically the direction Aaron had taken. I ran out of the store, but it was too late. I'd lost him.

Defeated, I went back to see Eduardo. He said, "I see him running out. So, you scare him good, eh?" He laughed and seemed pleased.

I was breathing hard. "At least now I know he's hiding something. And somehow he recognized me."

"And now I know what *you* looking for before." He thrust a bottle toward me that was as close to a large brown phallus as poor taste in marketing would allow. "Is call Adam Brun."

I smelled it. "That's the one."

Eduardo said, "Wait here, Astan. I find something for you." He dialed a number on the store telephone and spoke. "Hello, Gloria? Is me, Eduardo." He reminded me of a cat charming a mouse directly into its paws. "I know," he continued, "I just checking up on you, baby. Ha-ha-ha." Eduardo winked and nodded to me as he spoke into the phone. "Listen, honey, I need address for some person in the store. Can you do dat for me?" He covered the phone and whispered to me, "Gloria gonna help you. She tell me everyting in the store." Then he returned to the phone. "I know, honey, I sorry. I been busy. Hokay? It's Aaron in men furs. You know him." Eduardo scrawled something quickly on a sales slip. "Thanks, honey." He hung up and gave me the paper. "Is his address."

I looked at the paper. The street and number looked familiar, and in a moment I realized it was Calvin's address. "Thanks, Eduardo. At least I found out what he looks like."

"And what he smell like." His eyes twinkled. "Tell me, Astan, how come we never be marry?"

"Because I can't support your Eva Perón lifestyle."

"I don't care about that. You such a macho man."

I knew *that* was a lie. "Baby, when you put everything in my name, I'll marry you."

He flicked his wrist at me. "You such a bad boy!"

I left Neiman's feeling I was getting nowhere. And when I got back to the shop, I realized I'd forgotten Nicole's chocolate. Her response?

"I know you had a difficult night, Stanley, and that to forgive is divine. But to overlook this act of gross negligence would qualify me for sainthood."

She sent Ramon, one of the shampoo boys, out to get the forgotten chocolate. I didn't miss the twenty-dollar bill she slipped him as a tip, either. Oh, well. I was "family," so my favors came free.

It was just noon, but already I was frustrated and irritable. To top it off, the afternoon shooting session on the piers had been canceled. That meant my work wouldn't be appearing in the Sunday newspaper. (Just goes to prove that in my business, the breakthrough to celebrity or the toboggan to oblivion is a matter of whim, something on the order of a flea's fart.) The unexpected free time didn't compensate a bit. Strange as it may sound, I'd prefer to work when I've already planned on it.

I felt my crankiness growing. I plunked myself down at my station. As soon as Ramon left on his special mission, Nikki walked over and said quietly, "You had a visitor while you were gone."

"Who?"

"A sleek Italian cop."

"Lieutenant Branco?"

Nicole nodded approvingly.

"What did he want?" I asked.

"You're to call him immediately."

I picked up the phone and dialed the number he'd left, but Branco wasn't in. I left a message and said I'd call back later. Nicole sighed deeply and said, "That man is one hunk of Mediterranean meat. Is he yours or mine?"

I scowled at her. "He's straight."

"Ah, and such a long winter ahead. Perhaps I'll invite the lieutenant over for a warm, cozy evening. The fireplace hasn't been used for a while."

"Nicole, he's a cop!"

"Darling, nobody's perfect." She eyed me curiously. "Stanley, you're not jealous?"

"Doll, isn't it a bit gauche for you to want to date a guy who's eager to nail me with a murder charge?"

"I don't think he wants to do *that* at all."

"That's your nether brain talking, Nicole."

She twirled her pearls for a moment, then said, "Stanley, why did you lie to me?"

"What lie?"

"You told me your trip to Neiman's was police business."

"It was, kind of."

"The lieutenant didn't know anything about it."

"He wouldn't, since I didn't tell him. Nicole, I've made a big discovery about the police."

"How big is it?"

I faced her directly. "Doll, I can see you're in one of your swollen-moon phases, thanks to the lieutenant's visit."

"Stanley, you know that's physiologically impossible."

"I'm talking anatomy, doll."

"Don't be fresh."

"Don't be brain-dead."

"Just tell me then, what is this big discovery about the police?"

"I've decided that the best way to deal with them is simply to take matters into my own hands."

"Stanley, you're wrong. You have to work *with* them, not against them."

"But *they* suspect me! If I don't try to get myself off the hook, who's going to do it?"

"Stanley, you're blowing this all out of proportion."

"Nicole, you weren't there. I was. I am a suspect in Roger's murder. Remember? I told you last night. A *suspect*! Calvin is, too, but from what I can tell, they're only holding him for the drugs he was using."

"I'm sure they'll find the killer and everything will be fine."

"Thank you, Nancy Drew."

Just then Ramon returned with Nicole's chocolate. He was breathless from running, but he'd executed his mission proudly, like a loyal little dog. I half-expected her to say "Good boy!" and pet his head.

When he presented the fancily wrapped package, Nicole said to him, "Aren't you good!" and patted him on the head.

Psychic Stanley.

Ramon gave her some money, which was the change from the twenty-dollar bill. Then he quietly disappeared, and I was embarrassed at my earlier jealousy. Ramon, after all my doubts and suspicions, was still only Nicole's minion.

Nicole caught me eyeing the whole transaction, and she asked me slyly, "Would you like a truffle?"

I shook my head no.

She continued. "Stanley, I think you should stop this do-it-yourself crusade and cooperate with the lieutenant."

"Sorry, Nikki. It's equal-Steven. They follow the law. I follow my intuition. The more calcified they act, the more I want to prove my way is right."

"The temerity of youth."

"I'm not that young."

"Parts of you are."

I was certain that Nikki's new law-abiding morals were the results of Lieutenant Branco's recent visit, and her fickle allegiance only aggravated my bad mood. But then, some of my best ideas come when I'm in a morbid state of mind. (Must be another aspect of my innate Slavic perversity.) I needed to get out of the shop, and with an open afternoon ahead of me, I got a whim to go across the Charles River to Cambridge. I'd pay a visit to the offices of the Choate Group, Architectural Consultants, where Calvin Redding worked when he wasn't in jail.

5

DUST THE PLACE
FOR BLUEPRINTS

With so much time and the weather so cooperative, I risked taking the T to Harvard Square. (T is short for MTA, which is short for MBTA, which stands for Massachusetts Bay Transit Authority, which is Boston's ancient and chronically ailing public transportation system.) The Red Line subway has a station on Charles Street, and the best way there from the salon is through the Boston Public Garden. Even in the clear sunlight, everything in the garden showed signs of winter's impending gloom. Last night's rain had become a frost that killed what was left of the autumn flowers, leaving gray wilted blossoms on crunchy brown twigs. (Typical friendly fall weather for Boston.) Though the pond had not yet been drained, the Swan Boats were already drydocked for the oncoming winter, so the charm of the big white birds gliding their passengers serenely over the water was gone. Only the trees brandished a last flourish of life, with foliage streaked in blood-dense hues of orange, yellow, red, and green.

The walk along Charles Street was more pleasant, reminding me that Boston is at once quaint and modern. Real estate firms garnering commissions since the arrival of the *Mayflower* adjoined chic Italian *gelato* parlors; specialty brokers purveying Chippendale and Hepplewhite originals abutted trendy French *charcuteries*.

In the T station, the train arrived surprisingly soon, and the ride was fast and direct, unlike the usual interrupted journey with shuttle buses between stations along the route. Harvard Square was lively and full of students. The warm autumn sun encouraged many of them to don shorts and tank tops and even go bare-chested. I appreciated the tangle of legs and shoulders and faces of the more stalwart young Harvard men. After a brief loiter along Brattle Street, I got a cab. When I told the driver my destination, he said, "You goin' to the Choe-Ate Company?"

"It's pronounced Choate," I said. "Rhymes with throat."

"That so?" The cabbie snorted the viscous contents of his sinuses and swallowed hard. Then he swerved the car into the approaching traffic and we zoomed off. He continued, "That's where that faggot killer works, y'know?"

"Excuse me?"

"You seen the papers today?"

"Not yet." Actually I had seen the *Globe*'s tiny story, but I figured he'd speak more freely if I acted stupid.

"Oh, sure," the cabbie said. "It was in the *Herald* on the front page, the whole story about this fag killin'. Jeez, no one around here seen it. Don't anyone read the *Herald*?"

"Probably not in Harvard Square." I made a mental note to find a copy.

Suddenly we turned off Brattle Street and headed toward the Charles River, which I knew was the wrong direction. Then we made a series of sharp turns, as though we were in a maze. "Where are you going?" I asked. "It should be directly off Brattle Street."

The cabbie retorted, "Whaddya want? It's all one way streets and dead ends around here. I'm not tryna cheat ya." A dubious song, I thought. After twenty minutes of aimless swerving, we stopped in front of a high wooden fence of solid eight-foot planks painted a tasteful gray. The cabbie pointed to the fence and said, "It's in there. No cars allowed, so I gotta leave ya here." I paid him the exact amount and got out of the cab. He said, "Hey!"

I answered back, "I don't tip drivers who jack up the meter with extra mileage." He squalled off before I could even slam the cab door.

I followed the fence and found the entrance to the property. Inside was an immense three-story mansion from the late 1800s. The cabbie had lied. There was a parking lot, and it was filled with

German and Swedish luxury sedans. (Personally, I prefer the zest of an Italian roadster over those staid mobile lounges, but that could simply be my fascination with anything Mediterranean.)

I walked up a flagstone path bordered with neatly trimmed hedges. The pungent smell of recent landscaping reminded me of the persistent cedar and balsam aroma that lingered around Lieutenant Branco. There was also the smell of new paint, and once I got closer to the building, I was astonished to discover the whole structure was brand-new, not even a few years old. Talk about a trompe l'oeil!

The front entranceway was a big paneled double door painted bright red. I'd barely pushed against the right-hand door when it silently and automatically opened itself for me, and I entered a world completely contradicting the outside of the building. The interior was a cavernous skylit atrium surrounded by three levels of glass-enclosed offices. Two long, shallow ramps interconnected the three floors along each side of the building, and a glass elevator provided lift at the far end. Small trees and flowering shrubs were everywhere in sight, and the burbling sound of water cascading down a layered rocky fountain completed the effect of an enclosed tropical rain forest.

The receptionist was seated squarely in front of me as I walked into the open area. His simple desk—three slabs of oiled walnut, two vertical, one horizontal—allowed me a good look at his whole body. He was young, clean-shaven, and dressed à la preppy: khaki chinos, blue oxford-cloth shirt, silk rep tie, and soft brown Italian slip-ons with tassles on a low-cut vamp. Lavender argyle socks completed the look.

"Can I help you?" he asked with contrived politeness.

"I'm here to see Calvin Redding. The name is Harrington," I lied. "Carlisle Harrington."

The young man squeezed his thin lips even tighter and said, "I'm afraid Mr. Redding is unavailable today."

"But I have an appointment. He has some very important papers concerning my property in Dover."

The receptionist didn't answer me but pressed at a lighted panel built flush into the desktop in front of him. Then he spoke wearily into the air, and for a moment I thought he was talking to me. "A Mr. Harrington is here to see Calvin. Do you think you can help him?" I studied him closely and saw that he was wearing a nearly invisible headset and microphone. Then he said directly to me, "Ms. Doughton will see you. She's Mr. Redding's colleague."

Within seconds I heard a heavy door slam somewhere on one of the upper levels. I looked upward and saw what seemed to be an enormous eggplant wearing a tailored jacket and skirt emerge from an office on the second level. Rather than walk down the shallow ramp near her office, she waddled to the hydraulic lift at the far end of the building and descended that way. Then she hauled her bulky body the length of the skylit atrium toward me. She seemed bound and constrained by her tight purple business suit.

"Mr. Harrington?" She spoke with a low, rough voice, already out of breath from the slight exertion of walking.

I nodded. "Yes."

"I'm Jennifer Doughton. I work with Calvin Redding." Her voice sounded permanently hoarse from years of unfiltered cigarettes and bourbon. "You wanted to see him?"

I explained. "I'm remodeling a house in Dover, on Frog Pond Lane." (A wealthy client had once explained that the truly rich never refer to their domicile as a home. It's always a house, whether an English Tudor manor or a one-room-country-little-shack.) I went on, "The contractors are ready to work but they can't begin without the plans. Since Calvin is not available, perhaps you can open his office so I can get the papers."

She frowned and said, "That won't be necessary. We share the same office. I can find what you're looking for." She turned and I followed her. She stopped immediately and remarked, "There's no need for you to accompany me." Her voice was like the rasp of a dull file on hardwood.

"It's no trouble at all," I answered.

She paused and stared at me with suspecting eyes. When she finally moved her mass again, I walked alongside her toward the elevator. Annoyance appeared in her voice. "It's unusual that I haven't met you before. Calvin and I often serve the same clients as a team."

I chuckled casually. "Well, you see, Calvin is doing me a favor. We've been working on the plans for remodeling my house for quite a while, but most of the work has been done outside the office." Jennifer Doughton smirked, and I wondered if she believed me. I can usually tell by the eyes, but all I could see in hers was anger and hardness. She wasn't pleased with her life in this world.

We glided silently up one flight in the hydraulically controlled elevator. Once inside the office she and Calvin shared, she began a haphazard search through a big cabinet full of color-coded manila folders. Within minutes she was out of breath. She gasped heavily and said, "There's only one other place it could be," and she lumbered out of the office.

I saw my chance and I grabbed it. So what if one entire wall of the office was open plate glass and I was exposed? The question was, where to begin? I needed names and dates, so Calvin's calendar and phone directory seemed the logical places. But his desk was locked. Maybe he had everything computerized? I looked at the computer terminal near his desk. It was turned on, so I pressed a key marked ENTER. It beeped at me and displayed:

ENTER USER ID:

I typed Calvin's name, but that only caused:

USER AUTHORIZATION FAILURE. PLEASE TRY AGAIN.

I tried using his initials, then various combinations of his name and initials. Every try failed. I became frantic and typed anything, no matter how illogical. But all I got was beep-beep-beep. I was so engrossed that I didn't realize I wasn't alone anymore. What they say about big people being light on their feet is true.

"You need a password," she muttered hoarsely, directly behind me. Her voice startled me, but I covered my surprise.

"These computers are remarkable. I just couldn't resist trying it out." I turned in the chair to face her. "Maybe someday I'll learn how to use one."

Jennie said, "Maybe someday you'll come up with a better

story. There is no record of your contact with Calvin Redding. And furthermore, the property you described in Dover doesn't even exist. Now, would you like to tell me who you are and what you're doing here? Or shall I just call the police?"

I wet my lips and tried to speak evenly, though my heart was pounding. "I don't think we need the police."

"Then talk, mister, whoever you are."

After a horribly long silence, during which my cool pink skin had turned hot scarlet, I said, "Okay. I heard Calvin was in trouble. I'm a friend." My voice sounded dry and hollow, a sure sign that my nerves had taken over. It was mantra time. "I'm trying to get to his records and pull out any incriminating stuff before the police see it."

Jennie accepted this with a kindly smile. "How chivalrous!"

"So if I could just see—"

She snapped, "You're lying! I've worked with Calvin Redding for almost two years, and I know the kind of friends he has. None of them would be here trying to help him out."

"I'm not like the others."

She picked up the phone on her desk. "Patrick? Call the—"

"Okay, okay!" I pressed my finger into the phone cradle to stop the call. "The jig is up. I'm Calvin's hairdresser."

Jennie cackled. "You expect me to believe that!"

"It's the truth!" I snapped out a business card, but she ignored it.

"Look, mister, whatever you're trying to prove, you're too late anyway. The police have already come and gone. They've taken all of Calvin's papers with them."

Damn! That meant Branco had everything. "But I've got to find out what happened between Calvin and that guy who was killed yesterday."

Jennie brayed a raucous hee-haw. "I don't give a hoot about that. In fact, I hope Calvin's guilty!"

With those words everything between us changed. Suddenly big Jennie and I had more in common than I thought. "You mean," I said quietly and distinctly, "you'd like to see Calvin convicted?"

She lowered her eyes, and I noticed sadly that even her eyelids seemed flabby. My concern over "love handles" seemed a pathetic vanity compared to this woman's problem. Jennie said, "With Calvin out of the way my career might start moving forward again." She sounded almost sorry to have to say it.

"What do you mean?" I asked, benign as a father confessor.

She lit a cigarette. I was right—no filter. She filled her lungs a few times and left a soggy lip print on the cigarette end. (Nicole would have disapproved.) Then Jennie spoke. "Calvin breezed into town after touring Europe for a couple of years. He was supposed to be doing an apprenticeship over there, but it wasn't that at all. It was a vacation, the kind only people like Calvin can take."

"Meaning?"

"A lot of money, drugs, and sex."

"How do you know that?"

"I have ways of finding out things. Then he landed a job here as a staff architect. No drafting board for him, just directly to a staff title. And from there, he skips up to an associate's position. The title that took me ten years to *earn*, Calvin Redding got handed to him in less than two."

"Maybe he's just talented." I played devil's advocate just to keep her talking.

"Calvin Redding's talent hangs between his legs." Jennie's eyes were dark and mean now. "I'll tell you something, mister. There's a junior partnership coming up here, and Calvin and I are both in line for it. I've got the seniority and the proven past. I was working here when five people had to put in sixteen-hour days just to survive. I deserve that position!"

I gave her my compassionate therapist look, the look that meant, I understand. But I said nothing.

She went on. "The way Calvin sucks up to the boss, it's disgusting. And it's obviously just because Brickley has a name and connections."

"Who's Brickley?"

"Roy Brickley's the boss. But I'm talking too much."

"No you're not. Jennie, I wonder if we might be able to help each other."

She didn't answer but buried herself in a cloud of smoke. After a moment she said, "How can you help *me*?"

"I think we have similar hopes for Calvin's future."

"I thought you were trying to help him."

I shook my head so hard my hair fell out of place. "No way. I said that so you'd let me see his papers. I'm looking for incriminating evidence all right, but I don't want to protect him. I want to use it against him. I have a feeling he killed that ranger and I need proof."

"You change your story minute by minute."

"Jennie, the police suspect *me* in that killing, too, but I didn't do it. I've got to clear myself, and if it means convicting Calvin, well, that's fine with me."

An evil smile crept over Jennie's mouth. She wheezed heavily, then took a long drag from her cigarette.

"You don't like him much, either, do you?" she said.

"No, I don't. He exploits people. He thinks he's royalty. He doesn't do a thing for himself, much less for anyone else. He lies. He's cheap. He—"

"Okay, mister, you're convincing me. Maybe we *can* help each other."

A small victory.

"What do you need to know?" she asked.

"*Anything* about Roger Fayerbrock, the guy from Yosemite who was killed."

"How'd you know he was from Yosemite?" she asked.

"That's what he told me."

Jennie's eyes flashed on me. "So, you'd met him already?"

"Yes, in the hair salon yesterday."

She mulled this while she squinted at me through the acrid smoke. "All I can tell you is that Calvin brought him in here yesterday morning and bragged about the night they spent together. That was it."

"That's all? Nothing more?"

"I'm sure there's a lot more, mister, but one of the people who knows it is dead, and the other one is in jail."

I wondered who and where the rest were. "So this place *does* know Calvin's in jail?"

"Of course we do, but we don't go announcing it to our clients. It's not exactly a merit badge to have an associate in jail."

"Jennie, do you think Calvin could have killed Roger?"

"I wouldn't put anything past him."

"What would make him do it?"

Jennie banged her cigarette against an ashtray already mounded high with charred butts and dusty ash. "He probably said something honest to Calvin's face."

"But even Calvin wouldn't kill someone just for doing that. There has to be more."

Jennie closed her eyes, probably to keep the stagnant oily smoke out of them. "People have been killed for a lot less than telling the truth."

I nodded as though I understood, though I didn't. I offered her my business card again. "Will you call me if you think of anything else that might help?"

She took it in her plump, dimpled fingers and said, "I thought your name was Stan."

"I go by Vannos in the shop."

She wrote "Stan" on the card and slid it into the snug breast pocket of her jacket. "At least you got balls, which is more than I can say for Calvin's other tricks."

"Hey, don't get that idea! I never had sex with him. I never wanted to and never intend to."

"Another point in your favor."

"And thanks for not calling the police, Jennie. As I said, I'm already under suspicion, so I'm trying to keep out of their sight."

Her eyes had softened somewhat, and I got a glimpse of a keen intelligence working behind them. "Don't let the police bully you," she said.

I left her office and stopped near the reception desk to call a cab. While I was doing that, a handsome man walked by me. He looked like one of J. C. Leyendecker's Arrow Shirt men, but older, maybe fifty. He was in shirt-sleeves and slacks, both tailored to show off his muscular physique. I thought he looked damn good. He caught my gaze and he nodded politely. "Good afternoon," he said as he passed by. His cologne smelled like a citrus grove on a cool, dewy morning.

I overheard Patrick, the receptionist, say to him, "Mr. Brickley, that's the man who wanted to see Calvin."

Since I was the only other person around, I knew he was referring to me. I stopped my call and did a quick Dior turn to face the man. "Are *you* Mr. Brickley?"

He smiled cautiously. "Yes, I am."

I hung up the phone and went to him. Close up, I saw that his light gray slacks had subtle pinstripes of pink and apricot. A silk Hermès tie of slate blue and gold complemented a pale papaya-colored cotton shirt. "I'm a friend of Calvin Redding," I said. "I'd like to talk to you."

He paused a moment, unsure. Then he said cordially, "I'm sure I have a few minutes for a friend of Calvin. Let's go up to my office." He put his hand heavily on my shoulder. "What's your name?"

"Stan Kraychik."

He said, "That sounds Czech."

"It is."

We started toward the elevator, then stopped. "Why don't we take the ramps? That's better than the lift. I like to keep fit. Too many people these days are idle and don't appreciate the importance of physical activity and a healthy body. A healthy mind and a healthy body are codependent." Blah-blah-blah, he went. I sensed that his polished appearance was only the veneer over a suppressed chatterbox inside. I wondered what this physical culturist would think of my self-improvement campaign to learn to smoke.

His office was on the top level of the three-story building. Up there, through the top of the atrium, I could see part of a huge bank of solar panels facing southward on the roof. Most of the offices on that level had vertical blinds across the glass walls for privacy, unlike the offices on the second level, where all activity was exposed. Mr. Brickley settled himself behind a huge rosewood desk, while I sat in a comfortable side chair of the same rosewood, upholstered in mauve-colored leather.

He said, "How can I help you, Mr. Kraychik?"

"I'm trying to find out about a young man named Roger Fayerbrock."

Roy Brickley's face showed a flash of surprise that disappeared instantly. "I'm afraid I don't know the name."

"Perhaps you'd remember the face and body. Tall, light-haired, mustache, gentle voice. He was visiting from the West."

"Still no connection. What does this have to do with Calvin Redding?"

"I know that Calvin brought him here the other day, showed him around the place. I thought maybe you'd met him."

Mr. Brickley thought a moment. "Maybe I do remember him. You say he had a good build on him, eh?"

I nodded.

"I think I may remember seeing him."

"Do you know why he was here?"

Roy Brickley repositioned himself in his chair, then said, "I have no idea."

"You probably know that Calvin Redding is suspected of killing him."

The man pinched his mouth up, then spoke with a barb on his controlled words. "That's an outrageous accusation, especially of one of our associates."

"But it's true, Mr. Brickley."

He squirmed again and his chair creaked. Then he spoke with resignation, as though caught in a lie. "Yes, I know it's true, but it's only a suspicion, and I'm certain the police are wrong. The Choate Group believes, as I myself personally believe, of course, that such a thing is *not* possible."

"Of course."

"Nonetheless, I am distressed that one of our associates is in such a dire situation, since we *know* he is innocent."

"But—"

"I can personally vouch for Calvin Redding's character. My wife and I have entertained Calvin Redding on numerous occasions, and I can assure you that there is no possible way on this earth that Calvin Redding could physically harm another person."

It sounded like a statement prepared for the police and the reporters. I almost wanted to applaud, but instead I said, "It's too bad the police don't share your conviction."

Roy Brickley said, "I've already spoken with the police, and frankly, they don't even have enough evidence for a proper charge. They'll be dealing with Calvin's attorney shortly."

"For what?"

"Unlawful detainer."

"But Mr. Brickley, they do have evidence." A lie. "I've read the reports."

That stopped him. "How did you manage that?"

"It's public information, for a fee."

There was a loud knock on the door. Then it burst open and Jennifer Doughton hauled her massive bulk into the room. She jolted to a halt when she saw me, though her body rebounded a moment. She glared at me while she waved some papers and said to Roy Brickley, "These need your John Hancock before two o'clock."

He said, "Certainly, Jennifer. I'll see to it as soon as I'm finished here."

She turned and left the room, closing the door with a ponderous thud. Mr. Brickley said, "Well, as you can see, I'm a busy man, and I have quite a full schedule today."

I sensed that Jennie's interruption had broken the thread of our conversation, and that Roy Brickley was eager to be left alone, so I got up to leave. There's no reason in pressing people, especially if you might have to see them—and use them—again. I stood up and said, "Thanks for your time, Mr. Brickley."

"Not at all. I want Calvin absolved of this monstrous accusation as soon as possible."

"I'm determined to settle the matter, too."

He extended his hand, and I shook it. It was huge and strong. He said, as he held on to my hand, "By the way, how do you know Calvin?"

With no reason to lie, I told him, "I do his hair."

"Really! What a fortunate coincidence! My wife has been trying desperately to find a new hairdresser."

"There are plenty of us around," I said. "In my business you're either being discovered or discarded." His grip on my hand wasn't loosening.

"Calvin always looks good, and that's all the recommendation I'd need for your work. Where is your shop?"

"I have a card here . . ." I tugged my hand out of his, then got one of my cards. He took the card and examined it with his powerful fingers, like a boxer handling Venetian glass.

"Newbury Street. Good location. Near the Ritz, is it?"

I nodded.

"But your name isn't on here."

"I go by Vannos in the shop."

Roy Brickley wrinkled his forehead. "Why not your own name?"

"Stanley doesn't cut it in the world of fashion."

"Well, in the world of business, Stanley Kraychik would be a fine name. I hope we'll be meeting each other again soon."

"We probably will." I left his office and walked quickly down the two ramps to Patrick, the receptionist. "Can you call me a cab?" I asked in my sweetie-pie voice.

Patrick pressed his lips tightly together, then said haughtily, "There's one on the way, courtesy of Mr. Brickley." Was that jealousy I heard in his voice?

6

NO YOU CAN'T, YES YOU CAN

I got back to the shop around three o'clock. I walked by Nicole's table, where she was manicuring a customer. Without looking up or missing a single stroke of the emery board, she asked, "Did you see Lieutenant Branco?"

"Not yet."

"Well, Stanley, he called again. You're to report to him immediately."

"If it's so important, let him come to me."

Nicole laughed her gutsy laugh.

"What's so funny?" I asked.

"The cat-and-mouse routine you're getting into." She raised one eyebrow. "It's almost romantic."

"Don't project, doll. Your pelvic juices are backing up into your brain."

"Oh, Stani, admit it! You *do* find the lieutenant attractive."

"He's a cop!"

"You're evading the point."

"And you're projecting your libido onto me."

"I think you like him, just the teensiest bit."

"Get real, Nikki. I haven't had a date in months."

"Exactly my point, lover," she said, and laughed even louder than before. Her customer fidgeted uncomfortably, so Nicole laid down the manicure utensils. "Stani, if you could only see the look on your face!" she said with a squeal.

I looked in a nearby mirror and saw the usual puss: pink skin with the remnants of freckles, bright green eyes, reddish hair styled in a "regular boy's" cut, and a big mouth that fell easily into a dopey grin. The strong squarish bones and the mustache helped to counteract my tendency to fleshiness, or as I like to refer to it, my voluptuousness.

Nicole cried, "You're blushing like a third-grader playing Post Office on Valentine's Day." At this she shrieked, while her customer politely cleared her throat, but to no avail. Mirthful tears had filled Nicole's eyes.

"Be careful, doll," I said. "Your lashes might run, not to mention your client."

She shook her head through the spasms of laughter and explained, "This new stuff is waterproof."

"Any other calls while I was out?"

Nicole dabbed at her eyes. "*Whom* were you expecting?" She

emphasized the word for my benefit, which put her on the edge of another laughing fit.

"Just say yes or no, Nikki."

"Yes, darling. But he left no message. Said he'd call back." She resumed work on her customer's hands, applying heavy enamel to each nail in three expertly guided strokes from cuticle to tip—side, side, and center. "And, darling," she said as she dipped the brush into the creamy polish, "don't be cross with me. I couldn't laugh when I was modeling, but now I don't worry about wrinkles, and it feels so good."

"Especially at the expense of others."

"I wasn't laughing at you. I was laughing at your condition."

"You make it sound as though I'm pregnant."

The phone rang. The receptionist answered it and gestured to me. I picked up the receiver at Nicole's table and spoke into it, raising my voice an octave and applying a Southern drawl. "Stani's Curl-Up-N-Dye," I said breathily.

The voice was muffled and the line was noisy, but the message was clear: "Mind your own business or you end up like the ranger."

"Who is this?" I demanded in my normal voice.

"Just keep out!" Click.

"Hmph! Happy Halloween to you, too!" I slammed the phone down.

"Who was that?" asked Nicole.

"Someone with bad telephone manners."

"What did they want?"

"Nothing. It was just a crank caller."

Nicole continued manicuring her customer. "We get plenty of those."

I nodded. "No kidding. This one even tried to sound threatening, but it was halfhearted."

Nicole stopped her work. "Stani, are you serious?"

"Yes," I answered nonchalantly, not sensing any real trouble from the call. Then I thought a moment. They'd said "the ranger," so it was someone who knew I was involved in this mess. That narrowed it down to a specific handful. I asked Nicole, "Did we get the *Herald* today?"

"Oh! I meant to tell you about it. They've really outdone themselves this time. You're a costar with Calvin Redding."

"What do you mean?"

"Go read it." She nodded toward the newspaper rack in the waiting area. (Snips carries all the papers from Boston and New York on a daily basis. After all, theater folk from Manhattan want to read their "hometown" paper even while working in the provinces.)

I found the tabloidlike *Herald* all dog-eared and wrinkled. Today's edition had clearly been read throughout the shop. The caption was on the front page. It wasn't the main headline, but it was right under it. The writing was sensational and liberally interlaced with conjecture wherever the reporter had lacked facts. My name was there alongside Calvin's throughout. I looked like an accomplice. They identified my place of work, too. So much for privacy.

I returned to Nicole's station. "Business ought to pick up after *that* story," I said. "Why didn't they just write, 'Go to Snips and get your hair done by a murder suspect'?"

Nicole had finished with her customer, and the woman had departed. "Do you think she'll be back after our little scene?" I asked.

"Of course," answered Nicole. "She would never admit it, but she was thoroughly entertained by us."

"And that's part of our service here."

Nicole prepared her table for the next customer. "Stani, I'm concerned about that phone call."

"Nikki, considering that story in the paper, I'm sure it was just a stupid prank. Someone was playing 'scare the fairy,' and they had no imagination." I held the newspaper up. "Anyone who saw this could have made that call to me."

Nicole nodded. "That may be true, but what exactly did the caller say?"

"Just told me to lay off. And with the distortion, I couldn't tell if it was a man or a woman."

"Maybe now you'll agree that you should leave the detective work to the professionals. It might be safer."

"Nikki, I told you before . . . the pros are the ones who suspect me. Anyway, I don't feel any danger, especially from a call like that." I looked around the shop and noticed that Ramon, the shampoo boy, was absent. "Doll, I'm wondering. . . . *You* wouldn't by any chance have solicited someone—I'm thinking of a particular staff member—to make that phone call, just to put the so-called fear of God in me and get me off this case?"

Nicole looked offended. "Stanley! How could you! I'll confess to the occasional choreography of an event if it's not about to happen on its own, but I'd never stoop to something as common and cheap as an anonymous phone call."

"Then it was obviously someone with less class."

"Obviously. And I'm hurt that you could even think it."

"I apologize. But I know how much you want me to stop nosing around Roger's murder."

"True."

"But I need your support, doll, not another roadblock."

Nicole said, "I'm still hurt."

"And I apologize again, but, Nikki, honestly, I'm feeling so alone in all this, and I know it's only going to get worse."

"Then stop it all now."

"I can't. In for a penny, in for a pound."

"I'll pay you whatever it takes."

"Thanks, but money won't solve it. I suppose I ought to go see Lieutenant Branco now."

"Now *that's* a good idea! Work together with him."

"You're right doll . . . great idea! Play with the police!"

"I can think of worse playmates than the lieutenant."

"He'd be no fun, Nikki."

"How do you know?"

"He's the kind that never took his trucks out."

"What is that supposed to mean?"

"I'll bet the lieutenant was a very tidy tot, always afraid of getting his toys dirty."

Nicole cocked her head and arched one eyebrow. "Stanley, why do I get the feeling you're referring to something else?"

I winked at her and got my jacket. "Because I usually am, doll. I shouldn't be long."

"Did you check the book?"

"I don't have to. It's open, remember? My photo session was canceled."

"Well, make sure."

"Nikki, I'm sure!"

"In that case, take your time." Then her voice took on a lilt. "If the lieutenant wants to detain you for any reason, Ramon will help me close up."

Ramon, Ramon. Why was I bothered by Ramon? Was it because Nicole had sent him to Neiman's earlier for the chocolate I'd forgotten? Or because he was a sexy little Parisian who claimed to be bisexual? Or because I'd suspected him of making the phone call? Or because Nicole seemed to have a special interest in him? Was she tiring of me and preferring a younger confidante?

Nicole called after me as I left the shop, "Crabtree and Evelyn has ginger shortbread on special this week. Perhaps Lieutenant Branco would like a tin."

There it was again, that provocative tone of voice. "Sure, Nikki," I answered. "That's a lot butcher than flowers."

I heard her potent laugh as the door closed behind me.

I got a cab and headed across town to Station E of the Boston Police Department.

Station E was an old building that had been named an official historic landmark, so it qualified for city and state funds for restoration and preservation. Most noticeable in the recent work was the graffiti now gone from the noble Doric facade and columns. It had been sandblasted away, and the granite front had regained its ponderous authority.

I entered the building and strode by the desk sergeant, barely pausing in my airy rapid-fire delivery. "I'm-here-to-see-Lieutenant-Branco-he's-expecting-me." The sergeant didn't respond until I tried to open the door that led to the hall of offices. Then he snarled, "Come back here and state your business."

"I already told you, I'm here to see—"

"I heard what *you* said! *I* said state your name and the nature of your business."

I told him what he wanted to hear, while I silently reminded myself that the pushy technique I'd used in Neiman's and at the Choate Group didn't necessarily work with the police. He called Branco and told him I was there. Then he hung up and said, "You can go in now. Wait for me to unlock the door."

I went to the door without another word.

He said, "Did you hear me?"

"I'm to wait until you buzz me, Officer."

"You're kind of a smartass, aren't ya?"

"I am what I am."

After a long moment, during which I could feel the cop staring at my backside, he buzzed the door, but only briefly, as though trying to make me jump for it. When I didn't, he finally let me in. As I opened the door, I turned toward him and said breathily, "Thank you, ever so, Officer," then kicked up the back hem of an imaginary skirt and stepped through the doorway.

The hallway was wainscoted with natural mahogany, all stripped and refinished with clear shellac. Above that, the new plaster was freshly painted a grim pale ocher. Even my usual quiet footsteps clacked against the marble floor and reverberated against the shiny walls and ceiling. I found Branco's office and rapped my knuckles against the frosted glass panel set into the heavy oak door. From within I heard his strong voice order, "Come in!"

Branco's office faced the street. He was standing in profile near the window, looking through the top drawer of a tall file cabinet. His pleated trousers were nipped in closely at the waist and fitted cleanly over his haunches. I could almost see the sculpted hollows in his flanks. He didn't turn his head to acknowledge me but said brusquely, "Have a seat." I did. Then he said, "You been keeping out of trouble?"

"Oh, sure, Lieutenant. I never meddle."

Branco said, "I hope not." His voice sounded gruff. He turned his head toward me, then came and perched himself on the edge of his desk. One leg dangled precariously close to me in my chair. If this had been heaven, I would have nibbled on his calf, but instead, in the mortal world, I wondered yet again how Branco managed to smell like clean laundry in a pine forest. In a strange way, it was beginning to annoy me.

He brusquely intruded on my thoughts. "Care to explain the visit you paid to Calvin Redding's downstairs neighbor last night?"

"Are you tailing me?"

"Should we be?"

"It was just a social call."

"We happen to know that you met Hal Steiner just shortly before we arrived last night."

"So what? We were in the elevator together. Anything wrong with that?"

"Seems odd to pay a late-night visit to someone you just met."

"Oh, hell, Lieutenant, I couldn't help myself." I felt the fake Southern drawl creeping into my voice again. "There ah was in that cozy l'il ol' elevatah with a man all got up in leathah. What would *you* have done?"

Branco grimaced, shook his head, then continued. "Today we went to find Aaron Harvey for questioning, and the people at Neiman-Marcus told us that someone had already been there looking for him, someone whose description exactly fit your own." Branco looked at me sternly. "Now, it doesn't take advanced degrees in criminology to figure out what you're up to, Kraychik, and I want you to stop. Is that understood?"

"Sure, Lieutenant. Someone else just told me the same thing not twenty minutes ago."

"Who?"

"A charming disembodied voice on the telephone."

"Where?"

"At the shop."

"What exactly did he say?" His concern sounded almost genuine, or was he just using the crime side of his brain?

"I'm not sure it was a man," I answered, "but he said if I didn't keep my nose out of this, I'd end up like the ranger."

Branco thought a moment. "We'll get a trap on that line right away."

"Lieutenant, it could have been anybody who saw the papers. It's not that serious."

Branco slammed his hand on the desktop. "You don't know the kind of people you're dealing with!" After a moment's pause, he spoke more calmly. "We'd better get a trap on your home phone, too."

"Great. Does that mean you get to hear all my calls?"

"Mr. Kraychik, you don't seem to realize how serious this is. We're dealing with a killer."

"You have the killer in your hands. It's Calvin."

"Calvin Redding didn't make any phone calls today."

That shut me up.

"Now just keep out of this. And if you hear or see anything that might help us, you let me know immediately."

"Yes, sir! Except how am I supposed to hear or see anything if I'm cloistered like a nun?"

Branco heaved a long, exasperated sigh. "Look, what I mean is, you knew about Aaron Harvey. You should have told us about him instead of going to the store yourself and scaring him off. Now we've lost a key person."

"He'll turn up again."

"How do you know?"

"I know his type. He's a drifter. He'll go back to Calvin's place eventually."

"How do you know that?"

"Hal Steiner told me last night."

Branco grunted, then said, "That's all for now." He stood up and went back to the file cabinet as if to dismiss me.

"That's it? You just wanted me here to slap my hand?"

"I've got work to do."

"Okay. I'll go. Geez, your bedside manner is rough."

Branco snapped, "Isn't that the way your kind likes it?"

I answered quietly, "When you want to know about my personal life, ask me."

"I'll remember that."

Then the phone on his desk beeped. Branco picked it up, muttered his name, two yesses and a no, then hung up. "I've got to see the captain. You can go now." Branco's eyes darted from me to a packet of folders on top of the file cabinet. I caught the minuscule gesture.

"Oh, Lieutenant. I just remembered something important I have to tell you. I'll wait here for you."

He faced me directly with a serious look and said, "I'll be right back."

"No problem. I have time."

Branco picked up the folder from his desk—the one with my information in it—and left the office. Two seconds later I had the other packet down from the file cabinet and open on his desk. I pored over the police reports with laser speed, jamming the important points into my Slavic memory bank.

Found at scene of crime:

> One bow tie in toilet drain. [I remembered seeing two on Roger's body.]
> One crumpled glassine envelope containing traces of pure cocaine, also in the toilet.
> Leather luggage belonging to victim and containing miscellaneous clothing, toilet articles, and a rock climber's chock.

I wondered what a climber's chock was, then I went on.

Highlights of Calvin Redding's statement:

> Redding met Fayerbrock in a bar. They went to Fayerbrock's hotel. Next day Redding gave him the keys to his condo. Kraychik a witness to that. Fayerbrock went to Redding's place. Redding was back at work by 3 P.M. Left work at 7:30 P.M. Got home at 8 P.M. Kraychik was already in the apartment and Fayerbrock was dead on the bed.

"Son of a bitch!" I hissed, and continued reading.

Highlights of Harold Steiner's statement:

Aaron Harvey arrived at Redding's building around 2 P.M. Sometime after 7 P.M. a red-haired stranger arrived to see Redding. [That was me.] Later, police removed victim's covered body.

It was too bad Hal hadn't remembered the exact time I met him in the lobby. He would have been able to disprove Calvin's claim that I was already in his apartment at eight o'clock, which was actually the time I was leaving the shop.

Highlights of Jennifer Doughton's statement:

Redding brought Fayerbrock to Choate Group offices around 10:30 A.M. At 11 A.M. they left for lunch, during which Redding got his hair dyed. [Frosted, Jen, not dyed.] He returned to the office alone around 3 P.M. and left again at five. Doughton and Redding are amicable colleagues.

Fortunately, the police had been to the Choate Group before I had, so my visit wasn't in the reports, which is how I wanted to keep it. I continued reading.

Highlights of Roy Brickley's statement:

Redding is a major asset to the Choate Group. High-strung, but enormous talent. Future in the world of innovative architecture and design assured. Brickley was attending a convention of interior designers downtown between 2 and 4 P.M. Returned to Choate Group offices around 6 P.M.

The autopsy report:

Victim Fayerbrock is resident of Yosemite Village, California. Employed as a federal agent in the National Park Service. [The term *federal agent* had a coplike sound

about it, which surprised me.] Death caused by strangulation between 5 and 8 P.M. No drugs in bloodstream.
Rectum contained sexual lubricant, no trace of semen.
Victim had not achieved orgasm.

At least Calvin had played safe, I thought, but I wondered whether
he'd penetrated Roger before or after he killed him. I found some
other papers showing what else the police had found out about
Calvin Redding, including his lawyer's name: J. T. Wrorom. The
name reminded me of the musician and writer Ned Rorem, a gay
artist-hero. But what interested me was that four years ago Calvin
had been charged and found guilty of battery of a young woman.
He'd appealed the case, though, and was somehow acquitted. That
must have been just before he went to Europe, according to the story
Jennifer Doughton had told me. Shortly before that he'd been
busted for dealing cocaine and heroin in Provincetown, but he
pleaded incompetency from drug abuse and the charge was dropped.
One thing was clear—Calvin's past had enough active crime to
convince me that killing Roger was the next logical step for him. I
wondered how he was planning to slip out of this one, and I was
hell-bent on preventing it from happening.

Suddenly I heard footsteps coming down the hallway. I quickly
put the papers back in their folder and returned the packet to the top
of the cabinet, just seconds before Branco barged into his office. He
glared at me, then at the packet on top of the cabinet.

"Everything all right in here?"

I sat calmly in the creaky oak chair. "Sure."

"The captain saw you come in and wanted to verify something
he just heard about you."

"Didn't know I was so popular."

"Seems you were in Cambridge earlier today at the place
Calvin Redding works."

"Who told him that?"

Branco didn't answer me but went to the folder packet lying on
the file cabinet. He studied it carefully and lifted the cover, as
though looking for some clue of my mischief. "The captain believes
you might be Redding's accomplice, trying to cover his tracks."

"So he reads the *Herald*, too. Well, he's wrong. I'm trying to *clear* myself, and if that means convicting Calvin, so be it."

"Maybe you're just double-crossing Calvin Redding."

"Is that your idea? Or the captain's?"

Branco answered with a grunt. Then, for a few minutes, he stood silently at the file cabinet. I could tell something was bothering him. Something had happened after he'd left me to go talk with the captain. He sighed heavily, then spoke into the air, as though thinking aloud. "I'm not sure it's the right time to bring this up." He glanced again at the packet lying on top of the file cabinet before him.

"Spill your guts, Lieutenant."

After many minutes, Branco returned to his desk and sat down to face me. "I probably shouldn't even be discussing this, but there's no time and little choice."

"Throw caution to the wind, Lieutenant. I always do."

Branco toyed quietly with a pencil for a minute, thinking. Then he spoke. "I have a feeling, strictly personal, that this case might fade away unsolved."

"What!"

He nodded. "It's a feeling, but it's strong."

"Why?" I asked.

Branco paused, as though he'd already said too much but now realized he couldn't go back. "Let's just say that sometimes a case isn't given full attention because of the people involved."

"You talking protective immunity for someone?"

"I'm talking the captain doesn't feel too warmly toward the way some men choose to live."

"Meaning?"

The words came out of Branco's mouth haltingly. "You . . . Redding . . . the victim, Fayerbrock . . . all have a certain, er, common denominator, personality-wise, I mean." His eyes avoided mine. "You understand?"

"I'm not sure. You mean we're all success-oriented young men in the prime of our life?"

Branco grimaced. "It's beyond that."

"Make the leap, Lieutenant."

"You all three have a . . . You all like . . ."

"Flowers?" I said in my Helen Morgan voice.

Branco ran his hand through the dark springy curls on his head. "Jesus! You sure know how to get my blood boiling."

"Just say it!"

"He was gay! Fayerbrock was an officer of the law, but he was gay!"

"Lieutenant, job titles have no effect on the tendency. But I thought Roger was a park ranger, not a cop."

"National Park rangers *are* federal agents. And the death of another officer always involves everyone on the entire force to find the killer."

"Like a big family."

"Right. But somehow, in this case, that's not happening. Maybe it's because the guy was gay, maybe for some other reason. That's not clear. But from what I can see so far, this whole case is likely to vanish without an answer."

"But you don't want that?"

"I want to find the killer."

"You've got him already."

Branco shook his head. "No. We're holding Redding on a drug charge."

"But he should be charged with murder."

"We can't. His lawyer is ready to scream circumstantial evidence, so we can't hold him much longer without a proper charge. But what bothers me is that the captain isn't all fired up about it. He seems to be looking the other way."

"All because the victim was gay?"

"That's what it seems like."

"What happens when the case goes to trial?"

"It'll never get to trial without a suspect."

"So the justice system takes a major detour just because a murder victim was gay?"

Branco nodded solemnly. "It looks that way."

"But you want to pursue the case because it was another cop who was killed?"

Branco nodded again. "Except I don't like that word."

"Sorry," I said, knowing I'd have felt the same way if he'd used the word *fairy*.

Quiet seconds passed. Our eyes met.

"Lieutenant, why did you tell me this?"

"I had to tell somebody."

"So you trust me?"

"I don't know yet."

"So now what?"

"I want to continue the investigation on my own, but that means doing it without the captain's support, and I'm going to need all the help I can get."

"Aha! So you're wondering about asking a plebian from Boston's gay world—say me—for help. Am I right?"

"Yes," he said, sounding almost sorry.

"Then just say the words, Lieutenant. Some of us even understand English."

Branco sighed heavily, as though a tremendous task had been accomplished. "Your recent behavior, I mean the way you've been running around talking to people, could possibly bring information from your own community . . . information that someone like myself might not be able to obtain so easily."

"Have you ever wondered why that might be?"

"Look, this is hard enough to discuss without your constant wisecracks."

"Lieutenant, gay folks don't get exactly the same kind of police protection the so-called normal citizens do here. I mean, a few hours ago, I was a suspect in this case."

"You still are, technically."

"Damn it! Then how can you expect me to help you—do a *favor* for you—when you won't budge a micrometer in my direction? Why should I, Lieutenant? What's in it for me?"

Branco looked directly into my eyes. He'd learned somewhere early in his life that he could get what he wanted if he used his eyes the way he was doing with me at that moment. Then he said in a soothing, almost pleading voice, "Maybe between us, we can help change the way gay people are treated by the police in this city."

Cripes! A handsome Italian cop was resorting to common-vision persuasive tactics to get me to be his spy. What was I supposed to do? I averted my gaze, but it still didn't take very long to decide. With the willpower of a dandelion puff in the breeze, I figured, If I'm ever going to collaborate with the police, I might as well do it now, with Mr. Mediterranean here.

"Okay, Lieutenant. Say I'm interested. What's the deal?"

"It's simple. You just keep your eyes and ears open. Ask all the questions you want of anyone you want. When you find out something, call me immediately. But do *not* act on anything yourself!"

"So contrary to your previous admonitions, I can now meddle to my heart's content. Is that right?"

"No. Not meddle. Ask questions. Look around."

"But you won't try to stop me?"

"That depends."

"But I'm not a suspect anymore, right?"

"I won't look for reasons to book you, but I can't grant you immunity if sufficient evidence arises."

"It sure is a lopsided arrangement, Lieutenant, but if it means the pressure is off me, I'll do it."

"I'm only asking for your help. It's no more than that. You can call me whenever you have information, anytime, twenty-four hours. Here's the number for my private line." He handed me a card that read:

LIEUTENANT VITO BRANCO

HOMICIDE DIVISION

BOSTON POLICE DEPARTMENT

and showed his private telephone number. I took the card and remarked, "I suppose this seals the pact, eh?"

"I suppose so." He answered dubiously, as though he hadn't completely measured the risk involved. "One thing must be clear, though, Stan." I recognized the use of my first name to galvanize my trust. "This is all off the record. It's totally against regulations. The captain would have my ass."

Lucky captain, I thought. Then I took a bold step. I said, "Sure, Vito," just to keep us on an equal first-name footing. "I can understand that. You wouldn't want to be caught colluding with a gay hairdresser."

Branco winced.

"Lieutenant, what if Roger hadn't been a cop? Excuse me—a peace officer. What if he'd just been an ordinary gay person? Would you still want to pursue this case against the captain's wishes?"

Branco said, "Personally, I don't care how people live, one way or the other, as long as it's harmonious with others in society. The captain has his own opinions about what's right and wrong."

"How can you work for someone like that?"

"My job is to obey orders."

I thought a moment about what was happening and realized that a gentleman's agreement had transpired.

I got up and went to the door. "Well, I guess I'd better go dig up some Mata Hari drag."

"Just remember, I'll never admit to this discussion. If you spill any of this to anyone, I'll deny it. There'd be no question whose word would hold."

"I'll remember."

"You're on your own."

"Like any good spy."

With that, I left his office and headed back to the shop.

7

THE HORSE'S MOUTH

It was just after 5 P.M. when I got out of the station. I was about to hail a cab back to the shop when I noticed the rush-hour traffic was already petrified. There's nothing like being in a cab when the only thing moving is the meter. It would be quicker and cheaper to walk, so I did. The only problem was, with daylight saving time over, the sun had long since gone down, and I wasn't ready for the cold wind that blew around me, another reminder that Boston is a city where half a year is spent anticipating, enduring, or recovering from a phenomenon called winter.

While walking, I thought about what had happened in Branco's office. Two things bothered me. One was Calvin's report. He'd dumped suspicion on me simply by lying to the police. The other was Branco's cavalier attitude toward gay people, along with his mindless deference to the captain. As my annoyance increased, I walked faster, which helped dissipate the tension and also warmed me up. As an added consolation, the cars I passed on foot never caught up to me.

It was around five-thirty when I walked into Snips and Nicole jumped on me. "You're in trouble, lover-boy."

"Now what?"

She pointed to three glamorous young women waiting impatiently in the lounge area. With the photo session canceled earlier that day, I'd assumed my afternoon was free, and since I hadn't checked the book, I was solely to blame. I shrugged and went to the women. "Well, ladies," I whimpered like a pathetic puppy, "I apologize. I was in the South End and the traffic is hell." They smiled politely, if insincerely. "I'll be with you all in a minute." I went back to the desk, where Nicole gave me a look that implied I'd been up to no good. "Was the lieutenant happy to see you?"

"Cool it, doll."

"Oh, I'm cool, Stanley. But you're not."

"If you're referring to my highly charged aura, it's from the brisk walk back here in the cool evening air."

"I thought it was feminine hysteria."

"That is a sexist remark, doll. Gay men are prone to it, too."

I checked the book. One full color, one perm, and one highlighting. Yikes! With three jobs like that, I knew we'd all be at the shop until after seven o'clock. The only civilized solution was to make it into a party. I set the women up at three adjoining stations where I could work them in tandem, kind of like an assembly line. That way, my hands could always be busy on one while the chemicals worked their magic on the other two. Timing got a little tricky, but I managed. I am, after all, a professional. Later, when the critical work was done, Nicole brought out the liquor. The annoyance over my being late had completely vanished, and by the time I finished with them, the five of us were feeling pretty festive. All three women tipped me generously.

When they left, Nicole poured herself and me another drink and asked, "What *did* happen with the lieutenant?"

"Everything and nothing," I said. I didn't want to tell her yet about my special arrangement with Branco. I grabbed for her cigarette case, but she slapped my hand.

"Not tonight, Stanley. I've only a few left."

"What are friends for?"

"Anything but ruining perfectly good cigarettes. Now go on with your story." She lit a gold-tipped lavender cigarette.

"It's simple. Calvin Redding is trying to pin the whole thing on me."

Nicole blew the smoke out hard. "That's ridiculous!"

"I know, and I don't see how the cops are so blind to the kind of person he is."

"Dear boy, you have the advantage of being his hairdresser. You know things about him even his mother hadn't guessed."

"You may be right. But I'm not finding anything that's helping me clear myself. No matter whom I talk with, it's just more vagueness. I feel as though everyone is lying to me."

"Maybe they are."

"So, what do I do next?"

"Why don't you confront Calvin directly with his lies? Get it straight from the horse's mouth."

"In his case it's the horse's ass. But it's impossible. He's being held at Charles Street Jail."

Nicole thought a moment. "I'm sure they have visiting hours there."

I shook my head. "It's a jail, Nikki, not a Swiss spa."

Instead of answering me, she picked up the nearby phone, and, while holding the cigarette, called information. (Another Albright axiom of smoker's etiquette: Never rest a cigarette on an ashtray; either smoke it or extinguish it.) After a moment she said, "Charles Street Jail, please." Another moment. "The main number is fine, thank you." Then she hung up and dialed another number, and with a sultry voice she said, "Do you have visiting hours?" She might as well have been saying "Hey, there . . ." in a pickup bar. The rest of her conversation was interspersed with pauses. "You do? It's my nephew, Calvin Redding . . . Yes . . . He was arrested for drunken driving or something. . . . Adult Detention Unit? Thank you." Then she hung up the phone and said, "You're out of luck, dear. The visiting hours are from eleven to one."

"And since it's after seven . . ."

She inhaled deeply, then smiled mischievously as she let the last of the smoke curl out from her nostrils. "But they did say Calvin's attorney could go anytime."

We looked at each other, and I knew we were both thinking the same thing. I said, "Forget it, Nikki. I have plans tonight. My friend Wade has tickets to the ballet—"

"I'll call him with your regrets, Stanley."

"But, Nikki, I've never done lawyer drag before."

"Darling, it's easy. Just wear your dark suit and look harried. I even have an attaché case you can borrow."

"Not that pink thing with the loopy closures?"

Nicole looked down her nose at me. "*That* is my beach bag, Stanley, made expressly for me by a young designer in Nice. No, darling, I have a real attaché case." She went to the locked closet and came out with a fine cordovan case with soft handles. "It's from Mark Cross."

"Why do you have that?"

"For when I see my accountant. You're not the only person who understands the importance of the proper accessory."

"It doesn't matter, Nikki. I can't go through with this. Even if I do get past the guards, Calvin will tell them I'm a fake."

"Darling boy, Calvin will be so amazed to see you he won't say a word. Just make him believe you're there to help him."

"That's going to be a good act. He's only going to lie to me, anyway, so why bother?"

"You have to think positively, like a lawyer. If you help him, you get money. The more help, the more money."

"Is that what they call an affirmation?"

"Yes, darling. But in your case"—Nicole blew a huge cloud of heliotrope-colored smoke at me—"it's for free."

I picked up the attaché case and said, "Well, if I'm going at all, I'd better get going. Wish me luck."

"Call me if you need bail."

"For Calvin?"

"No, dearest. For yourself."

"Thanks, doll. That's a great send-off. Don't forget to call Wade about the ballet."

"Darling, I intend to go with him myself."

"That's swell, Nikki. What if I need you?"

"I'll inform my answering service where to find me."

"Enjoy yourself, then. Don't snore too loudly."

"I'll tell you all about it, darling."

I left the shop and headed home. I had a feeling that Nicole was purposely trying to undermine my commitment to the case. She knew I loved the ballet, and I knew she didn't care much for it. She wanted me off the case, yet she'd goaded me to visit Calvin in jail, while she took my place at the theater. She was in control, as usual.

Outside my apartment door I found a package from my mother

in New Jersey. Packed inside, as carefully as Fabergé Easter eggs, were homemade poppy-seed pastries, rolled and filled and shaped with my mother's very own hands. Though she had no idea I was involved in a murder case, I wondered if my mother sensed psychically that I was getting into "deep honey" these days. A gift from home meant she was thinking of me more than usual. I figured I'd enjoy the sweets as a reward later on, after I returned from my unpleasant mission at the jailhouse.

I quickly fed Sugar Baby, then changed into my charcoal gray three-piece suit. I looked great, but I did *not* look like a lawyer. Within fifteen minutes I was back on the street getting a cab to take me to the Charles Street Jail. A clunky old Checker stopped and I got in. When I told the driver where I was going, he said, "You don't look like you're dressed for jail."

"I'm seeing a client."

"You a lawyer?"

"Yes."

"Funny you're not driving yourself."

"My wife has the Jaguar tonight."

He let me off at the jail entrance. The bright lights within contrasted against the chilly darkness outside. I opened the door. It was like stepping out of the wings onto a stage. Too bad I'd hadn't rehearsed the part I was playing. It reminded me of those bad dreams where you have to perform something you know nothing about, like brain surgery on your mother.

Inside, a damp metallic smell greeted me. I walked deliberately to the front desk as though I belonged there, just like a lawyer. The cop behind the desk ignored me. I said, "I'm here to see my client, Calvin Redding."

The cop didn't look up from the sports pages he was reading. He just grumbled, "Sign in."

I looked around and thought, Sign in on what? There wasn't a piece of paper anywhere in sight, at least not one I could get to. I could feel panic rising in my shoulder blades, and I wanted to scramble the hell out of that place. Then the cop jabbed a clipboard at me. I filled in the form quickly, in the self-important way I imagined a lawyer would. My writing was completely illegible. The cop took it and examined it. He still hadn't looked at me. He swiveled in his chair and flipped through a file drawer full of folders and papers. Then he turned back to me with weary eyes and said, "I don't have your name here."

"I'm with the law firm that's representing him."

"What's the name?"

What *was* the name I'd seen on Calvin's police report? I could only remember J something. Seconds passed, and I knew it wasn't going to come, so I had to resort to the only thing I could think of. I had just begun to say "Stanley Kraychik" when Ned Rorem's handsome face suddenly popped into my mind, and the name "Wrorom" appeared on my tongue. It came out all together— "Sta-rorem."

The cop behind the desk said, "Huh?"

"It's Wrorom," I said with perfect elocution.

"Rome?"

"J. T. Roar-rum," I repeated, even more distinctly.

The cop twisted his head and gazed at me with a suspicious bureaucratic eye. Then he picked up the phone and dialed a number. "I got a guy here says he's a lawyer. Wants to see Redding in cell twenty-eight-B. Yeah. Hang on." He looked at the form I'd filled out, then squinted at my illegible writing. "I can't read the name here."

"It's Wrorom!" I screamed, trying to jam his Neanderthal logic circuits with my lawyer's persona.

"Okay, mister, okay." He said the name into the phone, then hung up and turned to me, still avoiding my eyes. "Ya seem kinda nervous, Mr. Rome. Have a seat there."

What would a lawyer do? Sit or stand? I decided to stand, and also realized it was good that I was so nervous. Who ever heard of a relaxed lawyer? After all, my client's life and my fee were at stake.

Then a big metal door opened and I heard a voice call out, "Rome?"

I walked to the door and met the guard who'd called my name. His badge said Sergeant Vadrone. He was young and dark-haired, with a brutish face and brown eyes. When he spoke to me, I thought he might smile and dissolve all the hardness about his face, but he didn't.

"You here to see Calvin Redding?"

I nodded.

"Follow me." He led me to a tiny room with glaring bright fluorescent lights. It had no windows and only the single door I'd come through. "Wait here," he ordered. A few minutes later he returned with Calvin. The guard asked him, "This your lawyer?" By the look in Calvin's eyes, I thought he would tell the guard who I really was. I returned his gaze and gave my head an imperceptible shake no.

Calvin said sullenly, "Yeah, that's my lawyer." The guard left us alone in the room.

Calvin muttered, "What do you want, Vannos?"

"That's a pretty lousy welcome, Calvin, considering I'm trying to get you out of here."

"Like hell. Where did you get my lawyer's name?"

"A little bird told me."

"Who?"

"I have my sources."

"Well, you ought to verify your information. My lawyer is a woman."

With sexist stupidity I'd presumed otherwise.

"Now, what do you want here?" he asked.

"Calvin, I told you, I'm trying to help."

He just glowered at me.

I said, "I think the police may have made a mistake."

"That's not what you thought last night."

"I was upset. I said things I didn't mean. And besides, I talked with your downstairs neighbor, and he says he remembers when you came home."

"So?"

"By his reckoning and the coroner's report, Roger was already dead when you got home. He's given you a perfect alibi."

"I don't need an alibi. I'm in here for a bogus drug charge, not murder." He looked at me suspiciously. I could almost sense him wondering whether I'd seen his report, the one that implicated me.

"Of all the people who might help me, you're the last one I'd expect."

I recalled Jennie Doughton's similar sentiments earlier that day. "Calvin, I'm helping you because you're a client."

"There's got to be more to it than that."

I gave him my heart-to-heart look. "I want to find out what happened to Roger. I want to know who did it."

"Why?"

"I just do." I felt smarmy discussing Roger, especially since Calvin was my own favorite for suspect number one. "When I found him dead, Calvin, I got irrational and thought you did it. But now I realize I was wrong, and I'm sorry. But I also realize you can help me find the truth. You were with Roger. You knew him."

Calvin shook his head. "You're so sentimental it's sickening."

"If it helps get you out, what do you care?" But I was thinking, I may be sentimental, pal, but I'm passing the noose back to you to get *you* convicted for what you did.

Calvin sat back and said, "Do you have a cigarette?"

"Uh, no." Damn! There he was, just about to cooperate, and me without cigarettes. "Maybe the guard—"

"Never mind!" He leaned forward again and spoke slowly through his teeth, as though talking to an obstinate child. "I already told the police the whole story." Then he paused, bothered about something. "Have *you* talked to them?"

"Yeah . . . ?"

"What did they tell you?"

"The police aren't exactly chatty, Calvin. That's why I'm here. I'm free and you're not, and face it, the police aren't going to help you the way I can." (What a line!)

"My lawyer is helping me just fine."

"But my services come free."

"Nothing is free for me."

My nice-guy act wasn't working, and I sensed I was losing my chance to get some facts out of him. Direct questions, that's what I needed.

"Calvin, who has keys to your place besides yourself?"

"No one."

"What about Aaron? I heard he comes and goes whenever he wants."

"Who *have* you been talking to?"

"I told you . . . Hal Steiner, your downstairs neighbor. Has he got keys, too?"

"What if he has?"

"Then he's a possible suspect along with Aaron."

Calvin put his chiseled face close to mine, too close. His breath smelled of artificial coffee creamer. He seemed to think the room was bugged, and looked around to make sure we were still alone. He whispered, "Aaron's not involved in this."

"How can you be sure? He could have gone up to your place, found Roger, and killed him in a jealous rage."

"Aaron's not the jealous type."

"Then maybe there was some other motivation. Where can I find him, Calvin?"

"What do you want him for?"

"Just to talk. Find out what he was doing that day. Calvin, he could be the killer. Why are you protecting him?"

"I'm not." Calvin watched me for a moment. It was clear we didn't trust each other. We had no reason to. But I figured that eventually he'd blurt out some atomic particle of truth, and I'd have something to go on. "Okay," he said, "you're right on one count. *Someone* did it. It wasn't me, and I don't know who it was, but maybe Aaron knows something. Maybe it even *was* him. But where you'll find him depends on who he's using." Whom, I thought, with a nervous tic. Calvin continued, "He works at Neiman's and sometimes he teaches jazz dance."

"Where does he teach?" My ex-lover was a *ballerino*, so that caught my ear.

"Wherever they'll hire him. He's all over town. Just don't tell the police."

"Why not?"

"He's already in enough other trouble with them."

Those little bits went into the old Czech data cruncher. Then I said, "Calvin, is there anyone who might be trying to frame you?"

Long pregnant pause. "No one. Why?"

"No one at work?"

Calvin scowled and spoke to me with slow staccato words, as though English were my second language. "This. Has. Nothing. To do. With. Work."

Point made.

"Okay, then answer another question. Why did you try to get rid of the ties on Roger's body?"

"Who told you that?"

"I read it in the police reports."

"I thought you said the cops didn't tell you anything."

"They didn't. I read the reports myself."

"All of them?" he asked nervously.

"Yup," I said. Calvin squirmed in his chair. Now he knew I'd read the lies he wrote about me. "So, Calvin, why *did* you try to flush the ties with the drugs?"

"Those were my fucking ties! If the police found them—"

"But they did find them, Calvin. You only dug yourself in deeper."

"I didn't do it! I don't know who did, but when I find out—"

"Nip it, Calvin. Why don't you just tell me what really happened and put the whole matter to rest."

"You're completely off the track."

"The guy is dead, Calvin! And I'm still wondering how and why you did it."

"I'm telling you, I didn't kill Roger! I came home and he was dead on the bed."

"And to celebrate, you just so happened to slip it to him from behind. Was he already dead when you put it in?"

"What are you talking about?"

"The autopsy report says they found lube in Roger's rectum. Someone had something up there."

"Maybe he used a dildo."

"Come off it. What happened? What else did you flush down the toilet? A used condom?"

Calvin got up and called the guard. "Take me back to my cell!"

"What goes around comes around, Calvin." The guard came in and led him away. I yelled after them, "And I'm helping yours come around!" But they'd already disappeared into the bowels of the prison.

When the guard returned to escort me back out, he said, "I thought you was his lawyer?"

I feigned grave disappointment in my voice. "I was."

"Wha' happened?"

"He lied to me." I shook my head judicially, like Perry Mason. "How can I help him if he betrays my trust?"

I walked home from the jail. I needed the physical activity to relieve the tension of performance. All I could think was, What a wasted effort! And I'd missed the ballet because of it, too.

It was cold and dark now, almost like the middle of winter, and it was only the end of October. As I crossed the last intersection before my block on Marlborough Street, a car revved its engine, the typical sound of a desperate Boston driver trying to get a motor going in the cold. That's what I thought until I heard the squeal of rubber and saw the car coming toward me. I froze in the crosswalk, blinded by halogen headlights. My legs were heavy and immovable. Two tons of metal raged toward me, but it all seemed to happen in slow motion. I could almost make out the marque on the car hood when a voice inside me screamed "Jump!" I pushed with every erg of strength in my legs. I was midair when the car sped by, then I crashed down to the pavement. I watched from the cold, hard ground as it swerved onto Storrow Drive and out of sight. "Asshole!" I screamed. I didn't even think to get the plate number. I was too relieved to be alive, and I thanked my springy Slavic limbs for saving me.

8

A GIRL FROM THE GOLDEN WEST

Next morning, Friday, I wore a long-sleeved shirt and bow tie to the shop. The sleeves were to hide the ugly scrapes all the way up my left forearm where I'd fallen on it last night, trying to avoid the reckless driver. The bow tie was . . . well, I had my reasons for wearing that. Nicole asked, "Is *that* this year's Halloween drag?"

I smirked. "No, doll. I'm just trying a different look." She wasn't convinced, and as I scanned the appointment book, she noticed the cuts on my hands.

"Stanley! Are you dealing with rough trade?"

"Nothing so interesting, Nikki. Just guerilla warfare with a Boston driver." I explained what had happened.

She said, "Did you report it?"

"No. I didn't get a make on the car or the plate number."

"So what? I want you to call Lieutenant Branco right now. Stani, that was almost a hit-and-run. You could have been killed!"

"Nikki, it's a thin line between life and death."

"Is that today's uplifting thought?"

"How was the ballet?"

"We left at intermission."

"With Rubinskaya dancing!"

"It was her understudy, darling."

"That's a consolation, at least. I guess even an *assoluta* gets tired of those white feathers."

I was booked solid all morning with difficult perms and complex multicolor work. When I'm that busy is usually when I get walk-in requests as well, and sure enough, within an hour a gray-haired woman walked in for a wash and set. I overheard her talking with Nicole at the reception desk. She was tall and full-figured, with just the slightest stoop in her shoulders. She looked in her late fifties, and her unwrinkled complexion and alert eyes indicated that her life, or her attitude at least, was not toilsome. Her voice warbled slightly as she spoke. "I want to have my hair done, and I'm to see Van . . ." She faltered and Nicole came to her rescue.

"You must want Vannos."

But the woman ignored Nicole's help and fumbled around in her purse. "Wait a minute, wait a minute! I know I have that card in here."

Nicole said, "It's no problem, Madam. I know who you mean. Just tell me your name and I'll check you off in the book."

The woman muttered random thoughts as she stirred about in her purse. "Now where did I put it? Oh, I don't have an appointment. I know it's in here."

Nicole looked concerned. "If you have no appointment, Madam, I'm afraid our walk-in business is Monday through Thursday only."

Finally the woman found the card. "Here it is! I knew I had it!" In victory, she waved the card in front of Nicole, then read it carefully. "I want to see Mr. Vannos. Is that right?"

"The 'mister' is often dubious," Nicole said, and looked to see if I'd overheard her.

I scowled back as I loosely rolled a long strand of blond hair for a body wave I was working on.

Nicole continued, "Madam, I'm sorry—"

"Yes, well my husband gave me this card. So here I am, and I'd like to have my hair set by Mr. Vannos."

"Madam, I understand!" An impatient edge had crept into Nicole's voice. "And Monday through Thursday that would be fine. But today is Friday. You need an appointment."

"Ohhhhhh." The woman sighed, suddenly crestfallen. "You mean I have to come back another time?"

I excused myself from my client, then swooped to the reception desk and faced the woman directly. "Are you Mrs. Brickley?"

"Oh!" she said, caught off-guard. "You surprised me!"

"Forgive me. I overheard you talking just now. I'm Vannos."

For a moment her eyes were confused. Then she remarked, "So *you're* the young man!" A moment later she smiled, almost like an afterthought. "Well, aren't you nice!"

From behind her, Nicole mouthed the words *Aren't you nice*, smirking as she did it. The woman continued, "I'm Vivian Brickley, and this woman says I can't have my hair done today."

Her eyes didn't quite focus on mine. She seemed to be looking at my ears. Perhaps she had ocular problems, or perhaps she was timid, or perhaps she was hiding something.

My voice slipped into its gentlest murmur. "Why don't you have a seat, Mrs. Brickley, and I'll see what I can do."

"Why, thank you. What a pleasant young man!"

Again Nicole mimed the words with a saccharine smile behind the woman's back. As Mrs. Brickley sat down, Nicole mumbled to me, "If she saw your act at Chez-Chez tonight, would she hold you in such high esteem?"

I retorted sotto voce, "Fishnet hose and pumps once a year do not a drag queen make. Nikki, she's married to Calvin's boss, and she may know something. I've got to squeeze her in."

"Stani, you are already overbooked with three people in the next hour."

"I can handle it, Nikki. It's only a shampoo-set."

"With that hair? That's a job for pin curls if I ever saw one."

"Watch today, doll, as Vivian Brickley discovers the wonder of the soft set."

"I'll have Ramon shampoo her."

"No! I'll wash her. Just tell him to get her into a robe." I wanted every moment of the woman's time to myself. Besides, I didn't appreciate Ramon's help lately. When he'd started as a shampoo boy, he knew his place with the customers. But once he'd gained Nicole's confidence and had a few clients of his own, I caught him occasionally courting my regular patrons.

Ramon escorted Mrs. Brickley to a dressing room. Meanwhile

I finished rolling the body wave I was working on. I put her under a dryer, then went to Mrs. Brickley, who was waiting in the shampoo area. As I approached her, she said, "Who is that woman at the desk? She almost kept me from having my hair done."

"She's the manicurist, but sometimes she forgets and thinks she owns the place." Nicole overheard me and looked up from her work. I winked back to assure her that her secret was still preserved.

I was guiding Mrs. Brickley to the shampoo sink when she suddenly balked. She seemed afraid of it. "I don't much like those things. They always give me a crick in the neck." I assured her that she'd be comfortable in this one. I padded the notch in the sink with a thick folded towel, so when I laid her head onto it, she said, "Oh, this *is* comfortable. You have a special touch, young man."

"I know," I said honestly, and proceeded to wet her hair. Its texture seemed a little dry, so I chose a moisturizing shampoo from the rack. As I massaged her scalp under the creamy lather, she giggled and remarked, "It smells like a strawberry patch, reminds me of growing up in California."

"Is that where you're from?"

She giggled. "I guess you could say that I'm from all over the world. I traveled a lot in my years."

"Vacations are nice," I said, trying to recall my last one.

The giggle continued. "They weren't vacations. They were assignments. I was a teacher in the foreign service."

"That's impressive!"

Mrs. Brickley laughed. "Oh, it was just a job. I wasn't one of the bigwigs. There was always that barrier between the diplomats' lives and mine."

I rinsed her hair and applied an almond-scented conditioner. She remarked, "I'm going to smell like a regular fruit salad by the time you're done with me." I told her the scent would barely linger. Then I rinsed her once more and wrapped a towel around her wet hair. I supported her head as I helped her up from the sink, and the simple courtesy seemed to surprise her. She giggled again and said, "Thank you! Usually they just leave me to grapple my own way out of the sink." Her word choice amused me.

I led her to my station. When she saw herself in the mirror, she chuckled. "I look like Mata Hari with a turban."

"When I'm finished, you'll look like a duchess."

But her words reminded me of my espionage agreement with Branco. For an instant I wondered if someone as mirthful as Vivian Brickley could be playing the same part for someone else.

I asked her if she wanted something to read while I briefly tended to my other client. Instead of answering, she pulled a copy of *The New Yorker* from her bag. "I always carry it with me," she said with a titter. I left her alone while I neutralized and rinsed the body wave, perhaps a little too quickly, but I was eager to get back to Mrs. Brickley.

When I returned to her, I began my work by combing and separating her hair into sections that would complement her features and the shape of her head. As I grabbed the first roller, she said, "Oh! Aren't you going to use pins?"

Damn Nikki! She'd pegged the woman right off.

"I'd like to try something different," I answered boldly, and oblivious to her concern, I rolled a lock of her hair around an anodized aluminum tube.

"But my other hairdresser always used pins."

I'm not your other hairdresser, I thought, and I don't have the time or the desire to do pin curls today. But I spoke secretively near her ear, "For you, Mrs. Brickley, I see something more daring, like an understated adventure."

She tittered again. "I must say my husband was right in recommending you to me. I don't remember when I had this much fun at the hairdresser."

I continued rolling her hair up. "Did you meet your husband on one of your trips?"

"Goodness, no! Not at all. He's spent just about all his life in New England. Doesn't like to travel."

"That must be awkward, since you seem to like it so much."

"It hasn't come up yet, actually. We've only been married, well, it's not quite a year yet. I guess you'd call it an autumn romance. We're still working out the kinks." She laughed.

"I can't imagine anyone having difficulty getting along with you. You're so cheery and optimistic."

"Well, I had doubts about marrying so late in my life, especially the first time, and to a *younger* man." She chortled now. "It's almost scandalous!"

I pretended to join in her laughter while Nikki mimed me with a mocking grin on her face.

Mrs. Brickley continued more quietly. "Of course, I'm jesting. Roy is not a *young* man by any means."

"He certainly appears youthful."

"Oh, heavens, yes! He loves to exercise. His physique is excellent. I'm sure he could have married a woman half his age, instead of one eight years older. . . ." Her voice trailed off with a doubtful, bewildered sound. "Of course, we *are* very happy . . . except that Roy has this idea to retire out West in a few years. I'd just as soon stay here in New England. We have a barn of a house in Cambridge and it's a perfect base for my wanderlust."

"If you can travel six or eight months of the year, Boston is a great place to live."

I continued wrapping her hair in rollers, and she read quietly for a few minutes. Then I asked her, "How long have you known Calvin Redding?"

"Oh!" she exclaimed as though I'd startled her. Then she answered calmly, "I met Calvin shortly after I married my husband last year, but I gather they'd known each other long before that. And you?" she asked.

"Calvin's been a client for about a year."

She put her magazine down. "And my husband?"

"Your husband what, Mrs. Brickley?" I didn't understand what she meant, and when I checked her reflection in the mirror, she looked displeased about something.

"When did you meet *him*?" she asked with a tinge of crossness.

"I just met him yesterday."

"And that was through Calvin?"

I paused, wondering what she was fishing for. Then I said, "Yes . . . indirectly."

"I see," she said, sounding unsatisfied. "*Where* did you meet him?"

"Calvin?"

"No, my husband!"

"At his office." Then, anticipating her next question, I said, "And Calvin was referred by a fashion model who is a longtime customer."

"I see." She seemed relieved to hear that, and everything else was sugar cake from then on. "Well, young man, I think it's admirable that you want to help Calvin Redding. It's absurd that the police suspect him of anything."

I lowered my voice to imply we were trading inside information. "I'm going to do whatever is necessary to find who killed Roger Fayerbrock and why."

Vivian Brickley adopted my hushed tone. "If there's any way I can help . . ."

"I'll remember that," I whispered back. Then I raised my voice back to a normal level and asked, "What part of California are you from?"

"My family is from Sacramento, but we have land in other parts of the state, too. Have you ever been out West?"

"No, but I want to go sometime."

"You really must. It's beautiful. Just being out there seems to expand the mind."

I didn't realize then that a subliminal suggestion had been planted. I wrapped the last roller. "There! You're ready for the dryer."

"Already? That's so much faster than pins."

"And even more effective, as you'll soon see." I called Ramon to put her under a dryer as I began working on my next customer, a color and cut. Mrs. Brickley would be ready for combing out in twenty minutes, which gave me just enough time to finish client A and apply the color to client B. Fortunately for me, client C was late, as usual, and hadn't arrived yet.

When Mrs. Brickley was dry, I quickly combed her out while she read quips from *The New Yorker* about improper English usage. I finished with a "sprunch" of soft-hold hair spray and said, "*Voilà!*"

She looked up from her magazine into the mirror. Her jaw dropped, and for a moment I was afraid I'd gone too far with her hair. But then she smiled and said, "Why, it's the way I've always wanted my hair done, but nobody's ever succeeded. Aren't you clever! You deserve an accolade for your work."

I appreciated the fifty-cent word, but all I'd done was use the natural springiness of her hair to find the best direction for the waves, rather than force them into submission with tight curls. I'd have to admit, for a mature woman, Vivian Brickley looked damn good, due in part to my ministerings, of course.

She got up from the chair and patted her hair. "It's so soft, too. Kudos to you, young man. I think I'll take myself to lunch now and read the rest of my magazine." She gave me a good tip and said, "That's a fine bow tie you're wearing." She left the shop in high spirits.

Within minutes Nicole came by my station. "Find out anything from Matron Jolly Jowls?"

I related the basic facts: Vivian Brickley was a retired private teacher, she and Roy Brickley were almost newlyweds, she came from the West, and she liked to travel.

Nicole pressed me. "That's all?"

"Well, she seemed very interested in knowing how I'd met Calvin and her husband. She suspects somebody of something, but I don't know whom or what."

"I'll tell you what I think, Stani. I don't trust the good-natured, doddering-older-woman act a bit. It's just a ploy to get what she wants."

"Nikki, that is an agist remark!"

"Open your eyes, darling. Vivian Brickley and I are the same vintage. Now, imagine us standing side by side. Which one would *you* believe on the witness stand?"

"Doll, don't put me on the line like that."

"Oh, you!" Nicole huffed impatiently. "She didn't fool *me* one bit!"

I went back to work. A few hours later, when I finished my last midday appointment, I had the receptionist call a cab for me. "To Cambridge!" I yelled across the salon.

Nicole heard me and glanced up from the fingernails she was covering with frosty peach-colored enamel. "Where are you off to now?"

"Back to the drawing board." I wanted to nose around the Choate Group some more, maybe find out why Mrs. Brickley was so interested in how I'd met Calvin and her husband.

"Don't forget your four o'clock appointment with Mr. Channel Eight."

"How could I miss my favorite butch anchorman?"

I grabbed my leather jacket and bounded out of the shop. When the cab pulled up, I told the husky driver my destination and handed her a twenty-dollar bill. "That's your tip, hon. Pedal to the metal!" She moved the cab through Newbury Street traffic like a Maserati and slid us onto the entrance ramp to the Massachusetts Turnpike. I quietly studied her close-cropped hair and the hint of a mustache on her upper lip while we broke the speed limit all the way to the Cambridge exit. From there I directed her to the Choate Group. When I got out of the cab I said, "If you wait here, there's another twenty to get me back to town on the same magic carpet."

Her work shirt had the name Bob stitched onto the pocket. She said, "You got a deal." Then she turned off the motor and pulled out a copy of *Leisure Life* magazine.

Today, Patrick, the receptionist, almost smiled at me. "Here to see Ms. Doughton again?"

"Exactly." I wondered what drug had caused his upward mood shift.

He beamed and said, "Your name again please?"

"Kraychik." I pronounced it clearly, "Stanley *Kraychik*."

Patrick looked confused. Perhaps he was remembering that I'd been Carlisle Harrington yesterday. "And you're to see Ms. Doughton concerning what matter?"

"The same as yesterday."

As he pressed buttons to call Jennie, I said, "That's all right. She's expecting me." I walked by his desk into the skylit atrium and went directly up the ramp to her office.

I stuck my head in the door to her office and asked, "Got a minute?" The air smelled of recently chewed peanuts.

"What do *you* want?" There was a wheeze in her voice, probably from large quantities of goobers consumed without a suitable beverage.

I said, "I got to see the police reports yesterday."

"So?"

"The story you told them and the story you told me don't agree."

She shrugged.

I said, "I want to know which version is the truth."

"My mother taught me never to lie to the police."

(Unlike my Czech grandmother, who warned me as a child never to tell them the truth. What would she have thought of her favorite grandson, Stanislav, named after a heroic Slavic warrior, now reduced to a Back Bay hairdresser who was a stoolie for the BPD?)

Jennie continued, "I see you got to meet the boss yesterday."

"Did he say anything to you afterward?"

"He'd seen us talking and asked me what you wanted."

"What did you tell him?"

"That's for me to know, isn't it?"

"I'm surprised he'd even care. I talked to him myself, after all."

"I think it's your manner," said Jennie, "the way you buzz around like a persistent flying insect. It's bothersome."

"Mr. Brickley didn't seem to mind. Actually, he seems like an easygoing kind of guy. But I wonder why his wife would care where I met him?"

"You know his wife, too?"

"I did her hair this morning."

"You sure do get around, mister."

"I meet a lot of people working with the public, Jennie. But, do you have any idea why his wife would care where I met Mr. Brickley?"

"Maybe it's all the time he spends at his gym instead of here at the drafting table, or at home at his conjugal duties."

"I would think she'd be happy with such a physically fit husband."

"I hear there's more action at his gym than what happens on the exercise equipment."

"Meaning?"

"If you don't know, mister, I'm certainly not going to explain it."

"Well, I don't see anything wrong with keeping fit," said Stanley the health-club hypocrite.

"Health is one thing, but those physical culturists take it to a perverse degree. I know it's hard to believe, but I was a size ten when I started working here. With the hours I have to work now, though, health clubs and regular meals are a luxury I don't have time for."

I looked sadly at the big woman who'd literally lost touch with her body. She lived at the other end of the same spectrum of those people who also measure their life's experience in pounds and inches—the fitness addicts.

"Maybe you work too hard, Jennie."

"Maybe some people don't work hard enough. In the end, someone else always has to make up for it."

Why did I think of the grasshopper and the ants?

Jennie went on. "Roy Brickley may be fit as an athlete, but he's a senior partner in this firm, and he can't even maneuver a French curve anymore."

Something about that sounded provocative.

"Jennie, I'm sorry to hear how hard your life is, but I still think we can help each other."

"Why don't you just give it up! Why should I even waste any more time with you?"

"Because if you can help me find information that convicts Calvin, you'll land up with that promotion instead of him. You can finally get even for all those times you had to work extra to pull his share of the load. Would you rather see him released and get that job from you?"

"Of course not! But what can I do about it?"

"Just listen to me."

She sat back and made the chair groan under the strain of her weight. "Go ahead. Talk. Waste some more oxygen."

I leaned toward her, hoping to seem more earnest. "You worked with Calvin, right? You saw him eight hours a day."

"Hah! On a good day he might put in four hours. Claims he's paid for what he knows, not what he does."

"Jennie, you have complete access to the computer. Go in there and read his calendar. Find out everything he was doing before Roger Fayerbrock arrived in Boston. You work here. You know where all the important stuff is."

She listened, but she didn't look convinced, so I continued the harangue. "The other day you said you had ways of finding out things. Well, now's the time to use them."

"You don't miss anything, do you?"

"I miss plenty."

"So you want me to spy for you, is that it?"

"People have done worse things to find answers." Was this espionage business contagious? I wondered.

"I can't do that!" she exclaimed. Her huge body jolted, then rebounded softly for a moment.

It was time to pull out all the stops.

"Jennie, are you just going to sit there and let this all happen to you? This is your chance, the big one, to take control of things around you. You can create a new life for yourself, but you have to *do* something." I was sounding like the promotional hype for a self-help program when a word from Mrs. Brickley's *New Yorker* popped into my head. "Jennie," I said, "this is your peripeteia!"

She rocked around in her chair. It teetered dangerously on its flimsy pedestal. Finally she spoke. "That's a big word." She pulled out a cigarette and lit it. "And I know what it means, too." She rocked herself in a cloud of smoke and thought a while. "Okay," she said. "You give a pretty good spiel. I'll look around, see what I can find."

"Good! You still have my card?" I asked. She nodded. "Just keep your eyes and ears open. If I don't hear from you soon, I'll be back."

"I'm not promising anything."

"Just think of that job."

As I was leaving her office, she said, "You're pretty brazen to wear a bow tie around here."

"Why?"

"Wasn't that ranger strangled with one?"

"So the story goes."

"The boss hasn't worn one since the killing."

"Does he usually?"

"He and Calvin both. They usually look like the Bobbsey Twins."

"Well, I wear them because they're fun." And, I thought, because they get different responses from people.

I left Jennie's office and trotted down the ramp. Coming up the ramp toward me was Roy Brickley. "Back again, eh?" he asked as his eyes admired my tie.

"I, uh . . ."

He smiled and said, "My wife just called from downtown. She's delighted with her new hairdo."

"I'm glad she's pleased."

"It's all thanks to you." He waved me off and walked forcefully up into Jennie's office. He didn't even question my presence there. Maybe he believed I really *was* on Calvin's side. For a minute, I watched Jennie and Roy Brickley through the glass wall of her office. She handed him a packet of papers, then she pointed to me. Mr. Brickley turned and looked, but he didn't acknowledge me. The two of them weren't saying much to each other, but I still wished I were a fly on the wall. When I walked out the front door, Bob the cabbette was waiting to whisk me back to the shop.

On the fast ride back, I thought about my pep talk to Jennie, and I thought about what *I* should do to change the course of events so far. I felt that I was getting nowhere. Everything was vague and frustrating. I needed to change my whole vision and do something. I needed to expand my mind. Those words jogged my memory, and that's when the answer came to me: Go West, young man. It was an extreme course of action, but it was time for *me* to take control now.

When I got to the shop, I nabbed Nicole by the elbow and dragged her to the back room. "Nikki," I said breathlessly, since my heart was racing, "I have an idea. I'm probably crazy—"

"You *are* crazy, darling," she interrupted. "What's happened to you? Your pupils are dilated."

"Nikki, I want to go to California."

"Certainly, Stani," she said calmly, as though dealing with a psychotic. "Next spring on your vacation—"

"No, Nikki. I mean now. Tonight. I want to go to Yosemite and poke around in Roger's end of the world."

Nicole was speechless.

I said, "It's the only choice I have right now."

"If that's what you believe, Stanley, then you *do* need a rest."

"Nikki, I'm not finding answers here. Nothing!"

"Stanley, you must drop this silly notion right now. It's ridiculous!"

"But the killer is still free!"

"That's not your concern."

"It is!"

"No, it isn't."

"So, what should I do? Just wait around until the next time Calvin comes in, then just frost his hair as usual? Is that your solution?"

"Even if Calvin *is* guilty, and even if he is *acquitted*, there's nothing you can do about it."

"But I'm sure there *is*, Nikki! There *has* to be an answer somewhere. Someone knows something. And if that person isn't here in Boston, then maybe they're out in California, where Roger came from."

"And don't you give me any line about Roger! I won't stand by and watch you turn your life upside down for a man you splashed around with for twenty minutes. I don't care what kind of fantasy he was for you."

"So you think I should just pretend nothing happened?"

"I think you should know when to accept things you can't change."

"You sound like that old prayer."

Nicole sighed in exasperation. "Stanley, if for no other reason, your running off to California is simply irresponsible. What about your appointments?"

"You can reschedule them, and Abbey can come in for the critical ones." Abbey was an old friend of Nicole's from New York who occasionally styled at the shop. "And Ramon can handle the

walk-ins. One dip and clip by him and they'll appreciate the value
of reserving time with me."

"Don't be so sure. He does very good work." Nicole paused and
looked me straight in the eye. "Well, as usual, I can see you have
your mind made up already, with everything all neatly planned. Just
how do you intend to pay for this little excursion?"

"Ah, Nikki, there's the rub. Most of it can go on plastic." Then
I gave her my younger-brother-in-trouble look. "But I'll need some
cash from the till."

Nicole hooted loudly. "You want *me* to finance a wild-goose
chase to California?"

"Only part of it, and it's not a wild-goose chase. Now, will you
help me?"

Nicole sighed heavily again. Then she shrugged. "What are
friends for?"

"Thanks, Nikki," I said, and hugged her. Immediately I called
my travel agent and made the arrangements. At least *he* was pleased
to hear I'd be traveling! I'd have to go standby, but if I got on, my
plane would leave Boston at eight o'clock that night and arrive in
California five and a half hours later at ten-thirty the same evening.
Already I liked the idea of a place where time was created just by
flying there.

After calling some friends to cancel my weekend plans—my
annual appearance at Chez-Chez—I spent the rest of my working
day anticipating my first trip to California. Sure, it was a serious kind
of trip, but I was also eager to see the part of the country where they
grew them like Roger.

Later, when I got home, Sugar Baby greeted me with a trill and
a stretch. I bent to pick her up and found an envelope lying on the
carpet. It had been slipped under the door. The note inside was
composed of letters cut out from magazines:

kEEp OuT oR YoU'll Be jOiNIng tHE rAnGeR

First I wondered which magazine the letters came from, then I
wondered who left it for me, and finally I thought, How melodramatic!

9
CALIFORNIA, HERE I COME!

With the balmy California weather I was anticipating for the next few days, I packed my bags for a tropical cruise. Anyone who's been to San Francisco knows what a delusion that was.

While I packed, I glanced occasionally at the note I'd found under the door when I came in. The words were so similar to the phone message from yesterday that I assumed they must have come from the same person. But, like the phone call, the note didn't frighten me so much as pique my curiosity. Whoever was pulling these pranks had seen too much second-rate *film noir*, and instead of scaring me, the threats seemed almost silly. I didn't understand their purpose. Still, I recalled every person I'd seen since Roger was killed, trying to guess who might be doing it. There was Calvin; his downstairs neighbor Hal Steiner; his lover, Aaron Harvey; his colleague Jennifer Doughton; and his boss, Roy Brickley, with wife Vivian. There were also others, like Nicole; my friend Eduardo; Lieutenant Branco, with all his cohorts; and various clients, but I was sure none of these had sent the note or made the call.

Nicole arrived to pick up Sugar Baby. She'd agreed to keep her while I was gone, in spite of her belief that animals do not belong in human dwellings. For her part, Sugar Baby, who is usually aloof and barely tolerant of other people, adores Nicole. They get along famously, and I often explain to Nicole that it's because they're so much alike, which she adamantly denies. In any case, Sugar Baby would be pampered with Alaskan crab and tournedos while staying with Nicole at her suite at Harbor Towers.

When I showed Nikki the note, she said, "Stanley, this is the second time someone has threatened you."

"It might be the third, doll. Remember that reckless Boston driver last night?"

"You don't think . . . ?"

"All I know is that someone is trying to scare me off, but their methods are so tacky, I can't take it seriously."

"The car was not tacky, Stanley."

"The idea of it was."

"You've called the lieutenant about this, haven't you?"

"I'll call him when the time is right."

"And when, pray tell, is that?"

"When I've got everything I can from the note."

Nicole said sarcastically, "Then maybe you should peel the letters off the paper and see if there are any clues on the back side." Immediately I grinned. "Oh, no!" she exclaimed, rolling her eyes, for she'd unwittingly given me an idea.

I went to the kitchen, and she followed. I cleared a space on the kitchen table and set it up as though I were about to perform microsurgery. "You'd better hold the cat," I said, "or she'll be up here trying to help me." Nicole picked up Sugar Baby and stroked her chin while I went to work. Within minutes, using my finest Swiss tweezers, I carefully peeled each letter from the page. It was almost as exciting as scratching a lottery ticket. I didn't find much, though. Most of the letters just had other printing on the back. Some were completely blank, one had a colored bit that looked like oiled wood, and another showed a chrome knob on a red-tile background.

"Not much to go on there," I said. "But if I'd done this note, I would have sent a photocopy of it. That way the recipient couldn't do what we just did."

"I always said you had a criminal mind."

"And if I'd told Branco about this the way you thought I should, we couldn't have destroyed it the way we just did."

Nicole snapped, "Why do you keep saying 'we'? I didn't lay a hand on that paper!"

"But you gave me the idea. Just be gracious, Nikki, and accept credit where it's due."

She grimaced. "What about fingerprints?"

"Even if the sender worked without latex gloves, the bond paper wouldn't take a print. The magazine paper might be slick enough, though." (I hadn't yet learned about the iodine-gas technique for finding latent fingerprints on *any* surface.)

"Can the cops tell when it was done?"

"Cripes, Nikki! How the hell should I know? I'll send it all to Branco before I leave. By the time he gets it, I'll be in California. Maybe I'll have found some *useful* clue by then."

Nicole suddenly became serious. "Stanley, I don't want you to go."

"Nikki, we've already been through this."

"I know, but now that it's happening, I really don't want you to do it."

"It's too late."

"No it's not. I have your traveling cash in my purse, and without that, this little escapade of yours will be difficult, if not impossible."

"Are you pulling rank on me?"

"Stanley, it's time to admit you're caught in a web of male ego. You've become irrational, and what you're about to do is dangerous."

"Nikki, I have to do this. Otherwise I'm one of those people who just sit around talking and thinking about what they should do rather than doing it for real. I'm tired of watching life being lived by other people. I want to go and I *am* going."

"You've been doing those affirmations again."

"It's my life!"

"Is your life about courting danger?"

"What should I do? Sit at home and read mail-order catalogs behind locked doors? *That's* safe!"

Our eyes stayed connected for a long, silent moment. Only

Sugar Baby's purring moved the air between us. She always responds when emotions around her are high. Nicole placed her gently down onto the kitchen floor.

"All right, Stanley. You win." Nicole reached into her bag and pulled out several banded packs of fifty-dollar bills. "Here! Go be a real man and get yourself killed. I'll keep the cat." She pushed the money into my hands.

I took it and did a quick calculation. "Nikki, that's two thousand dollars!"

She nodded. "It's a loan, not a gift. If you're diving into the jaws of hell, you'd better have enough money to get yourself out again."

I held her and hugged her a long while. "Thanks, Nikki. I was afraid you didn't love me anymore."

"I'm just concerned about this new John Wayne attitude of yours."

"Don't worry. You know women will always be my role models."

"I want you to call me when you get there, I don't care what time it is. And you call me every day, too, you hear? When you get back, I'll pick you up at the airport."

"Yes, Mum."

Then she dug into her purse again and pulled out a small lavender-colored vinyl case with a zipper around it.

"What's that?" I asked. "A douche kit?"

"It's my camera." She handed it to me. "You may need to take pictures."

I took the case and unzipped it. The small plastic camera inside was streamlined and smooth and lavender, just like the case. "It's so, uh, feminine," I remarked.

Nicole smiled. "It ought to be. I sent for it off the back of a Kotex box."

We said good night and she departed with Sugar Baby. Within seconds I felt really alone. I wondered why I *was* leaving town. By ordinary standards I should have been comfortable enough where I was. I had my job, my friends, my cat, my apartment, and my big empty bed. What could I gain by flying out West on a whim? If anything, my leaving town would only antagonize the police, and there wasn't even any guarantee of finding useful information out there. But that was all my rational, linear side talking, trying to convince me to be good, honest, upright, moral, and safe. My other side, the emotional, spatial, wildebeest part of me said simply, "Do it!"

I reassembled the threat note the best I could, then wrote a brief explanation of what I'd done to it. I added hugs and kisses at the end just to keep the whole thing breezy and light, then addressed it all to Lieutenant Branco. By the time he read it, I'd be in California. He'd have to come out West himself and physically abduct me to get me back to Boston. And with that happy thought, I called a cab and headed to the airport.

Luckily I got on the flight, but the takeoff was delayed over an hour. When the plane was finally airborne, I thought again about what I was doing and glumly realized that it was too late to change my mind. I did my mantra, using the word *surrender*. It was good preparation for a transcontinental flight, where you're forced to enter a collective frame of mind: You eat only after the food is cold, you move about the cabin at the captain's whim, and you watch a film when the first-class passengers are ready for it. So, I surrendered: I drank and dozed.

The plane landed in San Francisco well after midnight. I felt both eager and scared, but as I stepped from the plane onto the loading bridge, the cool, sweet night air thrilled me. I knew I was in a strange new city. Everything around me was new—the signs, the sounds, the smells. People seemed friendlier, too, more relaxed, even though it was so late.

I got a cab and headed into town. The driver had a sun-weathered face and a magnificent mustache. A cowboy hat lay on the seat beside him. He got us onto the highway quickly, but as we zoomed toward town, we drove directly into a thunderstorm. Within seconds the rain was hard and heavy, and visibility became nil. Other cars were pulling off the road until the deluge stopped, and my driver decided to do the same. He stopped the meter but left the motor running to keep us warm. Both gestures were considerate, which I took to be a good omen of West Coast hospitality.

We made small talk about the weather and how lucky I was that the plane had landed before the rain. Then, as he checked his logbook and the rain pelted and drummed against the roof of the cab, he said quietly, as if to himself, "It's a good night to be lickin' someone's balls."

The words shocked me. Was it a bold invitation? A Halloween ritual? Or just a callous offhand comment? I didn't know what to do or say. Here I was imagining San Francisco as the mecca of romantic love, and instead of courtship, a total stranger was discussing sex in the same breath as the weather. (I'd have to confess that another side of me was titillated by a handsome man stating his sexual thoughts so bluntly.) The cab windows were steaming up and our mutual silence became awkward. Finally the rain abated and we were back on the expressway into town.

My hotel had been recommended by a client who said it reminded him of a place where he'd once stayed in Berlin. I remembered the address easily because the intersecting streets were almost exactly the name of a great jazz pianist, Ellis Larkins. I pushed against the heavy brass door and entered the lobby. Even in my travel-weary daze I noticed the huge gilt-framed mirror hanging over a sculpted marble fireplace at the far end of the lobby. Potted palms were arranged on the two mammoth Persian carpets, and an electrified crystal chandelier spread soft light over the whole area.

I registered at the front desk. The clerk handed me my room key and flashed a broad smile, his big teeth too white and too straight to be natural. He led me to a small cagelike elevator and slid the gate open for me. With his body so close to mine, I sensed the aroma of musky leather and wondered where it came from. (Though leather always intrigues me, my heart prefers something more domestic, like the smell of laundry fresh off the line.) The clerk let the gate slide shut and waved to me as the elevator took me up to my floor.

When I got in the room, I dumped my bags on the floor and fell onto the bed. I checked the time. It was 1 A.M., which meant 4 A.M. in Boston. I picked up the phone and arranged a long-distance call to Nicole. The phone rang once, and Nicole answered without a hello.

"Are you all right?"

"Yes, Nikki." What a relief to hear her voice!

"How's the hotel?"

"Clean and simpatico."

"Room service?"

"I haven't had a chance to find out."

"Call me tomorrow." And she hung up.

I lay on the bed considering whether to go out and see San Francisco at night. Then I remembered the day of driving that faced me in the morning. So instead of painting the town, I surrendered to my travel exhaustion. I stripped and crawled under the cool, clean cotton sheets. There I was, a visitor on my first night in San Francisco, the gay capital of North America, where Halloween is a national holiday, and I was alone.

10

A SWEET LITTLE NEST SOMEWHERE IN THE WEST

Saturday morning I was up early to check out of the hotel. The same manager from last night was still at the desk, and he was also still full of nervous energy and eagerness. I wondered what drugs he'd taken to maintain the Mary Sunshine act for so long. When I told him I might be staying there again on my way back through town, he smiled with enthusiasm and said, "I hope so," with a twinkle in his eye. I had a quick breakfast at a small café nearby, then set off to rent a car.

At 8 A.M. the San Francisco sky was overcast, and the air cold and damp, not quite the balmy breezes I'd expected. I walked a few blocks to the car-rental agency. On the way I encountered what appeared to be three very sexy men returning home from the previous night's debauchery. As I neared them, I saw that two were a couple, and they had to physically support each other as they stumbled along. They passed, and a heavy smell of liquor and smoke followed in their wake. The third man tripped along behind them. He was engaged in animated conversation with himself. All three men were handsome specimens, but somehow they didn't seem so attractive up close. My romantic notions about San Francisco were about as accurate as my sense of the weather there.

At the rental agent there were two used cars available in my price range: a minuscule white coupe and a red ark of a sedan. I took the sedan. Nicole would have gone to a first-class agency and rented a snazzy convertible, but my New Jersey working-class mentality wouldn't allow such wanton luxury.

I was on the road before nine o'clock, but I unhappily discovered that the way to Yosemite didn't cross the Golden Gate Bridge. I had yearned to experience the mystique of that great symbol of the city. I promised myself that on my return through San Francisco I'd see the side of the city that really interested me: the old-fashioned Victorian charm and the relaxed approach to life that allowed like-minded men to live with each other as contented couples. I was still convinced that if such a place existed anywhere, it was in San Francisco.

After three hours of driving, I was on the final upward approach to the Yosemite Valley. (The "valley" is actually two thousand feet above sea level.) The narrow road snaked its way up the mountain sides, and I allowed myself brief glances into the gulleys and down the sheer cliffs that dropped just a few feet from the edge of the shoulder. Then it occurred to me that there were no guardrails, and I realized that disaster loomed just inches away. In my nervousness I must have unconsciously sped up. A large camper suddenly appeared on the narrow pavement coming the other way. The massive vehicle was barreling downhill, approaching me at a good clip. I could see the driver chatting with the passenger instead of watching the road. I hit the horn, but that only alarmed him, and he jerked the steering wheel. He aimed the goddamn camper directly at me! There was only another second. I saw the panic on his face. I felt my stomach go light. I swerved off the pavement and onto the crumbly shoulder at the edge of the sheer drop. I jammed the car to a stop.

Moments passed before I realized that I hadn't gone over the edge. I did some slow breathing to calm myself and bring my heartbeat back to normal. I turned around and looked out the back windshield to make sure the camper hadn't crashed, either, but it was continuing merrily down the mountain road, unconcerned over the brush with death it had caused me. I got back on the pavement and drove more cautiously. It was not comforting, that vision of my last breathing moment, hurtling over the edge into the yawning chasm in a rented used car, unshaven, and wearing old jeans.

The initial view of Yosemite is an expansive panorama of green hills and gray granite forming the V-shaped sides of the valley. A slender flume of water fell from a rock cliff over six hundred feet high. Even in its waning autumn force the waterfall was awesome. So this was where Roger had lived! As I passed among the granite monoliths that lined the valley walls, I felt that I had entered a place unbothered by time and history, almost like a holy place. That feeling wouldn't last long, though.

It was already 1 P.M., not too soon to find a place to stay. I tried the main lodge first, but with no luck. Just as well, I thought, since the place was busy with noisy tourists, even off-season. I headed toward the campsite on the east side of the valley. There I got a tiny cabin to myself. It was real quiet, which I took as another good omen. Once inside, I changed from my driving jeans to pleated black chinos. Since I'd be nosing around and asking questions, I wanted to look respectable.

Then came the question, Where do I start? For someone like me, that was obvious. The first stop was the local hairdresser. In a small town, that would be a good source for gossip and information about the town residents, and probably about the tourists, too. I'd also be more comfortable starting out my search among my own kind, *my* personal network. There was a place just outside the village, a humble little shop that reminded me of the businesses wrought by certain enterprising women out of their suburban garages. On the door to the shop, small black vinyl letters adhered crookedly to the painted glass panel and announced:

BEA'S BEAUTY PARLOR
OPEN M-W-F
NOON TO 5:00

It was one-thirty on Saturday. So much for that idea. Then I remembered the big hotel and figured that might also be a fertile source of small-town gossip. I got directions and found myself driving along a private road that led out from the back of the village center. The entrance to the hotel grounds was marked by a gigantic wrought-iron arch set on two great stone pillars rising from either side of the road. Split logs were arranged in a crescent on the black iron to spell out the name:

I'm sure the sign was intended to evoke the spirit of the Native American, but once inside, I found the soul of the Ohlone Hotel was all-American WASP. I was glad I'd changed my clothes, too, since guests staying at the Ohlone did not tour in denim. I was going to have to be "straight Stan" for a while. I avoided the desk clerk and went directly to the cocktail lounge. At two in the afternoon it was already full of wealthy white people sitting around drinking, laughing, and smoking. A clean-cut piano player amused himself with witty show tunes. I sat at the bar. One of the two bartenders saw me, and she hustled over.

"What can I getcha?" she snapped. She had long naturally wavy blond hair. Not much like a Native American, I thought, but she seemed feisty and interesting, maybe even cooperative.

"Beefy up with a twist," I said curtly.

She winked and turned to gather the makings for my cocktail. Then, like the best bartenders, she prepared the drink directly in front of me. She didn't shake or stir the gin. She just swirled it in a lot of ice, then strained it gently into a chilled martini glass. Finally she twisted the lemon peel *over* the glass so the icy gin caught the mist of tangy citrus oil.

I took a sip, nodded my approval, then asked, "Is there a hair salon in the hotel?"

"There's a guy named Leonard, but I doubt he's for you."

"Why not?"

She removed the setup for my drink. Then she cocked her head. "He talks a lot."

"That's okay." Just the kind I'm looking for, I thought.

She rinsed the utensils she'd used for my cocktail. "Most guys don't like him."

I shrugged. "I'm different from most guys."

"Are you?" she asked, and I wondered if she alluded to something else.

"Where can I find him?"

"His shop is on the mezzanine, and he lives here in the hotel, in one of the penthouse suites."

"Must be nice."

"Hey, y'know," she said as she toweled some wet glasses, "you don't look like you need your hair cut."

I ran my hand through my coppery hair, which had been barbered recently. "I guess I don't."

"You here on honeymoon or somethin'?"

Did she mean it? "Actually," I said seriously, "I'm here to find out about my friend, Roger Fayerbrock. Maybe you knew him. He was a park ranger up here."

The perkiness suddenly left her face. "Sure, I know Roger. Why? Is something wrong?"

"Well . . ." How was I going to tell her?

"You're talkin' about him like he's gone already. Is he okay?"

"I'm sorry to say no."

She blanched. "What happened?"

"He was killed in Boston."

She turned away abruptly and began washing glasses noisily in the sink under the bar. After a few minutes she returned and I saw that her eyes were wet with tears.

"I knew somethin' happened to him," she said, "with all those cops around his place." Her voice was shaky now.

"Anything you can tell me might help."

"There's nothin' much to tell. He wasn't the same ever since that big slide about a month ago."

"Slide?"

"We get rock slides up here almost every year. But this one bothered him a lot. He said there was somethin' funny about the way the rocks fell."

"Was there?"

"Who knows? He thought so. Then he gets it into his head to go to Boston." She hung wineglasses in an overhead rack. "How did you know him?"

"College buddies." I lied.

"Was he gay then, too?"

"I, uh, guess so." So she knew!

She stopped working and faced me directly. "Were you two lovers?"

"No." Oh, that I could have answered otherwise!

I made a move to pay for my drink, but she said, "It's on the house."

"Thanks," I said, and left her a tip worth twice the drink.

She leaned real close and spoke low. "You a cop?" I shook my head. Then she hushed her voice even more. "Detective?"

"Kind of."

"Roger was killed, huh?"

I nodded.

She said, "You know who did it?"

I nodded again with more conviction. "I think so."

"Are you gonna get him?"

"Absolutely."

"Good!" she whispered.

I left the lounge and strolled through the lobby. Then I jogged up the stairs to the mezzanine. I crossed a balcony that overlooked the main lobby and beyond that, the tall windows that opened onto the hotel grounds. At the balcony's end was a door with an engraved brass plate:

MR. LEONARD

BY APPOINTMENT ONLY

I pressed a turquoise button mounted in a silver frame on the woodwork. In a moment the door flew open and revealed a tall fleshy man with a headful of red hair styled in a poor imitation of the vibrant mane of the young Lucille Ball. He wore a flouncy caftan of purple and white raw silk. In the seconds that passed, I sensed him sizing me up just as I was doing to him. He sniffed haughtily and spoke with an inhospitable voice, "Can I help you?"

"I'd like to see Mr. Leonard."

"Do you have an appointment?"

"I just want to talk with him."

"You *are* talking to him!"

"Hello," I said, and extended my hand, which he ignored. "I'm a friend of Roger Fayerbrock."

The man's eyes bugged out and he said, "I'm with a client now."

"No problem. I'll just wait here till you're free."

"That might be inconvenient."

"I've got time."

"Inconvenient for *me!*"

He slammed the door in my face.

I was learning a lot about West Coast hospitality. I figured he'd have to come out sooner or later, so I planted myself on a padded bench outside his door and watched the foot traffic in the main lobby. Twenty minutes later a middle-aged man emerged from the door. His curly blond hair had the peculiar greenish tinge that I immediately recognized as ash-toned color applied to bleached hair. Any skilled colorist knows to use neutral tones after bleaching.

Within moments Mr. Leonard's head slunk out from the partially open door. "Are you still here?"

"I just want a few minutes of your precious time."

"Oh, all right! Come in! I'm bored anyway."

I got up and went inside. The afternoon sun shone through two wall-sized windows in his waiting area. A huge woven-grass water jug rested on a hand-loomed rug. Expensive and well-chosen artifacts were placed about the room. The guy sure knew how to spend his money conspicuously. He reclined on a chaise longue and smoked a pungent black cigarette. I half-expected him to hiss like a serpent that had just devoured its monthly meal. But instead he said, "What I want to know . . ." Then he created a cloud of smoke around himself before finishing, ". . . is how you found me."

"I told you, I'm a friend of Roger's."

"Yes, you did tell me. But it's strange I never met you before."

"I'm from Boston."

He accidentally swallowed some smoke from his cigarette and tried to subdue a cough that lurked in his throat. He finally croaked, "I see."

"I came out here to find out why Roger was back East."

"Since you're his friend, I should think you'd already know that."

"I didn't have a chance to find out before the, uh, accident."

Mr. Leonard sat up suddenly and nervously stamped out his cigarette in the earthen ashtray, but he failed to extinguish it completely, and a pathetic wisp of smoke rose from the corpse. Nicole would have cringed. "What happened to Roger was no accident!" he exclaimed.

"You know about it, then?"

"I can read! And I've talked to the police here. They claim that our dear Roger was in Boston on a drug run for crack and heroin, which is utter nonsense."

"How do you know?"

He stood up, went to a mirror, and fussed with his hair. "If you knew Roger at all, you'd know that he was obsessed with two things—health and conservation." He examined a nonexistent blemish on his sagging jowls. "There is no way in the world he was involved with drugs."

"Maybe he was a police decoy."

Mr. Leonard turned to me dramatically and lit another cigarette. I thought of Bette Davis. He said, "I should think your East Coast intellectual types could devise easier ways to break a drug syndicate than to import park rangers from Yosemite."

"Then why do *you* think Roger went East?"

"Darling," he said. (The word so charming on Nikki's lips was smarmy on his.) "I *know* why." He sneered and said, "You know, darling, you're a horrid liar. You don't know Roger from my anal pore. But you're bold, and that's certainly to my liking. I'm going to wager a little bargain with you."

Here it comes, I thought.

"I'll tell you why Roger went to New England if you tell me why you're here."

A bargain with this guy spelled trouble, but I'd come this far, and there was no turning back. "Okay," I said. "I told you already, and I'll tell you again. I knew Roger was in Boston, but we didn't get a chance to get together before he died, so I never knew why he'd gone there. But I think if I can find that out, I may also find exactly what happened to him. Nothing was turning up in Boston, so I thought I might find some answers out here. It's as simple as that."

"My, my! A knight yet lives," he said, and clucked his tongue. "Well, it's true that Roger dearest had a penchant for red-haired men. And yours is natural, which gives you the advantage over me. He never *would* look at me the way I wanted him to. And you're quite attractive in a strange sort of way."

"Thanks, I think."

"Yes, your eyes and your smile." Mr. Leonard paused and evaluated my bountiful derriere. "And *that* part of you would certainly have appealed to him. I imagine you and Roger had a great time together."

"Imagine is all I got to do."

"I seriously doubt that, but whatever . . ."

"You can doubt all you want, but now it's your turn to talk. You tell me why he went East."

Mr. Leonard took a huge drag on his cigarette. Then, as he let the smoke drift slowly from his mouth, he inhaled some of it back through his nose. He was such a cliché that I wished I could take a holograph of him back to Nicole. Maybe she'd appreciate me more. "Darling," he said, "Roger was a rock climber, one of those crazed people who clamber up and down cliffs, exercising their adrenal glands."

That explained the climber's chock the police had found in his bag at Calvin's place, the one mentioned in the reports I'd read in Branco's office.

Mr. Leonard went on, "The only drug dearest Roger was addicted to was his own goddamn lily-pure adrenaline."

"So why did he go East?"

"Darling, I'm getting to that." He puffed nervously now, barely taking the smoke into his lungs but creating a huge cloud around him. "Roger wanted to climb some mountain or other back there, something called the Old Mountain Man."

"Ol' Man o' the Mountain. It's in New Hampshire."

"Yes. That one. That's why he was back East. He'd seen a picture of the mountain and wanted to climb it. Just like your story . . . very simple."

If I could sing, Mr. Leonard would have heard an *aria di sorbetto*. That's how much I believed that little yarn. I said, "You know where his place is?"

Mr. Leonard nodded.

"I'd like to look around there myself," I said.

He got up and walked to the window and gazed out wistfully. "The police have already gone through everything, and then some. All of poor Roger's carefully guarded secret life was thrown into the blazing light of the law." He tried to look sad but he sounded gleeful.

I said, "Just tell me where it is."

"Of course, darling." He turned to face me. "But I must exact a small favor from you."

I smirked. "We just finished a round of that game."

"Face it," he said smugly. "I have what you want."

I could see that this guy was going to wield his petty power to the limit. "All right," I said. "One more time. Now what?"

"You are to join me for dinner this evening in my penthouse."

"I don't dine with strangers."

"But I am so seldom titillated here in the wilderness."

"I'm sure you get plenty of opportunity in a place like this."

"Yes, but there's an edge about you that I like."

I thought a moment, then said, "Okay, you tell me where Roger lives. If it's the truth, I'll have lunch with you, in the hotel dining room, tomorrow."

He smashed out his second cigarette. "You are a hard man!"

"Just tell me where he lives."

"Lived, darling, *lived*. He is dead. We are alive."

I wanted to smash his flabby bottle-bronzed face. I moved toward him, clenched my left fist, and yelled, "Just tell me, damn you!" It was macho travesty, but it worked.

Relief appeared on Mr. Leonard's face, as though he'd been awaiting the threat of violence. He answered quietly. "It's a small cabin near Mirror Lake. But it's all futile, darling. I told you, the police have already been there."

"They might have missed something."

Nervously he stuck yet another cigarette between his lips. As he spoke, it wagged there, waiting to be lit. "Just beware of the little dog. It bites."

"His dog is still there?"

"You'll see what I mean."

I left the salon and the hotel feeling dirty after my chat with Mr. Leonard. Poor Roger, to be ardently pursued by that! A hot shower was in order, but it was already after four o'clock, and searching Roger's cabin was more urgent. I headed toward the village to find my way to Mirror Lake.

11
THE LITTLE DOG
THAT BITES

When I stopped in Yosemite Village for directions to Mirror Lake, I learned that there was no road to get there, only hiking trails and bike paths. I'm not exactly a Sierra Club type, but I had no choice, so I rented a bike and pedaled my way. As it turned out, riding the bike immersed me into the quiet power of the valley, which I'd missed while driving the rented red whorehouse on wheels. I got to feel the cold, clean air rush across my face, and smell the trees, and hear peaceful forest sounds.

It was after five o'clock when I found Roger's place. It was the only dwelling on the lake, a small log cabin that was a perfect fairy-tale cottage tucked among the trees. A narrow covered porch ran along the front of the cabin and up the two sides. Each side had its own spectacular view, the names of which I learned later: Half Dome to the east, Mount Watkins to the north in front of the cabin, and Washington Column to the west. There were no police lines around the cabin, which surprised me. Perhaps the natural beauty of the valley was more important to the local officers than regulations about police lines.

I'm not sure what I expected to find in there, but I was certain of one thing—I had to get inside. I hoped to learn firsthand, with my own senses, who Roger was, and why he'd come to Boston. I stepped up onto the porch but didn't even bother trying the front door. Instead, I went around to the back of the cabin to try a window, but was quickly foiled by a huge picture window that made up most of the back wall of the cabin. Short of smashing the whole thing, I certainly wasn't going to get into the cabin that way. I peered through the glass, but a heavy opaque fabric hung inside, blocking any view.

I wandered around to the east-side porch, which was cast in shadow by the setting sun. Both windows there were also blocked with heavy cloth, but one had a chink through which I could see a bit of the cabin's dark interior. All I could make out was a bed. The sheets and blankets were thrown back, as though someone had recently slept there. I wondered whether Roger, like me, had left on a cross-country trip without making his bed.

The west side of the cabin glowed in amber light from the sunset. That's where I got lucky and found a window that hadn't been locked. I wondered if the cops had forgotten to secure it after their search, or maybe they'd never even noticed. Whatever the reason, I was grateful, and though a little voice warned me not to, I climbed through the window.

Once inside, I stood quietly still a few moments while my eyes adjusted to the dimness. The furniture was simple: a bed, a small nightstand, a square pine kitchen table with three straight-backed pine chairs around it, and a writing desk with yet another of the pine chairs. I searched the desk drawers and found nothing, no letters, no bills, no checkbook, nothing but unused stationery, some scissors, and an unopened package of imported liquorice toffee.

An enormous old armoire of darkened oak functioned as the only closet. I opened the door and the pungent smell of cedar rushed into my face. The armoire had been completely lined with strips of cedarwood, a natural moth repellent. The scent reminded me of Lieutenant Branco, and I wondered what he was doing at that very moment back in Boston. He was probably reading the mangled threat note I'd forwarded to him.

Hanging inside the armoire were twelve identical khaki-colored uniforms. Each shirt had a sewn-on patch with the insignia of Yosemite National Park, a mountain vertically sliced in half by a prehistoric glacier. Five gray neckties were all the type that clipped onto a shirt over the top collar button. I wondered a moment about the ties, then guessed that a clip-on necktie would release itself if an assailant happened to grab on to it, unlike a regular necktie, which could offer an attacker a good stranglehold.

Roger's record collection showed an inclination to jazz and country-western music. His books included biographies, collected essays, and ecological studies, along with some recent thrillers and romances. There was certainly more to Roger Fayerbrock than the handsome lug who'd visited the shop a few days ago, but still no clue as to why he'd gone to Boston.

I was gazing at an orderly stack of neatly wound ropes lying under a window near the small kitchen stove when I felt the floor move. I bristled in reflex and turned, but a monstrous weight was already on my back and shoulders, surrounding me and pressing me toward the floor. A strong arm slithered around my neck. Bear, I thought. Bear! But I realized it was only the scratchy sleeve of a wool jacket. Then a deep and ugly pressure appeared on the back of my neck, just below the skull, immobilizing me. It intensified until the setting sun flared brightly like manganese, then faded to nothing as my legs crumpled.

I felt a heavy nudge against my shoulder and heard a voice growl. "Hey! Wake up!" I opened my eyes and saw him leaning over me, his face inches from my own. His Asian eyes and features were dark against a tawny, youthful complexion. He stared at me uncertainly, then said, "Who are you?"

I shook my head, trying to clear it. "What happened?"

"I put you out for a little while." A faint scent of anise lingered from his breath. "Just tell me who you are." He was so close I could have kissed him. Instead I lurched to get up and run, but my hands and feet were bound. I felt no pain, though, so I guess he hadn't slugged me.

He smiled contentedly and said, "You're not going anywhere, so you might as well tell me what you want here."

His speech had the contrived informality of people who learn English from the Brits but who pick up their vernacular in the States.

"I was just looking around," I explained innocently.

"For what?"

"Nothing. Just being a nosy tourist."

He moved back and sat on the floor next to me. He was young, around twenty-one, with a compact, powerful body like a miniature sumo wrestler's, but without the fat. He had the face of a young warrior, and his short black hair shone with a bluish cast. His exotic dark eyes stared at me.

"You're lying," he said. "I already checked your pockets."

"Find anything you like?" I asked.

His eyes brightened slightly and divulged a certain inclination. He said, "Your name is Stan and you're from Boston. What happened to Roger?"

"Who's Roger?" I asked naïvely.

In a second he jumped onto me again, this time straddling my chest and gripping my collar. Through clenched teeth he snarled, "Where is he! What did you do with him?"

Though he was trying to frighten me with physical violence, I sensed that it was really all defensive bluster. I stupidly assumed that he was too cute to be dangerous, and that he was probably afraid of something, perhaps me.

I spoke as calmly as I could. "Do *you* know Roger?"

"I'm asking the questions!" He tightened my collar with his strong hands and I felt the trapped blood gathering in my scalp. So much for my defensive behavior theory.

"Okay, okay," I groaned, and he released me. "I met Roger last Wednesday, in Boston where I work."

"That's a lie! You kidnapped him." He grabbed at my neck again. "And now you're here to get me!" He squeezed hard. A blunt pain in my throat prevented air from passing and my eyeballs pulsed hard. I shook my head frantically. He squeezed harder, then released the pressure just enough for me to breathe.

I croaked, "Roger wasn't kidnapped."

"Is he all right?"

I shook my head no.

"What happened?"

"He's dead."

"You're lying!" he screamed, and slammed me back onto the floor. Then he got up and paced around the floor near me. Now I *did* hurt, but with his weight off me, at least I could breathe again. He hadn't quite mastered the velvet-glove technique.

When I got my breath, I said, "I'm not lying. That's why I'm here." My voice sounded appealingly mean and rough from having my throat wrenched. I kind of hoped it would stay that way.

He said, "How did you find this place?"

"You know a guy named Leonard?"

"Oh, him! Ms. Leona," he said, and he swayed his hips and held his wrist limply in front of him.

I nodded. "He's the kind that gives hairdressers a bad name." (And the kind I have nightmares of becoming.)

The young man looked astonished. "Are you a hairdresser?"

I nodded again.

He said, "You don't act like one, the way you broke in here."

"I'm one of the new breed." I wriggled the ropes clasping my hands and feet. "Can you untie me now?"

"Not until you tell me why you're here."

"I already told you, I want to find out why Roger went to Boston."

"Why?"

"I think I know who killed him." I pulled myself up to a sitting position. Those few sit-ups every morning finally came in handy. "And if I find out why Roger went to Boston, I can probably discover the killer's motive. Then I can nail him." It seemed I was giving the same tired explanation to everyone I met.

He weighed my words. "I want to believe you, but I don't dare." He appraised me as a smart puppy would, testing his senses to see whether I was trustworthy. After a few moments his eyes became dark and glossy. He looked away, then spoke as if to himself. "They all make it sound so dirty." Then he walked away from me.

"What are you talking about?" I asked.

He was at the window, looking out into the nearly extinguished sunlight. "There's no secrets, not in this place. Yosemite's small, and everyone thinks the same here. They think Roger and I were lovers."

"Were you?"

"We were friends," he answered quickly. "We did it together—a lot—but it didn't mean anything."

I wondered how people could insert or accept each other's body parts and then casually say it didn't mean anything. He continued explaining, as though reading my mind. "We just did it, that's all." He shrugged.

"How long were you together?"

"About a year."

"So, why did Roger go to Boston?"

"I don't know."

"You must know, if you were lovers."

"We were *friends!*"

"All right, friends then!"

He moved slowly toward the pile of ropes near the other window. He kicked at the ropes and said quietly, "It all started after the slide."

"What slide?"

"Over here," he said, looking out the window. He came back to me and helped me stand up. "I'll show you." He led me hopping to the west-side window. He pointed to a high cliff. "That's Washington Column. See that patch of rock that's clean and new at the top?" I peered carefully where his finger was aiming and nodded. He said, "That's where the slide happened last month."

"Wow!" I said as I realized how much of the granite column had fallen.

"Slides happen here all the time, but after this one Roger went crazy. Maybe because his view was ruined."

"Or maybe it was something else," I said.

The young man paused at my words. "Maybe." Then he said, "Roger was usually calm, but after that he was tense all the time. He was always making phone calls and writing letters. We didn't have much sex either, and when he did it, it was fast and rough. I could tell he was mad about something, but he wouldn't talk about it. He said he didn't want me to get involved."

"And this all happened after the slide?"

He nodded. "Then he went to Boston last Tuesday. The next thing, the rangers were all over here, then the state police from Sacramento came, and now you show up." He stopped suddenly with a look of fright. "I'm talking too much." He went quickly to the cabin door and opened it. "I'll be back," he said.

"You're not going to leave me tied up here?"

But he was already out of the cabin. I heard him lock the door behind him. He clearly intended to keep me hostage, but he forgot one thing. I was still standing and able to hop around. All I had to do was get the ropes off and I'd be free.

First, I tried to slide my hands down behind my rump, figuring I could get them to the front of my legs and use my fingers to untie the rope that bound my feet. But I couldn't get my wrists past my butt. Longer apelike arms would have helped. Then I figured, even with the rope off my feet, my hands would still be tied. So I concentrated on getting my hands free.

I looked around the cabin for a helper, something common and useful like a sharp knife locked upright in a vise. But the only thing I saw was the stove. Did I dare expose my bound hands—the only source of my worldly income—to an open flame? No way.

Then I remembered them. Scissors. There were some ordinary paper shears in the top drawer of the writing desk. And if there's one tool I can adapt to any situation, it's scissors. These would never cut through the thick nylon rope that bound me, but they would do just fine to loosen the fat knot around my wrists. I used my ten free fingers to get the scissors out of the drawer. Then I slid them, handle down, into one of my back pants pockets. It wasn't easy. My hands were, after all, bound together behind me. I had to do everything kind of sidesaddle, just like a lady. Once I finally got the scissors into the pocket though, they wobbled too much, so I had to pull them out again to try another plan. That's exactly when they jumped from my hands onto the floor. (I never *drop* scissors.) They didn't go far, though. I lowered myself carefully to my knees, and crept to where the scissors lay. I got them in my fingers again, but this time I wedged the blades under my belt first to stabilize them in an upright position. Then I slid the handle into my pocket again. Once the scissors were steady, I had to rest for a few seconds. I hadn't done that much torso-twisting since the one time I tried the video workout with you know who.

I studied the knots my young captor had used around my feet, and assumed he'd used the same kind on my wrists. Then I maneu-vered my bound hands over the point of the scissors until the blade tips penetrated the big bumpy knot. After ten minutes of careful prodding, one of the loops loosened a bit. I wriggled my wrists and managed to get my clever left-hand fingers into the knot. After that it was a piece of cake. Two minutes later I was free—and sore.

I left the cabin and quickly pedaled back to the village center. It was after eight o'clock and very dark. I knew there was no telephone in my cabin, so I called Nicole at home from a pay phone. I told her about Leonard and what had just happened in Roger's cabin.

"You get on the next plane and get back here right now!"

"But, Nikki—"

"No 'but Nikki.' This is the second time you've been assaulted. Now stop this nonsense and come home!"

"Nikki, I was trespassing. I broke into the place."

"I don't care. You're in danger. I'm calling Lieutenant Branco. This is ridiculous!" Then she was silent. I could hear her lighting a cigarette.

I breathed impatiently into the receiver, waited a few seconds, then asked, "Are you done?"

"I'm never done. I'm just resting." She exhaled and I could almost see the smoke swirling about her.

"Nikki, people up here knew Roger. Someone will know why he went to Boston."

"Then get them to tell you, then come straight home."

"But they're not telling me. That's just the point. The two people I met today are both hiding something."

"Stanley, does it ever occur to you that sometimes people *aren't* hiding something, that they really don't know these big secrets you've concocted, that what they're telling you is the truth?"

After a suitable dramatic pause, I said, "Never."

"I'm calling Lieutenant Branco right now."

I said, "Don't, Nikki, not yet."

"When should I call him? When your body is found in a snowdrift?"

"That could happen in Boston, too."

"Then come back and satisfy your death wish *here!*"

"Not until I've got something to bring back with me."

Nicole huffed. "Then find it quick! Call me tomorrow." She hung up. Sometimes a conversation with Nikki was truly satisfying.

I drove back to my room at the campsite. When I got in, I turned on the shower to heat it up. I'd just got my clothes off when someone knocked at my door. I called through the door, "Who is it?"

"It's me," said the door-muffled voice.

"Who?"

"From Roger's place."

I pulled back the window curtain and looked out. It was the young man who'd knocked me out at Roger's cabin. He was carrying a large white paper bag.

"What do you want!" I yelled.

"I brought you supper."

He held the bag up like bounty, and I thought of the Trojan horse. I would be a fool to open my door and let him in. But then, this guy probably knew more about Roger than anyone else I'd meet in Yosemite, and I'd be a fool not to wring some facts out of him. Also, without the disadvantage of surprise, I could probably hold my own with him. Besides, I was starving. And besides that, he was kind of cute.

I turned off the shower and put on my light robe, the one I'd packed for the tropical California weather, wherever that was. I opened the door and stuck out my head but kept my body hidden behind it.

He said. "I went back to the cabin and you were gone."

"I had a date. And I don't do bondage."

His eyes looked eager and happy for some reason. "I wanted to make sure you'd be there when I got back. That's why I left you tied up. Now everything is cold."

"There are easier ways to have dinner with me."

"I didn't think you'd trust me after I put you out like that."

"Who says I trust you now?"

"You opened the door, didn't you?"

He was right. "You might as well come in," I said.

He walked into the small cabin, then turned around and faced me as I closed and locked the door.

"Nice legs," he said after a quick appraisal of me in my robe.

"Thanks. And if we're going to be on such friendly terms, you might tell me your name."

He smiled as though he hoped I'd ask. "It's Yudi."

"Judy?"

"Yudi!"

"What kind of name is that?"

"I'm from Bali."

"I'm Stan."

"I know. Remember? I went through your pockets."

"Yeah, right. How did you find my cabin?"

"I saw you driving out of the village center. There aren't any other cars like yours in the valley. How did you untie yourself, anyway?"

"Cub Scout training."

Then he asked seriously, "Do you really have a date?"

I shook my head. "No. Why?"

"Just wondering . . ." He then pulled two takeout containers from the bag and put them on the bureau. "It's supposed to be barbecued chicken with rice and salad," he said, "but everything's all run together and cold now."

"It doesn't matter. It's still food."

The bag also contained two icy-cold bottles of beer, which I opened for us. I sat on the bed while we ate, with my robe demurely concealing the Czech family jewels. Yudi sat on a chair facing me. He had a curious grin on his face. My intuition told me what that grin meant, but I didn't want to pursue it, not now at least.

He asked, "Is the food all right?"

"Sure," I said. "Not exactly the all-natural wilderness diet I'd expect up here, but it's fine."

I could see my words register with Yudi. He responded, "Roger liked health food, too."

I said, "How did you meet Roger?"

He ate vigorously while he talked. "He was on vacation in Bali last summer."

I chewed and swallowed the tepid chicken, thinking there's nothing like food when you're hungry. "Your summer or our summer?" I asked, recalling Bali is south of the equator.

Yudi thought a moment, then nodded. "That's right . . . our summer, your winter. We met on the beach near the Sanur." Yudi shrugged. "Roger liked me, and he asked me to come back with him. He thought I'd have a better life here, maybe go to school, so I said yes. I had nothing holding me there. My family's all gone. Anyway, I was tired of carving wooden fish and painting frogs on tourists' sneakers. And Roger was my first American." Yudi's eyes became glazed, and I sensed that he was remembering with fondness all the meaningless sex he had enjoyed with Roger. I imagined his firm brown body lying on the warm beach sand, and I began to understand Roger's response to him.

"Yudi, where did Roger used to climb rocks in the valley?"

"Usually he goes, I mean *went* with Jack. Jack runs the climbing school."

"That near here?"

"Sort of, but don't go there."

"Why not?"

"Jack is crazy."

We said no more, but watched each other eat until all the food was gone. Suddenly Yudi stood up. "I'd better go now." He leaned toward me and kissed me on the cheek.

"What's that for?" I asked.

"I think you're nice." His eyes were warm and inviting. "And before, when I was tying you up, I *did* find something I liked in your pockets."

I sensed a rustle among the crown jewels. "Don't worry," I said, testing the sincerity of his sudden enthusiasm, "it doesn't mean anything." To my surprise, he looked disappointed, then quickly ran out.

When I finished my shower, it was after 10 P.M. I lay down to rest and plan my next move, but instead, exhausted by travel and adventure, I fell asleep.

12

HOW HIGH THE MOON

Sunday morning I was awakened by a gentle tapping on my cabin door. I got up and spread the plaid curtains slightly to look outside. Yudi's face was pressed hard against the window. He used his lips, nose, and tongue to make writhing pink shapes on the frost-coated glass. It looked like a bad "artistic" moment from a porn film. I opened the door and said sharply, "What do you want?"

"I thought I'd take you to Jack's climbing school."

"Who says I want to go there?"

"I could tell what you wanted last night," he said, his brown eyes lively even at that hour.

"Yudi, I'll find what I need on my own, thanks."

"Then I'll come along for the ride."

Yudi's tan skin glowed and his black hair glistened in the early-morning sun. I knew he was flirting, and I was vaguely irritated at myself for responding so easily.

I said, "Don't you have anything else to do?"

"Now that Roger's gone, I don't have a job."

"Why not?"

"I used to help him."

"With what?"

"Just . . . doing things."

That sure sounded like houseboy duties to me.

Yudi went on, "And school doesn't start until next January."

I surrendered. "Come back in half an hour," I said. "I have to shower and get dressed."

"Want some help?"

I smiled. "Maybe another time."

"You still don't trust me, do you?"

"You tie a mean knot, Yudi."

"I told you I was sorry. I didn't know what else to do." His eyes looked sad for a moment, then brightened quickly. "I'll come back in thirty minutes."

When he left, it was seven-thirty, and true to his word, as the second hand completed its thirtieth tour on the face of my trusty Timex, Yudi was at my door again. This time he had a bag of food with him. "Let's have breakfast in your car," he said. "I know a good place on the way."

The place Yudi knew about had a spectacular view of the famous El Capitan. I pulled the car off the road near the base of the awesome pale granite monolith. Yudi had brought two completely different breakfasts: for himself, a gorgeous glazed Danish pastry, all buttery and flaky, filled with apricots and raspberries and almonds; and for me, one very beige, bland granola bar.

"Why?" I asked plaintively. "Why not just two Danish?"

Yudi answered, "From what you said last night, I thought you wanted health food, like Roger."

"No!" I wailed. "I thought *you* ate health food with him."

"I did, but I hated it. I'd always sneak off to get the stuff I really liked. Now I don't have to do that."

Oatmeal for me it was, then. I tried to enjoy it, for Roger's sake at least.

We set off for the climbing school, the one owned and operated by Roger's buddy Jack. Yudi knew the way and guided me easily. On and off we talked about life on Bali and life in Boston. From what Yudi said, people in Bali seemed to embrace Nature, to love it and cooperate with it. I thought glumly of life in Boston, where we seemed in constant contest with it.

Just as we approached the school, Yudi yelled, "Stop here!" Then he opened his door and suddenly jumped out of the car. "You go without me. I'll meet you when you finish with Jack." He closed the door and waved me off. I was about to ask where we should meet, but he disappeared magically among the trees, just like a nature boy.

I drove on to the climbing school and left the car in the gravel-covered parking area. There was only one other car there, an old Chevrolet coupe from the mid-fifties, intact but poorly maintained. In the bright sun, the once-gleaming black paint now had a dull matte finish with bluish streaks, and the heavy chrome was pitted and peeling with rust.

The school was a small wooden shack. Through its open door I heard the buzz of country-western music from a radio inside. I knocked on the door frame, but no one answered. When I called out "Hello?" a voice shouted, "In back!"

I walked around behind the shack and saw a man about fifteen feet up above the ground, grappling the underside of a horizontal projection of overhanging rock. He looked like a gigantic fly, defying gravity and creeping along a ceiling. "Just practicin' my boulderin'," he said. "Don't get much chance durin' tourist season."

I watched him, amazed.

"What can I do for ya?" he said as he carefully crept and turned his body around to face me upside down.

"I . . . I'm trying to find out what happened to my friend Roger . . . Roger Fayerbrock."

The man stopped wrangling with the rock and looked down at me with his head tilted oddly, like a praying mantis. He had short-cropped gray hair and about a week's growth of grizzled beard. "Who sent ya?"

"His friend."

"The little Filipino?"

"He's from Bali, actually."

"Who cares where he's from? Can't figure why Roger ever got mixed up with him."

"He has a certain charm."

"That what ya call it? Charm?" His upside-down face sneered. "Plain ol' queer to me." And as if to add dramatic flourish to his statement, he let himself fall.

"No!" I heard myself yell as he dropped through the air.

But he landed easily and upright on his strong legs. "It's okay," he said, grinning. "Do it all the time." He walked toward me with an extended hand. "Name's Jack. Jack Werdegar. Folks call me

Wacky-Jacky." His strong wiry body appeared to be in its forties, but his skin was already so weather-ravaged that I imagined he wouldn't look much different in twenty years.

I shook his hand. His grip could crush anything easily. My palm came back covered with white powder. "Chalk," he said. "Need it for keeping a dry grip on the rocks. Gets real sweaty up there."

"I wouldn't know."

"Never climbed?"

I shook my head emphatically.

"Then how ya know Roger?"

"College buddies," I said, already feeling his abridged syntax affect my own speech.

"Huh!" he said with great doubt in his small shifty eyes. "Didn't know he went to college." He began methodically packing his gear.

I said, "I was wondering if you had any idea why Roger went to Boston recently."

He looked up at me with a suspicious glance. "Far as I know, went to climb Ol' Man o' the Mountain."

"That's what I heard, but he didn't take any climbing gear with him back East. Isn't that strange?"

"Nah. Pick up what he needed there." He stopped organizing his gear and faced me. His shifty gaze met my steady eyes. "Rumor says Roger got himself killed back there."

I nodded. "It's true. That's why I'm here."

He grunted. "You a cop?"

I shook my head no.

He said, "Rog never got to climb the mountain?"

"No."

"Too bad. He was a good rock man."

And good dream material, too, I thought soberly. "Jack, I heard that slide on Washington Column really bothered him."

The man bristled. "Little pansy tell ya that? Can't trust him, y'know. Imagination runs wild."

"I've often been accused of the same thing."

"Ya not like him, are ya?"

"Does it matter?"

"Guess not. Ya don't live *here* at least."

That was a cheery welcome-wagon attitude. I persisted anyway. "Why did the slide upset Roger?"

"Don't know nothin' about rocks, do ya?"

"I had a collection when I was young."

Wacky-Jacky laughed. "Best way to learn is to get on 'em."

"Doesn't appeal to me." There it was again, the contagious speech pattern.

"Take ya on an easy slab. Probably love it. Most guys end up hooked on the buzz they get. C'mon. Ya're already wearin' sneaks. Get ya by on an easy slope."

"No," I said, backing away slightly. "I'm fine right here."

He hoisted the coils of ropes over his shoulder. "Suit ya'self. Ya wanna talk, ya come to my place, and my place"—he jerked his thumb toward the cliffs overhead—"is up there." They looked extremely high and far away.

"Thanks, but I'm sure we can talk just as easily right here."

"Suit ya'self," he said again, and headed toward the shack.

I saw my opportunity walking away. "Wait!" I yelped.

"Yeah?" he said, turning.

"You said an easy one, right?" I asked tentatively. What choice did I have?

He grinned. "Sure! Ya gonna love it!"

He went into the shack and brought out a nylon web belt.

"Put this on." He pushed it into my belly. It had metal rings and pins and clips hanging all around it, along with hanks of nylon rope.

I attached the belt around my waist. I felt like a telephone lineman. "I thought you said we'd do an easy one."

"We will. Just two pitches."

"Pictures?"

"Pitches, man! Pitches! That's the climb between two flat places."

"Why not just say slope then?"

"Nah! Slope is different. Slope is . . . slope is . . . slope is the whole thing."

"So, many pitches make a slope?"

"Ya got it. Hey, ya're smart."

"Thanks, but if it's going to be so easy, why do I have to wear all this stuff?"

"Always gotta have some friends with ya, no matter how easy the climb."

"Friends?"

"That's what we call the safety gear, 'cause when it saves ya life, man, it's ya *friend*." Then the guy named Wacky-Jacky looked me over and winked. "Besides," he added, "I like the way it looks on ya." He cackled. "Better roll up ya pants, too."

"Why?"

"Makes movin' easier."

I did as he suggested and carefully rolled the legs of my baggy khakis up. He approved heartily. "Get 'em up higher. Yeah, like that. Hey, good legs!"

"So people say."

I noticed, though, that he wasn't wearing the same kind of equipment he'd foisted on me. When I asked him about it, he said, "I got the clips on my belt here." He proudly showed me the metal hardware around the heavy leather belt on his jeans. "For the kind of climb we're doin', this'll hold just fine in an emergency."

"Emergency, Jack?"

"Don't worry, kid. No one's gonna fall."

"Hope ya right," I said doubtfully in his vernacular.

"Let's go!"

I was wary of his enthusiasm, but I wanted him to talk, so I humored him. I figured I would find out what I wanted before we started the actual climb. Then I could back out at the last minute. Besides, I had no intention of ruining my new ecru leather sneakers frolicking about on the rocks.

I tried to question him as we walked, but all he said was, "Gotta be quiet now. Goin' to church. The rocks are like church." My plan to talk now and back out later obviously wasn't going to work.

We arrived at the base of a steep hill of smooth granite. Close up, it didn't look threatening, but it didn't look easy to climb, either. Jack took a rope and passed it through one of the metal rings around his belt. He attached the other end of the rope to one of the rings on my belt. "Now we're safe," he said with a wink and a laugh.

He turned to begin the climb up the wall of rock. He said, "Watch me go up. Then, when I'm up there on that ledge, I'll give ya the signal to start. Just do it the same way I do. Keep ya hands and feet flat on the rock and ya fanny in the air. And don't look down!"

Sounded easy enough. I just wasn't prepared for how smoothly and deliberately he moved, crawling quickly on all fours up the slope. When he was halfway up, about thirty feet, he called back to me, "See how?"

"Yeah, Jack. But I think I'm changing my mind."

"Aw, c'mon! Ya don't want me to drag ya up here by the rope, do ya?"

"Uh, no."

He continued climbing up the rock to the first ledge. He attached the safety line to a rock up there, then pulled the rope so that it was taut. "Okay!" he called down. "You climb up now. Don't worry. I got the rope secured."

My moment had come, so I launched myself up the rock. If nothing else, I've got good legs and feet, so I used them to clamber up the granite the way Jack had done. It was easier than I expected, especially with the extra grip my new sneakers provided. I pulled myself up onto the shallow ledge where Jack was, then stood up to survey the scenery with him. We were probably sixty feet from the ground, and even at that elevation, the view of the valley was different. The granite felt warm and strong, almost friendly.

"It's really beautiful," I said. "Unspoiled. I hope it never changes."

Wacky-Jacky said, "Still some holdin's down there."

"Holdens? Are they related to William Holden?" Hell, we *were* in California.

Wacky-Jacky made a face. "Holdin's! *In*-holdin's!"

I shook my head. "I don't understand. What's that?"

"Private land," said Wacky-Jacky. "The owners are still *holdin'* it."

Holding, I thought. *In*-holdings. Still didn't make sense to me. "You mean there's private land here? In a National Park?"

He nodded. "Sure."

"But it's protected, right? I mean, they can't build on it or anything, can they?"

"All kinds of rules s'pose to protect it, but ya never know."

I imagined some dreadful condo project with swimming pools and tennis courts and wire-link fences. "That would be a tragedy," I said, looking out o'er purple mountains' majesty.

"Old, old fight. Still up in the air." Then Wacky-Jacky winked at me again. I was hoping it was a nervous habit and not a courtship ritual. "Let's get goin'," he said. "One more pitch. But ya're the anchor now." He positioned me like a wedge between two rocks. "Now don't move till I tell ya."

"Why not?"

"So's in case I fall, man, I don't go no further than where ya' standin' here."

"Oh," I said. Great! Now I had my life *and* his to worry about.

He began climbing the second pitch, which looked much steeper than the first one. The simple flat hand and foot technique that had worked earlier no longer sufficed. Jack yelled back as he climbed, "Watch me! Look where my hands and feet are goin'. Ya gonna copy me!"

"Fine," I said, but I detected a serious note in his voice. When he finally reached the ledge at the top, he secured the rope again, then yelled down to me, "Okay, yar turn! Put ya hands and feet where I put 'em. Jus' stay relaxed and alert!"

Sure, I thought, but my hands had become sweaty just watching him go up before me. I took a deep breath and headed up the granite slab. I tried to mimic the method Jack had used to get up the second pitch, and for most of it I was fine. At one point I lost my footing and slipped back a few feet. I felt myself grappling madly along the rock, but then the safety rope stopped my downward movement.

"Y'all right?" Jack yelled.

"Just testing the line!" I yelled back, but I thought I'd died and been reborn in those seconds. Now I knew what these rock climbers were after: that surge of life-after-death energy they got when they *didn't* die. And people call the things *I* do unnatural!

But the real moment of truth came near the top of the pitch, where I would have to pull myself up onto the ledge. The rock became vertical for a few feet before curving slightly outward from the wall up there. I didn't quite know where to make my next grip, and I made the idiotic decision to look down. I saw that I was over a hundred feet from the ground. All at once my guts got light and a unpleasant tingle spread across my shoulders. I closed my eyes. Mantra time. Then I heard Jack yelling, "What's goin' on? Hey! Ain't no time for a nap!" I opened my eyes, but there was no way in hell I was going to move.

He hollered instructions from where he was kneeling securely on the ledge directly above me. "One hand up here. C'mon guy, let's go! Do it!"

"I think I'll just stay here for a while."

"Can't! Gonna wear ya'self out squeezin' the rock like that."

It was true. I was holding on so tightly that the fingers on both my hands were white and trembling already. He said, "C'mon fella. I gotcha on the safety line. Just put one hand up here with me."

"Help me!"

"Better if ya do it ya'self."

Damn you, I thought. I don't have to prove I'm a man this way. This was probably supposed to be some kind of rock climber's rite of passage, but all I knew was I hadn't learned anything about Roger, and now I felt I was on the verge of plummeting fifty feet to the first ledge, then crashing another sixty after that, safety rope or not. The valley didn't seem so beautiful now.

Wacky-Jacky continued coaxing me. "One hand up here, palm down." He patted the ledge above me, as if to make it more homey. "Move it up here smooth and easy."

Okay, buster. I'll be a man. In as casual a gesture as I could manage dangling one hundred feet above the ground, I released one shaking white hand, reached up high above my head, and slapped it palm down onto the ledge above me. "Good," he said, beckoning me with his fingers. "The other one. C'mon, buddy."

Moving my other hand was going to be worse, though, because even if I dared to move it, I'd also have to shift both my legs at the same time. At that one moment, all my weight would be supported by the lonely hand, which was already grappling for dear life up on the ledge. Jack coaxed me. I took a big breath . . . then *reached* and grabbed with everything in me! Finally I had both palms on the ledge, wobbling in terror. "Now just walk up the rock," he said.

"No way, pal!"

"A baby could do it, I'm telling ya! One foot in front of the other."

I tried, inch by inch, to do as he said. He cooed softly, "That's it, boy. Easy does it. Come to Papa."

"Papa-Shmapa! Now what?" My ass was hanging out into the air, and my legs were bent so that my knees were up near my chest.

He said, "Big breath, boy. Ready?"

"Help!" I gasped.

"Jee*zus!*" he yelled. "Look at that big ol' rattlesnake nippin' at ya butt!"

It was do or die, so I did. I pushed down with everything I had in me and scrambled my legs up onto the ledge. I collapsed on the narrow ledge, breathless and speechless. I was home safe!

He laughed. "Ya really got pumped there. Good thing ya didn't fall ya first time up. Mighta ruined ya for climbin'."

"Not to mention living."

"How ya feelin'?" he asked.

"Alive!" I gasped.

"That's the rush. Ya get to like it, then ya want *more.*"

"Where's that snake?"

Wacky-Jacky laughed loud and long. "Ain't no snake! Fooled ya!" Then he knelt down beside me and spoke low. "Y'know what'd be real nice right now?"

"A double martini."

"I mean somethin' that'd let ya know how alive ya really are?"

"I'm feeling pretty alive right now, thanks."

He murmured, "We let off up here."

"What!"

"It's great."

"Here? On the rocks?"

"Sure. C'mon."

"I'm fine, thanks. I'll just rest for a while."

"Suit ya'self. I'm gonna."

He stood up and faced away from me, out toward the vast wilderness. From behind I could sense him unfasten his jeans and open them. He muttered to me, "Hey, don't get me wrong. I'm just havin' a little fun."

"It's all right, Jack. Do what you have to do."

"Just don't get the wrong idea."

"Not at all, Jack. People are always spilling their procreative juices around me."

I could sense him unfurl himself from his white jockey shorts. I tried to ignore him and concentrate on the valley below, but I couldn't help sensing him next to me, teetering at the rock's edge as his body swayed in anticipation of the impending release. It was grotesque. I mean, *my* idea of kinky sex is satin sheets at the Ritz.

It was then that I noticed how scuffed my new sneaks had got in the skirmish to get up on the ledge. Damn, I thought! I leaned forward to examine the damaged leather, and while doing it, I accidentally moved the safety rope attached to the belt on Jack's jeans, which were already slipping lower on his hips. I don't know how it happened, but the minuscule tug on the line must have been just enough to alter his precarious balance. It was as simple as now you see him now you don't.

I heard him yell at exactly the moment I felt the line spring taut next to me. Fortunately, he'd secured the rope, so he didn't fall far. I looked over the edge and saw him hanging upside down in a state of *demi-dishabille*. His shirt had fallen over his face, so all I could see was his torso, his white jockey shorts, his legs, and his jeans, now gathered around his ankles. He wasn't moving.

"Jack?" I said. "Are you all right?"

From under the shirt his voice sounded frightened but under control. "Is the safety line secure?"

I checked it on the rock behind me. "Yes, it is."

He spoke with care. "Listen. My belt is slippin' from my jeans. If I move, I'll lose the safety line. I fall on my head, I'm done. Ya gotta help me."

He was right. The place where the safety line was attached to his belt was moving in small, almost invisible steps, I gulped. "Uh, okay, Jack. Just tell me what to do."

Jack measured his words. "I can't see, dumbo! I can't move. *You* gotta do it. Ya're on ya own. Just grab my ankles. I'll do the rest."

"Sure, Jack. It's going to be okay." I'd never had a person's life in my hands before—their reputation for fashion and style, perhaps, but never their life. But at that very moment, a perverse thought occurred: Jack hadn't yet kept his part of the agreement we'd made earlier. He hadn't told me about Roger and the slide. No time like the present, I thought.

"Uh, Jack?" I said innocently.

"What! What are ya waitin' for?"

"Jack, we never got to talk about Roger."

"What!" The rope slipped a half-inch. "Shit!" muttered Jack.

"So I was wondering—"

"Damn you! What are ya ramblin' about?"

"Jack, talk nice to me," I said with the gentle persuasiveness of a toddler's television host. "Tell me why that slide bothered Roger so much."

"What! You grab my ankles now!"

The rope did a baby slip.

"Jack, I want to help you, but first you have to help me."

"Grrrrraaaagh!" went Jack.

Slip, slip went the rope on his belt.

"Why did Roger go to Boston."

"Damn you! Damn! You!"

"Jack?"

Slip.

"Okay! Okay!" he said. "Ya got me by the balls."

"Not quite, Jack."

"Take my ankles and I'll tell ya."

"Say it first."

Slip, slip.

"I *hate* ya!" he yelled. Then, a moment later, with a savage growl, he said, "Roger thought someone blew up them rocks on purpose!"

"So! It wasn't a natural slide?"

"No!"

"And that's why Roger went to Boston?"

"Damn, yes! That's why!"

"What's in Boston?"

"I don't know, damn you, fucker! *Grab my ankles!*"

"Okay, Jack."

I grabbed on to his ankles, and the instant I did, he curled himself up and grabbed on to the safety rope himself. Then he pulled himself up onto the ledge. He looked at me with a mean glare. "That wasn't fair," he said.

"I had to know, Jack."

He stood up and refastened his jeans.

I said, "Didn't you at least enjoy the rush, the one you weren't expecting?"

He breathed heavily for a few moments, while he reattached the safety line and felt good old terra firma under him again. After a few minutes of quiet fuming, he looked at me, and to my surprise, he smiled. "Y'know, buddy, maybe ya right." Then he put his arm around my neck and pulled me toward him. "I sure wasn't expecting *that* kinda rush. And now that I'm up here safe and sound with ya, I confess it *was* real nice."

"Jack, I wasn't really going to let you fall." But I wondered how a person could be on the verge of death at one moment, and at the next be thanking you for the excitement of it. Was I unwittingly into heavy S/M?

Getting down from the rocks was extremely easy since there was an alternate hiking route on the other side of the mountain. When we returned to the climbing school, Jack shook my hand and said, "Thanks again for the rush, buddy. Ya oughta try climbin' more. Ya're a natural."

"I'm still afraid of heights."

"Nah, ya get used to it. Come by anytime, take ya up again."

I'm sure you would, I thought.

It was after two o'clock when I got in the car. I drove back out to the main road, and felt a burning soreness in my fingertips as I handled the steering wheel. Then it clicked, and I knew what had caused those strange calluses on Roger's fingertips: the rocks.

As I drove from the school, I looked around for Yudi. I wondered if he'd seen Jack and me in our Folies Bergère number up on the ledge. I assumed he'd be watching out for me along the road. He couldn't miss spotting the big red clunker I was driving in that natural setting. I reached the main valley road without finding him, so I backtracked all the way to the climbing school again, but with no luck. I gave up and drove into the village, hoping to find him along the way, but it didn't happen.

Instead of searching any longer, I drove to the Ohlone Hotel to keep my luncheon interrogation with Mr. Leonard. Now that I was armed with more information, I wanted to find out just how much he knew. Yudi would have to understand that I didn't have time for hide and seek.

13

LUNCH WITH THE SWELLS

When I returned to the Ohlone, I went directly to Mr. Leonard's salon on the mezzanine. Instead of politely using the doorbell, though, I acted like a cop and banged loudly on the door. Then I tried to open it without waiting for an answer, figuring I'd barge in like a he-man. Of course, the door was locked, and my act was ruined.

I started pressing the doorbell repeatedly until I heard footsteps on the other side of the door. Moments later, the door latch buzzed and I went inside. Mr. Leonard was lounging by the window in a billowing caftan of turquoise and cobalt-colored raw silk. The fabric was strangely gathered at the bustline to create an illusion that his chest measurement was bigger than his waistline. In the sunlight, his dyed hair glowed like an orange shag rug. The enormous rose-tinted lenses of his glasses were beveled and shaped like lotus petals. He was giving himself a manicure, and his technique was abominable. He sawed at his nails with the file instead of pulling it gently across the edge of each nail in one direction only. He looked up nonchalantly and said, "You've come back."

I just stared at him.

"Did you find Roger's cabin?"

I nodded.

"And was it exactly where I told you?"

I nodded again.

He removed his glasses. "So you owe me a favor," he said smugly.

I stared without saying a word.

"When can I exact payment?"

"Now," I said finally. "Lunch."

"Well! I like a man who clears his debts." Mr. Leonard picked up the phone and punched in three numbers. "Donald? Leonard. I'd like my table set now. Yes, I know the dining room is closed, but I have a guest whose schedule is somewhat, er, inflexible. Yes, Donald, I understand. Thank you, Donald." He hung up, then cocked his head toward me and raised one eyebrow. I think he was trying to be sexy. "Why don't you go down to the dining room and wait for me there. Donald, the maître d'hôtel, will seat you and select the wine. I'll join you shortly."

I left him and went downstairs to the main lobby, but I had no intention of sitting and waiting for him. Instead I returned to the cocktail lounge where I'd got my first lead on Mr. Leonard yesterday. I wanted to thank the barmaid who'd helped me, but she wasn't on duty. So, instead, I wandered through the Ohlone's lobby. I found the main parlor, a gigantic hall designed for serious lounging. At each end of the room was a colossal stone fireplace large enough to walk into. The fieldstones reached right up to the ceiling, as did the tall windows running along either side of the huge rectangular room. The top four feet of the windows were fitted with panels of geometrically shaped stained glass in shades of red, orange, gold, blue, and green. The multicolored glass filtered and scattered the sunlight into dazzling rainbows.

When I was sure I was late and Mr. Leonard would be waiting for me, I strolled casually into the cavernous dining room. The place was empty except for his lone body, seated at a table tucked into an alcove of bay windows at the far end of the dining room. I told the headwaiter, who must have been Donald, that I was Mr. Leonard's guest. He nodded obligingly and led me to the table. The dining room windows also stretched from the floor to the ceiling thirty feet above. Instead of stained glass on top, they offered a vast panorama of the valley walls outside. Seated beneath this grandeur was my host. He'd changed from his control-top muumuu to tan slacks and a blouson overshirt of hunter green linen. He did not seem pleased to see me.

"I expected you to be here for me!" He'd recently doused himself with sweet floral cologne, which instantly irritated my sinuses.

"I was looking around the hotel," I answered coolly. "Guess I lost track of the time. Sorry."

He fluttered his eyes coyly. "You're forgiven."

Donald poured red wine for me, and I asked him for a menu. Mr. Leonard interrupted. "I've already ordered for us."

"How do you know what I like?"

"Dear boy, you must trust me. I never allow the menu to limit me. The kitchen staff understands my taste."

I'll bet they do, I thought. "I'm not a boy," I said.

"Darling, it was a compliment to your youthfulness."

I sipped at the wine and found it agreeably dry and fruity. Points for Donald and the California vintner.

Mr. Leonard jabbered for a while about his past, how his talent was never appreciated in New York or Los Angeles, so he set himself up at the Ohlone and catered to rich tourists. When I asked him where he'd learned his color technique, he snarled, "With my eyes! They are the only true instruments of my art." I wondered when he'd last had a spectroscopic examination.

Then he said, "So you found Roger's place exactly where I said?"

I nodded. "I already told you that."

"And there was nothing there, as I predicted, right?"

I swirled my wineglass gently for a dramatic pause. "Wrong," I said. Then I faced him squarely. "There were lots of things."

Mr. Leonard drank some wine. "Really?" He tried to sound indifferent, but I could tell he was dying to know what I'd found in Roger's cabin. "Tell me," he said.

"Roger was an avid rock climber."

He shuddered slightly. "Oh, that nonsense! I already told you he was always crawling around up there, trying to prove what a man he was." Mr. Leonard's words recalled my own similar opinion about the sport, and I decided to change my attitude immediately.

I continued, "I also found out that Roger was really upset by the recent rock slide on Washington Column."

Mr. Leonard's eyes narrowed. "Who told you that?"

"Someone I ran into there."

"Ah yes," he said with relief. "Yudi." His eyelids relaxed. "Roger's little dog. I warned you about him."

"He's more like a puppy, actually."

"Then he hasn't bitten you yet."

"Don't assume too much," I said.

Mr. Leonard arched an eyebrow. "Care to elaborate?"

I shook my head. "You don't seem to like him, though."

"Darling, I dislike any rival. He, like you, got to enjoy Roger's flesh, a privilege I was never allowed."

"There are no rules with objects of desire." Nikki's philosophy seemed appropriate at the moment.

"Does that include me and you?" he asked. He indicated the two of us with a limp gesture of his hand, while the diamonds on his watch glittered in the sunlight.

"No," I said. "Desire does not apply to us."

Mr. Leonard bristled. "Well, that Yudi's a rotten little liar, anyway. Don't believe a word he says."

Our lunch arrived. Cubes of fresh salmon had been marinated, skewered, and grilled, then dressed with a sauce lightly flavored with tarragon and balsamic vinegar. Two vegetables accompanied the fish: broccoli flowerets sprinkled with olive oil and fresh lemon juice, and a gratin of pumpkin spiced with cardamom.

Donald removed Mr. Leonard's unfinished glass of red wine and replaced it with a clean smaller glass into which he poured a crackling cool white wine. He was about to do the same for me, but I discreetly touched the base of my glass. "I'll stay with red, thanks."

Mr. Leonard shrieked, "Not with the fish!"

I calmly answered, "Where I come from, anything goes."

He glared at me, shook his head, then popped a big chunk of salmon into his soft mouth. He chewed sloppily, leaving his lips open as he maneuvered the food within. "Mmmmm," he said. "Superb, as usual."

I started with a broccoli bud. The olive oil was vintage stuff, definitely cold-pressed from fine green olives. Despite my feelings about Mr. Leonard, he was right about one thing: The food was simple and superb.

I said casually, "Roger thought the rocks were blown up."

Mr. Leonard's eye popped open. "Who told you that?"

I smiled enigmatically.

"Damn little Filipino, I bet!" he snapped.

"Why does everyone think that? Yudi's from Bali."

Mr. Leonard shrugged. "Same thing. So *he* told you?"

I shook my head. "No. It was a guy named Jack."

"Jack who!" Mr. Leonard's fork plopped quietly into his pumpkin gratin.

"Runs a climbing school around here."

He quickly composed himself. "You do get around, darling." He picked up his fork and ate the pumpkin adhering to it, as though he'd intended to pick it up that way in the first place.

I took my first piece of salmon. It was delicately glazed and crusty from the grill, yet the flesh inside was moist with flavorful marinade. Someone in that kitchen knew what they were doing, and I was enjoying the results.

I asked, "Did Roger ever talk to you about the slide not being an accident, that someone had purposely caused it?"

Mr. Leonard was trying hard to appear blasé. "Anything that touched Roger's sacred valley upset him, but the idea of someone purposely blowing up Washington Column is nonsense, of course." He took some wine into his mouth and sloshed it around for a while.

I thought he might even gargle with it. Finally, after he swallowed it, he said, "It's true that Roger dearest *did* carry on a bit, writing letters, calling people, trying to be the hero of the land, and all that."

"Letters to whom?"

"Eh?" A nasty eye peered over the rim of his wineglass and a ruby blazed in the ring on his pinky finger.

"Whom did he write to?"

"Well, I'm sure *I* don't know. That was *his* little obsession."

"But if he wrote so many letters, where are they now?"

Mr. Leonard stared at me, trying to maintain a poker face, but the effort gave him away. "I imagine the police confiscated everything," he said.

"Why should they? Roger was a victim, not a suspect."

In response Mr. Leonard cocked his head coquettishly and shrugged one shoulder. "Darling, I really don't know."

We ate quietly for a while, but through it all I could sense him scrutinizing me and brooding about something. It was all I could do to keep cool with his eyes boring through my clothes and into me. Finally, he slammed his fork down and said, "What are you *really* doing here? What do you want? You must be after something. Everybody is."

I continued eating and answered him flippantly. "I told you before, I want to find out why Roger went to Boston."

"What good will that do?"

"Let's just say I'm settling a personal matter." I paused to savor a morsel of fish, then continued, "I already know who killed him."

"You do?" His mouth dropped and I witnessed a rather unattractive mélange of broccoli, pumpkin, salmon, and wine inside.

I nodded. "I just need some hard evidence to convince the police."

Mr. Leonard returned to his food, but then suddenly looked at his watch. "You'll have to excuse me," he said, and motioned for Donald. "I've just remembered, I have an appointment now. Please finish without me."

"I've had enough, thanks." Actually, during lunch I'd realized what I had to do next, and there was no more time to waste sitting around with this guy. I'd already found what I wanted to know anyway. By his responses, I knew Leonard was involved somehow with Roger's trip to Boston, and he was lying badly about it.

Donald arrived at our table and politely offered coffee and dessert. I said, "Just the bill, please."

Donald smiled back graciously. "It's already been taken care of."

Mr. Leonard interjected, "It's a peace offering for my being so testy, Stan. You don't mind if I call you Stan, do you?" he asked with a leer.

How could I ever explain how *much* I minded?

"Thanks," I said, "but I don't want any favors."

He continued, "But, Stan, I told you before, I get so little opportunity for stimulating company up here. I'm afraid I've forgotten all my social graces. So please accept this lunch as my personal gratitude for your presence."

I stood up. "Fine. Thanks, Lenny," I chirped.

He tried to muffle a belch.

I said, "I gotta go now, too . . . lots to do." I extended my hand reluctantly. It seemed the least I could do, since he'd probably dropped over seventy bucks for lunch. But when Mr. Leonard grabbed my hand, I regretted it. His paw was clammy. He clenched my hand hard and yanked me toward him, pulling my face close to his.

"Come to my penthouse tonight," he said with breathless desperation. "Please!"

It was all I could do to keep my voice calm, with my hand clenched uncomfortably in his. I spoke distinctly, with a cool even tone. "Thank you for lunch. I have things to do." I tried to pull away, but he drew me even closer. His sweet cologne mingled with the smell of grilled fish on his breath—not exactly an aphrodisiac. I placed my free hand on his bare forearm as if to confirm the handshake. Then in one deliberate motion, I dug my fingernails into his skin and yanked my other hand free.

As I hurried away from the table, I heard him hiss at me, "Bitch!"

14

TREES BEARING FRUIT

The four o'clock sun cast mauve, pink, and yellow streaks across a pale blue sky. Nature seemed beautiful and serene in Yosemite, yet the people I was meeting there seemed unbalanced and bizarre. (And country folk think *city* folk are strange!)

I drove the rented red ark out of the Ohlone Hotel parking lot and turned onto the main road back to my cabin, wondering where Yudi was hiding and where he would turn up next. No sooner had I thought it than I saw him sitting on a rock among the trees just off the road. Perhaps he really *was* a forest sprite who responded to people's thoughts.

He waved to me, and I pulled the car off the road onto the shoulder. Instead of coming to the car, though, he signaled me to get out and go to him, so I did. As I approached, he put up one hand to stop me, then moved his finger to his lips to silence me. In a moment I saw why. A small bright yellow bird with black wings fluttered toward him. Yudi put his index finger straight out like a perch in front of him, and as though in an animated film, the little bird chirped and lighted on the outstretched finger. Yudi tested the creature's tenacity by swinging his hand in a slow and ever-widening arc. The bird flapped its wings to maintain its balance, then finally flew off his hand. From a crumpled paper bag near his feet, Yudi took another crumb and placed it on his finger. Within seconds the bird returned, but this time just snatched the crumb and flew away.

Yudi said, "He must have seen you."

"The face that stopped a thousand clocks."

"That's not what I meant."

"Do you always feed animals like this?"

"Sometimes."

"How do you get a wild bird to be so tame?"

"He knows I won't hurt him, so he's just being natural." Yudi picked up the paper bag and twisted it into a tight cruller as he asked me, "Did you climb with Jack?"

"Uh, yeah . . ." I wondered again if he'd seen us together up on that ledge earlier today, with Jack indulging his acrobatic exhibitionism.

"I thought so. When you didn't come back soon, I knew he took you up. Roger and he were always up there."

Yudi's use of *he* prompted me to ask where he'd learned English. "A man from England lived in Bali," he answered. "But Roger helped me with the American slang." (Just as I'd suspected.)

"Yudi, why doesn't Jack like you?"

He stood up and stretched his limber young body. The tan skin of his belly peeked out between his shirt and jeans. He caught me staring and smiled mischievously. "Jack thinks I made Roger have sex with me, but it was really the other way around. Roger started the whole thing. I only did it to thank him for bringing me here from Bali."

That was quite a different song from the "it didn't mean anything" protests Yudi had given me yesterday.

I said, "Jack told me Roger went to Boston because he thought the slide wasn't natural, that someone had blown the rocks up on purpose."

Yudi said, "It's true."

"You knew it, too?"

"I knew that Roger *thought* they were." His dancing eyes showed that he enjoyed misleading and teasing me.

"Why didn't you tell me that before?"

He shrugged. "I didn't think of it." Then he said, "I can smell Ms. Leona's perfume on you."

"I had lunch with him."

"Is that all?"

"Why?"

"It doesn't matter. You can do whatever you want. You don't owe me anything, not after how I treated you yesterday." In spite of his words, though, he looked hurt, as though I'd broken a pledge and had given myself to Mr. Leonard.

"I'm telling you, Yudi, nothing happened. We just had lunch and talked."

"Where?"

"In the Ohlone dining room."

"What did you talk about?"

"Roger, of course."

"And me?"

"And you, and Jack, and the slide."

"Don't believe anything he said."

"Why not?"

"Leona is the worst liar in the valley."

"He said the same about you."

"But *he's* a liar."

I recalled a similar argument between me and Branco about my story versus Calvin's, and also a similar conclusion. It was time to act on the idea I'd got while dining with Mr. Leonard. "Yudi, can you take me to the slide?"

"You want to go *there?*"

I nodded. "I want to see what it looks like."

"You can't get to it." He looked frightened. "It's all roped off."

"But I bet you know a way."

"No. The rangers are everywhere."

"Even tonight? Off-season?"

I watched him think a moment before asking, "What do I get if I take you?"

No free rides. "I'll buy you dinner."

"And then?" His eyes teased and allured.

"One step at a time, pal." What was going on? I wondered. Suddenly I was Queen for a Day and the three valley men I'd met all had sex on their mind.

"All right," Yudi said eagerly. "I'll take you, but we should put on dark clothes first. I'll go change and meet you in the village center later."

"I can drive you home."

"No."

"It's on the way."

"No it isn't."

"It's no trouble."

"No!" He made a gesture to hug me, then stopped himself. "I'll go rent the bikes before they close. I'll meet you at the bike shop around eight. It'll be dark enough by then." He left me standing among the trees.

On the way back to my cabin I stopped at a pay phone to call Nicole. It was almost six o'clock, and with the time-zone difference, she should have been relaxing at home on a Sunday evening. She was home all right, but she wasn't relaxing. She picked the phone up on the first ring.

"Nikki?" I said.

Her voice was anxious. "Thank god you've called!"

"Why? What's happening?"

"Lieutenant Branco paid me a visit today, at home!"

"*Chez toi?* What did he want?"

"He was looking for you and he was ripping mad."

"Must have been that packet of sweet nothings I sent him." I was referring to the mangled threat note.

"That was one thing, and he also found out that you visited Calvin in jail, and he knows you've skipped town."

"Who told him?"

"Darling, how should I know?"

"Well, he can't do much about it now."

"Wrong, Stanley. He gave me a message for you."

"Yes?"

"He said if you don't report to him in Boston, in *person*, by nine o'clock tomorrow morning, he's putting out a search on you."

"Come on!"

"Those were his exact words. Stanley, he's serious."

"You didn't tell him where I was, did you?"

"Of course not! I told him I had no idea where you were, and that I was annoyed with you, too, for running out on me . . .

which I *am*, Stanley. I think you'd better get back here before you have a police escort."

"I can't leave now, Nikki. I'm on to something. There was a big rock slide up here—"

"Stanley, come home now!"

"I just need one more night, Nikki. I'm on my way right now to have a look at the rock slide."

"What are you talking about?"

"There was a big rock slide up here, and from what I've heard, Roger thought someone deliberately caused it. It wasn't natural."

"And your vast experience with unnatural acts will tell you something tonight?"

"Anything that helps explain *why* he went to Boston may point to the killer's motive."

"Stanley, you are obsessed with this."

"No, doll, I'm focused. That's the new term for it." I heard her exasperated sigh over the phone line. "How's Sugar Baby?" I asked, hoping to ease the tension rising between us.

"Right now she's waging war with a champagne cork."

I envisioned my favorite cat tossing the cork high into the air, then springing up to intercept it midflight. "Do you think she misses me?"

"Don't change the subject. You'll see her tonight."

"I will?"

"Yes, Stanley, when you come home. Or have you forgotten the lieutenant's warning already?"

"When I'm done out here, Mother, I'll be back."

"Tonight, Stanley. He wants you in town tomorrow morning."

"I can't, Nikki."

"Call him, then, and explain that to him."

"Oh, all right! But I'm coming back tomorrow anyway. I don't see what difference a few hours will make."

"Just call him, and call *me* back as soon as you know your flight." She hung up as usual, without saying good-bye.

I figured I'd call Branco later, after my adventure with Yudi. I'd have more to tell him, and maybe he'd be more sympathetic. Then

I figured, Why bother to call at all? I'd be back in Boston tomorrow even though it wouldn't be exactly in the morning. That logic, however, turned out to be unsound.

When I got to the village bike shop later, Yudi was waiting for me. He'd put on black jeans and a black sweatshirt, with black sneakers and a black leather bomber's jacket. Maybe it was my nerves, or maybe it was the moonlight, but Yudi looked more desirable than I wanted to admit. Two bikes were resting against a nearby tree.

"Let's go!" he muttered testily.

"What's the matter? You sound annoyed."

"I changed my mind. I don't think this is a good idea."

"Everything will be fine," I said, wishing I could believe my own words.

Yudi looked down at the ground and kicked at the dirt with the toe of his sneaker. "Roger went out to the slide a lot, and look what happened to him."

I tried to sound courageous and sure of our mission. "Yudi, *someone's* got to find out what really happened. If we don't do it, who will?"

He didn't look convinced but got on his bike anyway.

We rode along the bike path, past the Ohlone Hotel and on into the woods. We went all the way to the end of the path, then started walking. It was completely dark now, and we had only the light of the near full moon and our flashlights. Yudi led the way.

"Don't use your flashlight except for one second," he said. "The light really shows up here."

We walked cautiously through the darkness. Save the occasional soft crunch of redwood needles under our feet, the quiet forest air was almost disturbing. Having adapted to the urban noise of automobiles, raucous neighbors, and canned music, I'd forgotten the heightened awareness that absolute quiet can bring.

Through the darkness ahead I perceived what looked like a fence made of light-colored cloth, faintly visible in the moonlight.

When we got to it, I found that it was a wide belt of yellow Mylar imprinted every few feet with the warning:

DANGEROUS AREA

DO NOT ENTER

The two-foot-wide band of plastic sheeting had been wrapped around the trunks of trees and stretched throughout the forest. It glowed eerily in the moonlight.

"It's not much of a deterrent," I remarked.

Yudi said, "What's a deterrent?"

"Something that prevents something else from happening, like fences blocking the way."

He considered my words a moment, then asked, "Or condoms preventing disease?"

"Yeah, or conception, even."

"Deterrent," he said again as we ducked under the yellow plastic. We walked on for another fifteen minutes and I wondered whether we'd ever reach our destination.

Then suddenly we were upon it, and my fretting vanished in the wondrous vision before us. Massive hunks of jagged black granite rose up in the bluish moonlight, some half the size of a Back Bay brownstone. I looked up and saw the pinnacle of Washington Column in the moonlight. I wondered how such huge and horrible boulders had ever stayed up on top.

Yudi said, "It's amazing, isn't it?"

"Pretty impressive."

"What are you going to do?"

"I want to look around, get the feeling of it. The size is overwhelming. I've never seen anything like this before."

"They've all been here already, the rangers and geologists. They all said it was a natural slide."

"But Roger didn't believe them, right?"

"No. But they looked everywhere for clues. If there's anything left, it's under those rocks, and nothing will ever move them."

I walked cautiously about the rocks, studied them, touched

them, smelled the air, listened. Everything had the calm past-tense energy of a monstrous deed already accomplished and irreversible. I had my first moment of doubt as to whether I'd get anywhere with my quest for answers. For a change of perspective, I turned around and looked back into the forest we'd walked through. As my gaze rose toward the sky, I saw something shine for an instant in one of the trees. I grabbed Yudi and hissed, "Down!" I pulled him to the ground with me, then yanked him along as I scrambled behind a nearby boulder.

My sudden actions had confused him. "What's wrong?"

"There's someone with a gun in one of the trees," I said. "I saw it."

"Are you sure?"

"I'm sure."

He poked his head above the rock. "Which tree?"

"Get down!" I yanked him by his leather jacket and pulled him back next to me.

"I think you're seeing things."

"I tell you, there's something metallic up there."

"So are we just going to sit here?"

I thought it might not be such a bad idea, considering his leather jacket smelled so good.

"I don't want to get shot," I said.

"Maybe it's something else."

I thought a moment. Maybe he was right.

He peered out over the boulder and said, "Which tree?"

I peeked over the edge with him and scanned the trees. As I honed in on the branches where I'd seen the glint of metal, I looked hard and saw no shadow of a human body. "It's okay, I think. There's no one up there now."

We stood up and walked cautiously to the tree. I looked straight up into the branches. Sure enough, something still glistened up there in the moonlight. I motioned to Yudi to come and look. As he did, he said, "I think I know what that is." The next second he was shinnying up the trunk like a monkey.

"Wait!" I said.

"I can get it!"

He disappeared into the branches, where he rustled around for a few minutes. Then he called out, "I see it!"

"What is it?"

"I'm going to get it."

I hollered, "Don't touch it!"

"Ssh! How can I get it then?"

"Use something to hold it. There may be fingerprints."

The air was quiet for many minutes. I said, "What are you doing now?"

"Taking the shoelace from my sneaker."

"Why?"

"I'm going to lasso it."

"That's good. Just keep your fingers off it."

"Okay, okay! I heard you!" he whispered loudly.

More quiet minutes passed. Then from the tree he muttered, "Pissnpoop!"

"What happened?"

"I missed again. I have to get closer."

I heard the branch groan above. "Be careful, Yudi!"

Some rustling, another woeful creak, then, "There! Got it!"

"What is it?"

"It's a climber's chock." The word jangled my memory. "There's something funny stuck in it," he said.

"Don't touch it!"

"*I'm not touching it!*"

He rustled his way back out to the trunk, then crawled down until he was ten feet off the ground. He let go and landed with a soft "ploomp" on his sturdy legs. The chock dangled from the shoelace he held between his teeth. He crept on all fours to my feet, then sat up like a dog offering his master a present. I patted him on the head and took the prize from his mouth. I examined it carefully. It resembled a large hollow metal nut with holes drilled through its walls. A gray puttylike substance had been pressed into one of the holes. I dangled it in front of my nose. It smelled musty.

Yudi stood up and looked at the chock. "What do you think that stuff is?"

"I don't know, but I know who will."

"Who?"

"This is a little souvenir for a cop back in Boston. He'll know what to do with it."

"Why don't you just give it to the police here?"

"Because I need this as ransom to clear my name."

"But then you have to wait until you go back home."

His remark clarified what I had to do next. "Yudi, I've got to go back tomorrow."

"But you just got here!"

"I know, but this is exactly what I came for." I dangled the chock in front of us. "*This* is hard evidence."

"What about our date?"

"Date?"

"Dinner. You promised me!"

I shined the flashlight on my watch. It was impossible to get back, wash, and change before the hotel dining room closed. In the darkness Yudi couldn't see my flush of embarrassment. "Will you take a rain check?" I asked meekly.

He sighed irritably. We both realized that I'd not be taking him to dinner soon, if ever.

We made our way back to the bikes, then rode to the village, flashlights blazing. I offered to give Yudi a lift to his place, but he said sullenly, "I can walk."

Awkwardly, I put out my hand. "I guess this is good-bye for now," I said.

"Can't you just stay another day?"

"Not if I don't want to be dragged off by the police."

"What do you mean?"

I confessed, "I'm technically a suspect in Roger's death. I skipped town to come out here and nose around. If I'm not back in Boston by tomorrow, I may be arrested."

"So you are involved!" The whites of his eyes glowed in the moonlight.

I nodded seriously. "I am, Yudi. But I'm innocent, believe me."

"I was right all along." Tears began to roll down his cheeks.

"Yudi, it's okay. I liked Roger. That's why I'm here."

"You're a liar, just like everybody else!" He turned and ran away from me into the trees. I felt like a cad.

15

SHOW ME THE WAY
TO GO HOME

The next morning I was up with the sun at six. I called Nicole to tell her the drastic change in plans. It was nine o'clock back East, so I knew she'd be just opening the shop.

"I'm on my way," I said. "And I've got something for Branco."

"Did you call him to explain that you'd be delayed?"

"No need to, doll. I'll be arriving around eight tonight."

"I'll be there."

The next plane out of San Francisco departed at noon that day, which gave me only six hours to drive from Yosemite to the city, return the car, and get to the airport. So much for my tour of romantic San Francisco.

I hauled my bags out to the car, and saw the first omen of a long, bumpy ride home: It had snowed during the night. As I approached my rented clunker, though, I saw that it had been magically cleaned off. On the trunk lid sat the culprit with a suitcase on either side of him.

"Hi!" said Yudi. He waved energetically, as though we'd arranged to meet like this. He'd clearly recovered from last night's disappointment. Yudi had what you'd call a resilient personality.

"You look like you're going somewhere," I said.

He nodded quickly. "San Francisco airport."

"Funny, that's exactly where I'm going."

"I know. That's why I cleaned off the car."

"How did you know?"

"Easy. I called the airline. I knew you'd take the first plane to Boston out of San Francisco, so I just got up early to wait here for you."

"But why the bags?"

He jumped off the trunk and faced me directly. "I've never been to Boston."

"Wait a minute, pal! You're going to Boston?"

"Why not? I don't need a visa or anything, do I?"

I shook my head, more in irritation than in response.

Yudi said, "What's wrong?"

"There's too much for me to do when I get back. I can't be your host."

"I'll find someplace to stay."

"You have money?"

Yudi nodded. "Roger always had cash for emergencies—for me, too. I won't bother you, except for one dinner. You owe me for taking you to the slide last night."

He was right. Besides, there was no law prohibiting him from visiting Boston, so once again I surrendered, and told him to get in the car. Then I discovered that I felt strangely happy to have him with me.

When I returned the cabin keys to the campsite office, the woman at the desk told me that snow chains were required to drive in the valley. I explained that I was leaving Yosemite anyway.

"You still have to put them on," she said. "It's the law."

I said okay but had no intention of doing it. Through all the Boston winters I've endured, I've never needed chains. I wasn't about to start now.

Yudi and I began the long drive out of the valley. We saw small drifts of snow gathering here and there, but nothing worth worrying about. After another ten minutes or so, when the wind and snow picked up a little, Yudi said, "I think you'd better put the chains on."

I answered sharply, "I know about snow, and this stuff does not require chains." But soon after the ascent out of the valley, we crossed the snow line, and the roads became an unplowed, slippery mess. The car began to respond sluggishly to my steering directions, then it ignored them altogether. Finally, it moved sideways into the

oncoming lane and refused to climb forward any farther. I stopped
the unroadworthy vessel before it completely blocked the way.

Yudi said, "I told you to put chains on back there."

"Thanks, Yudi. You were right. I was wrong."

I opened the trunk, hoping there'd be chains in there. All I
found was a pile of rusted links in a plastic bucket. I showed them
to Yudi. "Are these chains?"

He nodded bleakly. The wind blasted a gust of cold, wet snow
onto us. Forty-five precious minutes later, we were both streaked
with orange and black stains, and soaked with sweat and melted
snow. Not one car had passed in either direction during that time,
but at least we'd got the chains mounted securely on the back tires.
We were about to get in the car when Yudi said, "Maybe we should
change."

"Where?"

"Here, I guess."

He was right. We'd be miserable if not sick after riding for four
hours in cold, wet, dirty clothes. So up on the mountainside, amidst
the snow-laden trees and rocks, we stripped. His smooth brown body
contrasted appealingly against the white snow and the red car. He
turned his back toward me as if to hide his privates, not realizing he
was showing me the side I prefer. We put on dry clothes and
continued on our way. On the other side of the mountain, the road
was miraculously clear and dry, but Yudi explained that it wasn't
unusual. I pulled into the first gas station and had the chains
removed from the tires. While the mechanic worked, Yudi and I
drank coffee and chewed on stale pastry, both from vending
machines. Somehow, sipping the bitter brew together, I didn't mind
it.

We arrived in the city and I returned the rented car. We took
a shuttle bus to the airport and got there only twenty minutes before
the plane was to depart. I'd hoped the flight would be delayed, as
they usually are. It wasn't.

At the airline counter we got in separate lines, since I already
had a ticket. When my turn came, everything went smooth and
easy. I even got a seat on the aisle and charmed the agent into
reserving the seat next to me for Yudi, who was still buying his ticket

with another agent. Everything was going hunky-dory. We'd make the flight!

Then two large men wearing ill-fitting dark suits were suddenly pushing behind me at the counter.

One of them said clearly, "Mr. Kraycher?"

"Possibly," I answered. "Whom do you want?"

"Come with us."

"Huh? Who are you?"

They both flashed badges. Unlike the people in movies, I read what the badges said. The two guys were federal airport police. Damn! "What about my flight?" I asked.

"We'll see you get back to Boston."

They grabbed me, one at each arm. One of them already had my carry-on bag in his other hand. Branco's souvenir, the climber's chock, was in that bag. The men pulled me away from the counter. I saw Yudi coming toward me. I shook my head no to warn him. He caught my cue and walked by as though he didn't know who I was. Then I said loudly, so he could hear me, "What about Nicole? Nicole is meeting me in Boston. *Nicole!* She won't know what happened to me!"

The two men dragged me roughly away from the crowd waiting in line. I turned back and saw Yudi standing with his two suitcases, totally bewildered. I shouted, "Snips Salon! *Snips*, on Newbury Street!" So what if the shop gained undeserved notoriety? I was desperate.

One of the men yanked at my arm and said, "Keep quiet!"

They took me through an unmarked door to a small room. Inside was a pale green vinyl sofa, two nubbly orange chairs, and a Formica-topped table with an electric coffee maker. The coffee smelled burnt.

I tried to speak boldly. "Care to tell me what this is all about?" But my voice quivered in fright.

"We got orders to take you back to Boston."

I realized what had happened and tried to explain, perhaps a bit too breezily. "That's Lieutenant Branco, I'm sure. He's a friend. He wanted me back there by this morning, and I was delayed, but as you both can see—"

"Save your breath, buddy. We don't know and we don't care."

Next thing I knew, one guy handcuffed my right hand to his left. First thought: What if I have to pee? Fortunately, I'm left-handed, so at least the cop wouldn't have his hands in my nether regions. Of the two clods, the one hooked onto me smelled worse, like cigar smoke and fried food.

"Don't I get a call or something?" I asked.

"Plenty of time for that in Boston."

"But—"

"Hey, mister, I don't know what the hell you did. All's I know is I got a job to do, and you're the goods I'm taking to Boston."

Meanwhile the other guy was going through my carry-on bag. He found the climber's chock, protected in plastic wrap and carefully wrapped in a gauzy cotton shirt I'd intended to wear to a white sandy beach somewhere in California. He examined the chock through the plastic wrap. "Don't touch that!" I screamed. He was about to unwrap the plastic, and I lost all self-control. "It's evidence! There may be fingerprints on it, so keep your bloody mitts off!"

I guess my words were a little too strong for him, because he looked as though I'd just insulted his masculinity. He put the chock back in my bag and walked over to me, clomping his heavy feet on the scuffed linoleum.

"You fuckin' faggot!" he said. He grabbed me by my jacket and spit in my face. The glob hit me right on the lips. My left leg twitched instinctively. The muscles coiled up, ready to strike. It was one of the hardest things I ever resisted—not dispatching a healthy kick to his groin.

I said, "If you think I'm going to try to kick you just so you can slug me, you're wrong." I sensed that he wanted to hit me, but I figured he wouldn't dare do anything, since I was handcuffed to the other cop, and technically defenseless. But guess who got the last laugh?

He pulled his right arm back at hip level. I tightened my belly, but it wasn't strong enough to protect me as he lunged toward me.

"Don't!" yelled the cop who was handcuffed to me.

But the other one smashed his fist into my guts.

"Smartass fairy!" he muttered.

I crumpled toward the floor, dangling from the handcuffs. The spasms in my stomach jerked my body around for a few minutes.

I groaned. "Should've kicked you when I had the chance." Then I spat up blood onto the hard, dirty floor. The cop who'd hit me left the room and slammed the door. Through the pain I wondered what I'd done to deserve it.

Once the worst agony subsided, I thought about what to do next. The answer was clear, since I was still chained to a big smelly brute: nothing.

The flight to Boston was horrible. We were in the last row of the cabin with the heavy smokers, and I was jammed in against the window. It was humiliating to be handcuffed to an oaf who drank beer and belched and didn't even chew his food. Any well-bred deb knows that causes flatulence.

During the film I had plenty of time to think. Ever since Roger's death, all I'd done was try to find out what had really happened, and to clear my own name. Branco had even encouraged me, and I thought we had an unwritten agreement. But now, just because I didn't show up exactly on time in his office, he resorted to brute force. The Lone Ranger had turned on Tonto.

I wondered where Yudi was. Had he even got on the plane? If he had, why wasn't he at least looking for me? Or was he afraid they'd get him, too?

The plane touched down at Logan Airport twenty minutes early, due to unusually strong tail winds. It seemed even Mother Nature wanted me home in a hurry. My clod of a traveling companion told me we had to wait until the entire plane unloaded before we could leave. When we finally got off, I saw both Branco and Nicole waiting at the gate. They stood near each other, looking like adversaries for the same quarry. Branco stepped forward and intercepted my escort, the pigpen, with me attached. I'm sure my face registered disillusionment and rage, for in my eyes at that moment, Branco was just another cop.

They disconnected the handcuffs. The smelly cop said to Branco, "I'll go make my report," and he vanished into the crowd.

Nicole came up and hugged me. "Stani! What happened? You look awful!"

I held her tightly and sobbed into her ample bosom. "One of those jerks assaulted me."

"What! Lieutenant, did you hear that?"

I glared at Branco and said, "Why did you do it?"

Branco kept his voice level. "We had to get you back here fast, so they put you in protective custody."

"Protective custody! The only protection I needed was from the two palookas you sent after me."

"The only way to guarantee your return was to use special agents from California."

"They were special, all right. How'd you find me out there?"

Branco's eyes dropped. "I suspected where you'd gone, but when you called your shop this morning, it was a cinch to find you in San Francisco. We had a trap on the phone where you work, remember?"

"Too bad I forgot," I said.

"Let's get going," ordered Branco.

I held on to Nicole's arm as the three of us walked from the gate. Then I remembered Yudi. I still didn't know if he'd even got on the flight.

"Wait," I said. "Someone else should have been on that plane." I was about to ask an airline agent about the passenger list when Yudi emerged from a nearby men's room. He looked terrified.

I called out to him. "It's okay, Yudi!"

I saw him looking at Nicole and Branco.

"They're friends," I said. "Well, *one* of them is." Branco gave me a stony stare.

Yudi came to us. When he was close enough to me, he asked quietly, "Did you see him?"

"Who?"

He looked nervously at Branco, then shook his head. "I'll tell you later. What did those men want with you?"

"It's a long story, Yudi. I'll tell *you* later." Then I introduced him to Nicole but ignored Branco.

Yudi asked Nicole, "Are you his sister?"

She said, "Probably."

We got outside and Branco said to me, "I'll take you in my car, Stan."

Nicole remarked icily, "Haven't you done enough for him, Lieutenant?"

Branco said, "I have to talk to him, in private."

"It's okay, Nikki," I said.

She grimaced and continued walking with me and Yudi. She stopped at a shiny new convertible, illegally parked, and took some keys from her purse.

"What's this?" I asked.

She opened the trunk, and Yudi and I threw in our bags.

"You'll be driving this for a while," she said.

"Why?"

"You haven't solved the case yet, have you?"

"No."

"Then you need a car."

"Who's paying for it?"

"It's a transportation expense for the shop."

Matter settled. At least Nicole was still on my side.

To my great joy, I saw Sugar Baby standing up on her hind legs and peering out through the driver's window. "You brought her!" In seconds we were reunited. Sugar purred noisily and licked my cheek. Yudi watched everything with reserved amusement, but I could see that something was troubling him.

I got in the cruiser with Branco, while Yudi and Nicole and Sugar rode together in the convertible. Once Branco got the cruiser moving through traffic, he said, "Is it true, what happened with those agents?"

"Lieutenant, you put me in with a fag-bashing homophobic cop."

"Stan, I hope your imagination isn't exaggerating again. That's a serious accusation."

"I know, damn it! But I was beaten, and it was entirely without provocation."

"Tell me exactly what happened."

I recounted the whole ugly incident to him. Then Branco said,

"I'll make a report tonight and see that he's put on probation. If you want to press charges—"

"You bet I do! Christ, it was those two against me, and I was handcuffed! I should've kicked the SOB! Vito, why did you do it? Why did you sic them on me?"

Branco drove in silence. Was it because I'd presumed to use his first name? Was it a bit of remorse? Was he capable of such a feeling? He clenched his jaw and I watched the muscles grip and release. Finally he said, "The captain got wind of your little excursion out there. He wanted you back here fast."

"So you set a time and date and that was it."

"That's not how it happened, but my ass was on the line."

"I was on my way home!"

"I know, but the law's the law."

"Cripes! You'd probably divorce your wife if she folded your underwear the wrong way."

"I'm not married."

"Your girlfriend, then."

"You keep out of my personal life!"

"But it's all right if you wreck mine!"

"By leaving town, you put yourself under suspicion again."

"For something I didn't do! I suppose *your* past is lily pure, with no smudges?"

Branco clenched his jaw again and didn't say anything until we came up out of the airport tunnel. Finally, he spoke. "Stan, when the captain found out you'd skipped, he ordered your extradition."

"Who told him I was gone? You?"

"No, and I don't know who. I tried to intercept the order, but I was too late. Fact is, the captain thinks I've been too lenient with you, and he's thinking of taking me off the case."

"So, are you blaming me for that now?"

"No, but for your own safety, you shouldn't have gone. You don't realize the danger you can get in snooping around the way you do. I know I asked for your help, but I meant for you to talk with people, not fly across the country."

"But I wasn't in any danger out there."

"You could have been and not realized it."

I wondered, Did he really care? Or was he just trying to appease me and convince himself that he wasn't groveling under his sacred cow, the captain? I sulked the rest of the way home.

When we arrived at my building, Nicole had just finished parking the rented convertible in a loading zone in front. Branco said, "I'll leave you now, but you report to me first thing tomorrow morning, is that clear?"

"Yessir!"

"And you'd better tell Ms. Albright to move that car. I don't want to give her a ticket for the parking violation."

"Lieutenant," I said, "it's a loading zone. We are un*loading* bags from the trunk. Can't you bend the rules just a little, just once?"

Branco pulled his lips tight.

I said, "You have to come upstairs anyway. I have something for you. It's important."

"I don't have much time." He sounded impatient.

"Lieutenant, I promise it'll be a quickie."

Nicole carried Sugar Baby in her arms, while Yudi and I carried our luggage. Branco followed. As we neared my apartment door, Sugar began clawing at Nicole's jacket, trying to get down.

"Something is making her very nervous," she said, throwing a cold glance at Lieutenant Branco.

I tried to unlock the dead bolt on my door. Something wasn't right there. "Nikki, did you come in while I was gone?"

"No. Why?"

"The dead bolt's not locked, and I always set it."

"You did leave in an awful hurry, Stani. Maybe you forgot?"

"No. I distinctly remember locking it." The instant I opened the door, I knew someone had been in there—the air felt strange.

"Uh-oh," said Yudi as Sugar Baby jumped onto the sofa and puffed her short fur out like a porcupine. "She's scared of something."

I quickly went through the apartment. On first appearance things seemed generally all right, but on closer examination, every single item in my place had been moved or touched. Shoes in my closet were rearranged by color instead of style, towels in the bathroom had been refolded in halves instead of thirds, pot lids were seated tightly instead of being left ajar, normally scattered magazines were in neat piles, book spines had been aligned exactly to the edges of their shelves, rather than pushed in slightly.

"I've had visitors. Too bad I wasn't here to receive them properly."

Branco had watched me during my search. He said, "You have a keen sense for detail, Stan. You seem suited for this kind of work."

"It's my Slavic heritage. Haven't you see those embroidered doilies and paper collages the old Czech women make and sell at the church bazaars?"

"No," he answered uneasily, crossing his arms and shifting his weight onto one of his strong legs.

"Details for days," I said.

Nicole asked, "Anything missing?"

"As far as I can tell, no. But everything's been pawed over."

Nicole said, "I don't know about the rest of you, but I could use a drink. Would anyone else like a hot toddy?" Yudi and I nodded. Branco said no, and Nicole disappeared into the kitchen.

Yudi was sitting on the sofa petting Sugar Baby and whispering into her ear, making it twitch. "It's all right, kitty. It's all right." It seemed that he was trying to comfort himself as well.

Meanwhile, I wanted to dunk the whole apartment in a vat of industrial-strength disinfectant. It felt dirty from the invasion of a peculiar stranger who had stolen nothing but who had still violated my privacy.

Branco took a report on what had happened. Then he said to me, "You might as well know, we released Calvin Redding yesterday."

"What! You put *me* in irons and let a killer go?"

"Take it easy, Stan."

"Something's weird, Lieutenant, when a visitor to Boston ends up dead on the bed of his host, and the host is immune to a murder charge."

"Stan, I already told you back before you left—we were holding Redding on possession of drugs, and the bail was paid, so technically he's free for the moment."

"Lieutenant, that drug stuff is a decoy. From what I learned about Roger, he wasn't into the kinky stuff that fascinates Calvin at all."

From the sofa, Yudi piped in, "Roger was old-fashioned."

Branco nudged me toward the front window. He faced us away from the center of the room and spoke low, so that Nicole and Yudi couldn't hear us. "None of that matters now, Stan. They have another suspect."

"Who?"

"Aaron Harvey."

"Why him?"

"Calvin Redding admitted that Aaron was blackmailing him."

"So?"

"Redding refused to pay him."

I thought a moment, but it didn't make sense. "You mean Aaron Harvey killed Roger to get back at Calvin, because Calvin wouldn't pay him? That's a convoluted motive, Lieutenant, if that's what you think."

"I don't think anything. It wasn't my idea. I told you, I may not even be on the case anymore."

"Do they have Aaron in custody?"

"Not yet."

"And meanwhile our great system of justice lets Calvin Redding wander the streets, just because someone else came up with his bail. Who paid it, anyway?"

"That's confidential."

I shook my head. It was all disappointing news, but I surrendered (again!) to the fact that the police would continue blundering until some tyro gumshoe like me showed them the way and light.

Nicole brought the hot toddies from the kitchen, and I remembered the souvenir I'd brought from Yosemite for Branco.

"Lieutenant, I found something that might help explain why Roger was in Boston in the first place." I dug through my carry-on bag and got it, then proudly handed him the climber's chock in its plastic bag.

Branco took it and examined it as though it were a prize fish. "Where'd you get this?"

"Found it hiding in a tree up in Yosemite. Actually, Yudi rescued it after I saw it. I saved it especially for you."

Branco actually smiled, then nodded toward Yudi. "Thanks," he said. "This is good evidence, Stan. I'll take it to the lab tonight."

I asked, "Is it like the one that was in Roger's bag?"

Branco's eyes flared open. "How did you know about that?"

"I, uh . . ." I had to look away from his harsh gaze. "Hell, Lieutenant, I read it in the report in your office."

When I looked up at him, his eyes were narrow and angry. He said, "I knew that the day you did it." He turned to leave, but then added, "I'll explain to the captain that you didn't know how to contact the proper authorities out West, but you're back now and you've reported to me. There shouldn't be any trouble from him."

I followed him to the door and lowered my voice so the others wouldn't hear. "If you *are* taken off the case, Lieutenant, what about our . . . arrangement?"

Branco chewed at his lip and stared at me. Then he said secretively, "You still call me."

He said good night to Nicole and Yudi, then he left. I realized he hadn't made the slightest apology for the pain and distress the order for extradition had caused me.

Nicole finished her toddy and asked me whether I'd need the rented car that night. I shook my head. She said, "Then I'll drive it home, if you don't mind. You can pick it up at the shop tomorrow."

Yudi added, "I'd better go now, too." He asked Nicole, "Can you take me to a cheap hotel?"

Instead of answering him, Nicole gave me a questioning look. I took her cue and said, "You can stay here, Yudi. There's room."

Yudi answered brightly, "I promise I'll find a place tomorrow."

Nicoled kissed me, then Yudi. "Good night, boys," she said, and as she walked out the door, Sugar Baby scampered after her. "Oh, Stani, the cat!"

"It's all right, Nikki. Looks as though she'd rather go with you. Glad to see how much I was missed."

"She can stay with me, if you like."

"I think it's out of my hands and into her paws."

Nicole picked Sugar up and walked to the elevator. "Good night, darling."

"Night, doll."

I closed the door. Yudi and I were alone. I smiled tiredly at him. "I'm exhausted. I'm going to bed."

"Me, too," he said, but he still had that hesitant, frightened look.

"Yudi, is anything wrong?"

He opened his mouth to speak, then shook his head.

"Well then, for sleepies, there's my bed and there's the sofa."

His eyes looked into mine, inviting and beckoning for a moment, then they looked nervously around the living room, then back into mine with a warm, receptive gaze.

"I'd better sleep on the sofa."

"Oh," I said, somewhat surprised. I'd expected him to choose my bed, and after the violent day I'd had, I really needed the physical comfort of a warm friendly body next to me. Even Sugar Baby had deserted me. But instead, I set up the sofa for him, and we went our own ways.

Later during the night, though, he slipped into my room and sat on the edge of the bed. I woke up and asked, "What's the matter?"

Long, quiet minutes passed in the shadows caused by the nighttime glow of city lights outside my bedroom window. Yudi sighed heavily and said, "You know what?"

"What?" I said, hoping for an erotic revelation.

"I saw Jack on the plane."

"What? Are you sure?"

"I think it was he. I was looking for you when I walked by him."

"Did he see you?"

"No. He was asleep, so I couldn't tell exactly, but it looked like him."

"Did you see him coming off the plane?"

"No. His seat was way behind mine, so I ran off the plane and hid in the men's room. I didn't want him to see me."

"I wonder what he's doing here."

"Maybe it wasn't he. Maybe I was confused by everything that happened today, with you and those men." He moved closer to me.

"Stan," he said with a faint waver in his voice, "There's something else I want to show you . . ."

"I know," I said, and pushed the blanket down to uncover my chest and my sore belly, and to invite him even closer.

"But I'm not sure it's the right time."

"It is if we both agree, Yudi."

"It's about Roger."

Ah yes. Roger. Suddenly, I felt awkward exposing my naked torso to him. I modestly pulled the blanket back up and asked, "What about Roger?"

Yudi was quiet. Then he shook his head and said, "I'll tell you later."

"And meanwhile?"

"Meanwhile what?"

I rested my hand on his thigh and said, "Why don't you stay here by me tonight?"

He stood up abruptly and moved away from the bed. "I'd better go back to the sofa."

"Don't be afraid, Yudi."

"I'm not afraid of you." He seemed to be pleading with me. "I'm afraid of myself."

He left me alone in the darkness of my room. After all his flirtatious, innuendo-laden words and behavior, I finally made a move on him, and he bolted.

What a homecoming! My last waking thought was that I should have stayed in San Francisco, changed my name, and married the first man I met, even if it was a "fellatious" cowboy cabdriver.

16

WHATEVER YOU'RE THINKING, IT'S WRONG

Early the next morning I woke with a start from the sound of the apartment door closing. For an instant I thought, Where am I? Then the facts clicked in—the clock said 7 A.M.; it was Tuesday; I was in Boston. I wrapped a sheet around myself and shuffled into the living room. Yudi was gone. The sofa had been returned to its normal lounging state, and a note was on one of the cushions:

Whatever you're thinking, it's wrong.

Had my clumsy sexual advance last night scared him away? All I'd wanted was company, not a marriage contract. I was already seeing the consequences of this dalliance. Yudi was young, he was from another culture, and he'd been Roger's lover. On the other hand, Roger was dead, Yudi was alive, and so was I. Unfortunately, that logic reminded me of Mr. Leonard's words. More important for the moment, though, was that Yudi was gone, and he didn't have a key to get back into my place. I hoped he'd remember the shop's name and where it was. He could always go there.

I called Nicole at home. She picked up the phone and grumbled, "It's too early."

I quickly told her what had happened.

"Wasn't he with you?" she asked.

"No. He slept on the sofa bed."

"That's too bad. Where did he go?"

"I don't know."

"You weren't too forward with him, were you? He seems rather timid and untamed."

"No, Nikki. I hinted, but I didn't push."

"Well, dear, you can't worry too much. He *is* an adult, after all."

"I'm not so sure about that, and he certainly doesn't know his way around Boston."

"He can speak English." Then her tone became more businesslike. "What time are you coming in today?"

"Nikki, it's Tuesday, my day off, remember?"

"Usually, yes, but you were gone Saturday and yesterday. The other staff had to cover for you."

"But I need more time to work on the case."

"And the shop needs the income, Stanley."

It was rare that Nicole used her ownership of Snips to call the shots, so I felt I ought to comply. "All right, I'll come in. If Yudi shows up there before I do, tell him to wait there for me."

"Fine, dear. Just tell me what time I can book you for."

I checked the clock again. It was just after seven. "Say eleven to be safe."

"Why so late?"

"I want to pay a visit to Calvin Redding."

"Are you still on that? Stanley, they've let him go."

"I know, Nikki, and now I'm going to wring the facts from his lying neck."

"Stanley . . . Oh, never mind! I'll see you at eleven," she said, and abruptly hung up.

As I proceeded into my morning ablutions, I had the sensation that something was physically missing from the apartment. It wasn't Yudi, since we'd barely been together. Then I realized that Sugar Baby wasn't bothering me for her breakfast as usual, and I remembered she'd stayed with Nicole last night. I hoped *she* was enjoying herself, at least.

I showered and had a quick coffee, then left for Calvin

Redding's place. I got there around nine, but I knew he started work at eleven, so he still should have been at home. I didn't want to warn him of my arrival, so instead of ringing his doorbell, I waited outside the front door until someone came out on their way to work. Then I just smiled and slipped in before the door closed.

I knocked firmly on his door. No answer. I knocked louder, but still no response. What to do? I figured I'd drop in on Calvin's downstairs neighbor, Hal Steiner. Maybe he'd seen Calvin. Maybe he'd invite me in for coffee. Maybe something else.

I had to ring his buzzer twice before I heard activity behind the door. Someone inside said, "Who's there?" but it wasn't the deep bass register of Hal's voice. I wanted to know who it was, and I had to think quickly.

"Shreve's," I said. "I have a special delivery for Mr. Steiner."

I heard the dead bolt being released from inside, and the door opened a crack.

"What is it?" the stranger asked.

I kept myself out of sight. "I have the Victorian kaleidoscope you bought last week. You have to sign for it."

Whoever it was closed the door and undid the safety chain. Then, at the very moment he opened the door again to accept the nonexistent package, I rammed myself past him into Hal's apartment. All a simple matter of microsecond timing.

The stranger turned out to be Aaron Harvey, Calvin's lover, the dark-skinned jazz dancer I'd seen at Neiman-Marcus. He was wearing the same silky robe Calvin had worn the night Roger was killed.

"What are *you* doing here?" I asked.

"I could ask the same of you."

His eyes glowed with hostility, or perhaps fear. Whatever the reason, he couldn't escape by running away from me now, not dressed like that. The air was laden with his spicy cologne, along with another familiar smell—leather. That's when I noticed the leather pant legs hanging below the hem of the silk robe. I wondered if they were chaps, and what else, if anything, Aaron wore with them.

"What do you want?" he said hoarsely. He seemed more alarmed than angry now.

"I'm looking for Calvin. Where is he?"

"I don't know."

"Why did you run away from me at Neiman's?"

"Because you're trouble, man."

"You don't even know me."

He paused a moment. "I know you. You're one of Calvin's tricks."

"You're wrong there, but aren't *you* a little nervous messing around with a killer?"

He smiled confidently. "He won't hurt me."

"Don't you think—"

"Hey, Mister Stan, where do you get off pushing yourself in here and asking *me* questions?"

"You know my name?"

"I told you, I know you. And I don't like talking to you. In fact, I'm going to call the police."

I pointed to the phone. "Go ahead. Ask for Lieutenant Branco and give him my regards. He'd be delighted to know where you are."

Aaron started for the phone, then stopped. He smiled, but it was all for effect. His heart wasn't in it. "Okay, man," he said. "So it wouldn't be cool to invite the police here. Now why don't you just get out."

"I'll leave as soon as you tell me where Calvin is."

"Why do you want him?"

"He's going to tell me why he killed that ranger."

Aaron sneered, then snickered, then burst into a noisy laugh. "Man, he'll never do that!"

"Don't be so sure."

He laughed harder and shook his head. "Calvin didn't kill that dude!"

"What?"

"You're going after the wrong guy!" He hooted with laughter.

"How do you know?"

Aaron immediately snapped into seriousness and his eyes

glowed with rage. "I know because I know, and it wasn't Calvin who did it."

"Then who did?"

Aaron's face now spread into a broad sinister grin, and I sensed uncomfortably that the man standing in front of me was unstable. Was it possible that *he* had killed Roger in a fit of jealousy? Branco seemed to think so.

"I know what you're thinking," he said, "and you're wrong. True, I *am* weary of Calvin, but I'm no fool. I wouldn't go killing a man just to get Calvin put away. I know a good deal when I see one, and as *you* know . . ." He paused, and with a broad balletic sweep of his arm, indicated Calvin's suite immediately overhead. ". . . Calvin is a good deal. So I sit pretty, man, and don't lift a finger or *lay* a finger on anybody. Life is sweet."

"But you know who did it?"

"I know what I know."

"Sounds like you're blackmailing someone, Aaron."

"Your vernacular is crass, and you are not welcome here, so why don't you leave now."

"I get the feeling there's someone else around."

Aaron planted his strong bare feet firmly in the carpet. "There's nobody here but me."

"I'll just go have a look," I said, and walked past him.

He tried to stop me, and the guy was damn agile. But I've got agility, too, plus those twelve or so extra pounds I'm always trying to shed. Now it all came in handy. He stood in front of me to block me, which made it real simple. I moved to his side and crouched low, then slammed one arm behind his knees and knocked him off balance. He fell into my arms. His body was surprisingly light, but then, he *was* a dancer. I used my legs and whole body to lift him up and throw him down hard onto the floor. He made a loud rough cough when he hit the floor, and I knew I'd knocked the wind out of him.

I moved quickly through Hal's apartment looking for the infamous "other" room he'd mentioned the first night we talked. I finally found it, and waiting for me in there was a stunning surprise. I mean, I was stunned.

He was hovering in midair, suspended from the wood-beamed ceiling by four long, shiny chrome chains. The chains were attached to a matrix of leather straps that bound his naked body. His wrists were tied together above his head. His mouth was gagged with a broad leather belt.

"So we meet again," I said.

It was Hal. He looked at me with mild amusement. I quickly unfastened the gag so he could talk, and was surprised to withdraw from his mouth a long leather phallus attached to the leather strap. I wondered how he could breathe. Ah, the mysteries of life.

"Nice to see you," he said, as casually as though we were chatting in a supermarket aisle.

"What the hell is going on here, Hal?"

"I should think that's obvious. Would you like to join us?"

"Thanks, but it's not my idea of a kaffeeklatsch. Do you know where Calvin is?"

"Obviously not here."

"I thought you said you never made it with these guys."

"Not with Calvin. But as you can see, Aaron and I *are* . . ." He smiled. ". . . familiar." He seemed relaxed and was enjoying himself. "Why don't you stay?" he asked. "There are skins in the closet. I'm sure there's something for you." His eyes were inviting and his equipment was tantalizing. The guy was built for sex, lots of it. And here he was, trussed up and ready to serve a willing taker. Was that me? Is that what I wanted?

I felt a slight rustling in my groin. "I've got work to do, Hal. But I'll certainly keep you in mind." It was probably one of the stupidest things I ever did, but I left him there, unused.

Back in the living room, Aaron was now slumped against the sofa. I opened the door to leave. "See you around, Aaron," I said. "You might want to find new digs, now that I know where you are."

He groaned. "I'll get you for this."

I arrived at the shop around ten o'clock. Nicole seemed pleased that I'd arrived earlier than I'd promised. She greeted me with a kiss and a small white paper bag. "What's this?" I asked.

"I'm sorry I snapped at you earlier, Stani. You have a full

schedule ahead of you, and I thought you'd need the energy." It was an almond-filled croissant.

"Thanks, Nikki."

"Any word from Yudi?"

"Christ! I forgot about him! He didn't show up here?"

"No, dear. How did your visit with Calvin go?"

"He, uh, wasn't home." She didn't need to know what else I'd seen there. "Nikki, did you drive that rented convertible here?"

"Yes, dear, and don't change the subject."

"I want to go to Cambridge and see if Calvin's at work."

She frowned. "Not *now*, Stanley. You have a customer coming in at eleven."

"Nikki, I *have* to do it now. With the car I can go and be back by eleven."

"I rented that car to help you, not to lose you."

"I promise I'll be back in time."

"If I know you—"

"Doll, if I'm late, just reschedule me." I took the bag and headed out the back door. "And thanks for the snack." Sure enough, the white convertible was parked in the alley. I got in, dropped the top, and headed onto Storrow Drive, which runs alongside the Charles River. With the morning traffic past, the drive to Cambridge was easy. In the bright sun the trees along the riverbank glowed orange and yellow and red. If nothing else, autumn in Boston was colorful.

I pulled into the Choate Group parking lot and jogged to the door. I thought it might be too early, since any hour before 11 A.M. is almost dawn by Cambridge architectural time. Patrick, the receptionist, sat at his desk reading an expensive European fashion magazine. He barely acknowledged me. I leaned over his desk and tipped his magazine down. "Tell Calvin Redding that Vannos is here to see him."

He looked up lazily at me through his oversized horn-rimmed glasses. "Is that your name today?"

"That's who I am every day."

"Whoever you are, Mr. Redding is not here."

"We've done this dance before, sweetheart. I know Calvin's

here, so I'll just go have a look for myself." I started toward the offices.

"I wouldn't advise that," he said.

I turned back to him. "Excuse me?"

"If you enter without my consent, I will consider you a trespasser."

"Then why don't you make life easy for both of us and just consent?"

At that moment a gravelly voice echoed within the open atrium. "Patrick, it's all right! Let him in."

I looked through the open space of the lobby and saw Jennifer Doughton's soft bulky body leaning over the second-floor railing. She waved to me. I discreetly waved back. "Hi, Jennie."

Patrick said, "You can go in now."

"Thanks, Patty-love," I said, then trotted across the atrium and up the ramp to where Jennifer was standing.

She wore a lint-speckled black skirt and a dark knitted top that had begun to pill. A tiny particle of moist potato chip clung to her chin. She spoke low and her eyes moved excitedly. "I'm glad you came. I tried calling you, but they said you were out of town."

"No matter. I'm back now. Where's Calvin?"

"He's not here."

"Where is he, then?"

"When he was released, the boss gave him time off to rest." She sniggered. "As though he needs it, with his work habits."

"Do you know where he went?"

"Probably the Caribbean."

Jennie's words created an annoying montage in my mind, with Calvin lying on a sunny beach, languidly sipping a piña colada, his body laden with cocoa butter, while I raced around the country trying in vain to convict him of murder.

Jennie continued nervously, lowering her voice even more. "But I've got good news for you. I found some incredible facts about that ranger's visit here in Boston."

That was music to my ears. "Tell me," I said.

"I can't talk now. I'm meeting with a major client any minute. Can you see me later, after work?"

A little warning bell sounded inside my head, but I answered, "Sure. Where and when?"

"Harvest Lounge in Harvard Square, say around seven tonight."

"I'll be there."

"Good. I'm honestly relieved you came by. You won't believe what turned up." She waddled back to her office double-time and left me feeling bothered. Even though she'd found something, I still didn't trust her.

As I headed toward the ramp to leave, I heard a familiar voice behind me ask, "How was your vacation?"

I turned and saw Roy Brickley approaching me.

"It was fine," I answered, perhaps too quickly.

Dark gray pleated pants showed off his waistline. I envied Brickley's trim midriff. After all, he had about twenty years on me, yet *his* belly was flat. He shook my hand and smiled, but it was one of those designer smiles.

I asked, "How did you know I was gone?"

"My wife called your salon, and they told her you were out of town for a while. We assumed you were on vacation."

"Did she need anything?" I asked, wondering if Mrs. Brickley had really called the shop.

"Nothing urgent. Just more praise for your work, but I imagine you're used to that."

Not these days, I thought.

"Where did you go?" he asked.

"I was in New York. Hair stylists' convention."

"Really?" Brickley's left eyelid twitched for an instant.

I said, "I was hoping to talk to Calvin Redding today."

"Oh, that's too bad. He's not here. He's taking some time off to recover from the stress of the past week. We have three big contracts coming up soon and I need him eager and bright."

"Do you know where he went?"

"No idea. Perhaps to New York . . . just like you."

"It's a nice place to visit," I said, catching the inflection on his last three words. He knew I was lying.

He nodded and smiled again. "I must get back to work. It's good to see you, and thank you again for what you did with my wife's hair. We're both very happy with her new look." He turned and headed up the ramp to his office.

Cripes, I thought, it was only a lousy shampoo and set!

I walked back through the bright open atrium toward the entranceway to the building. As I passed the receptionist, I blew him a kiss and said, "See you later, pumpkin." He scowled.

I drove back to Boston, breaking the speed limit all the way. There was one more stop I had to make, even if it meant being late for my eleven o'clock appointment at the shop. So what if the damn police hauled me in for speeding? I was going to see Branco anyway, to tell him what I'd just found out about Aaron Harvey and Calvin Redding.

There were no parking spaces near the station, so I pulled into one of the empty bays reserved for the cruisers. Hell, how's a responsible citizen supposed to cooperate with the cops if he can't even park near the station? I waved energetically as I charged by the desk sergeant. "Branco!" I said with brusque authority. "He's expecting me." Today my cocky attitude seemed to work, and the sergeant buzzed me in through the locked door that led to the rest of the station. Little did I know that Lieutenant Branco really *was* expecting me.

He was seated behind his desk: chair tilted back, hands clasped behind his head, legs up on the desk, bent slightly at the knee. For a panoramic view of his business region, the pose was without equal.

"Good you came in, Stan. Saved me coming after you."

"You wanted to see *me?*"

He nodded. "You were supposed to report to me this morning, remember?"

I'd forgotten. "I guess I thought after our talk last night—"

Branco interrupted me. "Where'd you get that climber's chock you gave me?"

"I told you, I found it in a tree near the slide site in Yosemite."

He looked through me, trying to detect the faintest trace of a lie on my face. Then he sat straight up in the chair and faced me directly, a stance that meant all business. "The stuff on that piece of metal is a material called Rezon. It's a plastic explosive that detonates through resonance. It's under top-secret development at M.I.T." I knew Branco was referring to the prestigious Massachusetts Institute of Technology, in Cambridge.

I asked, "How did it get on a climber's chock in the Yosemite Valley?"

"Good question. I was wondering if you had any friends, maybe a customer who works in the labs over there."

"Come off it, Lieutenant. I did not put that gunk in that chock."

"Somebody did. And it seems unlikely that the Rezon went all the way out West just to come back here in your luggage. Maybe you stuck it on the chock just before you gave it to me."

"That's absurd! I have no reason to pull that kind of prank."

Branco stared at me. "No telling how far you'd go to incriminate Calvin Redding."

"Why bother now, since he just skipped town."

"When?"

"I just came from Cambridge. He wasn't at work."

"That doesn't mean he's skipped town."

"You're not even tailing him, are you?"

"What do you expect, Stan? I can't put out an APB because a guy doesn't show up for work."

"You did for me."

"That was different."

"Sure was. *He's* a killer and I'm a goon."

"You're entitled to your opinion."

"Have you found Aaron Harvey yet?"

Branco shifted in his chair.

"Well, Lieutenant, if you move fast, you'll find him with Calvin Redding's downstairs neighbor, Hal Steiner."

"How do you know that?"

"I saw him there this morning, during one of my secret 'gay probes' for you."

Branco picked up his phone and ordered a crew to pick up Aaron at Hal's apartment. While he talked, I noticed a small frame on his desk. It contained an old black and white photo of a man, a woman, and a small boy together. The man was fair; the woman dark-featured, with Branco's eyes; and the boy was a miniature version of the very cop seated before me. They were on vacation somewhere warm and sunny with mountains. Italy maybe, long ago.

Branco finished his call and said, "Thanks for the tip. And there's something else I want to tell you about."

"I'm all ears."

"You ever hear of a guy named Jack Werdegar?"

I weighed Branco's intentions in asking the question. "Name sounds familiar."

"It ought to. He says he knows you."

"Oh, right," I said jovially. "From Yosemite."

"That's the one. He's here in town."

"Really?" So Yudi was right—Jack had been on the plane. "You've talked to him, Lieutenant?"

"He has to report to us anytime he comes to Boston."

"Why?"

"He used to live here, but he had some trouble a few years back, got into a barroom brawl, ended up killing a man. He was charged with manslaughter but got acquitted on self-defense. Went out West for a new start. I just thought you might like to know who your friends are."

"Uh, thanks, Lieutenant." What would Branco have thought of my recent wilderness adventure with the guy, skipping up and down the rocks at Yosemite?

"By the way, Stan, how are you and your other friend getting along?"

"Which one?"

"The little one you brought back with you."

"Damn! I keep forgetting! He disappeared this morning. He hasn't come by here, has he?"

"No. What happened last night?"

"Nothing!" I spat back. Boy, my defenses were up, and it showed. I breathed a minute, then continued. "He left my place this morning and I don't know where he went."

"Maybe you ought to be pay more attention to him and less to Calvin Redding."

I felt my face redden. "Maybe I could, if Calvin was still in custody."

"Stan, how many times do I have to tell you, we don't have evidence for a murder charge." The edge on his voice and the glint in his eyes told me he was becoming more impatient with me.

"It's all there, Lieutenant! Calvin was there. Roger was dead on his bed. They were both naked . . . the drugs . . . the ties."

"That's all circumstantial evidence."

"I thought you guys thrived on that kind of stuff."

Branco just grunted.

"Lieutenant, what *would* it take to make a charge?"

"For this case, a suspect with a lousy lawyer and no connections."

"But it's obvious it's Calvin. I don't know why you don't just charge him."

"I've already explained the situation to you. If I charged Redding now, I'd be going directly against orders. That's grounds for suspension."

"What about finding the killer? I thought that was important to you."

"It is, but frankly, I'm not convinced Redding did it. Otherwise, I *would* take action."

"Easy to say, Lieutenant. Safe. And you'll still have your job." I stomped out of his office and slammed the door. I drove off with tires squealing. It was like a scene from a prime-time television soap opera, and I was proud of it.

17
MISTER SANDMAN, BRING ME A CLUE

I was already late for my eleven o'clock appointment, so I figured it wouldn't make much difference if I zipped by my place on the chance that Yudi might be waiting there for me, or at least have left me a note. But it was in vain—there was no sign of him.

When I got to the shop, I was still revved up from all the fast driving, which had originated with my histrionics with Branco. I hurried in through the back door and went to the front desk, where Nicole was quietly going over the appointment book. Even I could hear the excited edge on my voice when I asked her whether Yudi had materialized there at the shop while I was gone. She responded with a dull "No."

"And, Nikki, do you recall if Vivian Brickley called here at the shop while I was in California?"

"No, Stanley, I don't recall. You see, when you're not here, it's very difficult to manage the shop myself, and I can't keep track of your personal phone calls as well. She may have called, but I didn't speak to her."

"But I think she *didn't* call, Nikki. I'm trying to verify . . . ." Then I noticed Nicole's eyes glowering impatiently. "Never mind," I said. "But I have to leave early tonight. I thought you should know."

"Fine, Stanley," she answered coolly, and I wondered why she accepted it so calmly, since it meant she'd have to close the shop without me, again.

"Don't you want to know where I'm going?" I asked.

"Only if you care to tell me, dear," she said blithely. At that very moment I saw something that both shocked and sickened me. Ramon, the shampoo boy, was working at *my* station with one of *my* regular customers. They were laughing and teasing each other like secret lovers, while I, the cuckolded spouse, looked on in despair. I had been neglecting my home and now I saw it disintegrating before me.

Nicole said, "I'm sure Ramon can help me close up."

"Or open up," I snapped back, then instantly regretted the double entendre. One of my worst imaginings was that Ramon would eventually replace me as Nicole's lead stylist and confidante. Now it seemed to be coming true.

She removed her reading glasses, looked directly into my eyes, and said, "Stanley, I realize that you are under tremendous stress, more than I've ever seen you in, actually. And I'm sure that explains the remark you just made, as well as the prima-donna attitude you've recently adopted. Now, I'll continue to help you as much as I can, but frankly I do not condone what you are doing, nor how it's affecting your work. I have a business to run here, and lately you have been more of a liability than an asset."

I said nothing, realizing that explanations were futile.

Nicole continued, "Ramon will be finished shortly, and you can take your next appointment at your station then."

I bowed my head and shuffled away sulkily. I knew Nicole was right. How much longer could I pretend that I was Perry Mason without serious consequences to my job and my friendship with her?

A short time later, I reclaimed my station, and Ramon returned to his own work in the shampoo area, but I noticed a smug grin appear on his face whenever he caught my eye. Once I was with my customers, though, I was all happy talk, busy fingers, hello doll, kiss-kiss.

And what a welcome sight when one of my favorite people arrived for her weekly appointment! Mallory Framson stood five feet exactly and weighed ninety-five pounds to the ounce. Her sparrow-like size belied her regal deportment, burnished like fine silver by eighty years of glorious living, most of it as a concert pianist and teacher. Mallory insisted on having her thick white hair styled the same way every time—bobbed and brushed back away from her face. On someone else it might have created a stark, boyish look, but on Mallory it reflected her progressive energy, which was always moving forward in time and space.

The rest of the afternoon went fast. Around six o'clock I said good night to Nicole and made for the back door. She followed me there, then grabbed me and hugged me hard. "Stani, I was foolish to say the things I did earlier. Forgive me."

"I'm the fool, Nikki. I've brought it all on myself."

"Let me help you."

"I wish you could, but now it's become personal. You were right . . . it's part of my obsessive nature. Until I find out how and why Calvin killed Roger and then prove it to Branco, I won't be able to stop."

"Stani, be careful, please."

"I'm trying." I got in the car and drove home again to check on Yudi. There was no sign of him anywhere, so I glumly set off for Cambridge and my rendezvous with Jennifer Doughton. As I drove, I recalled how Yudi had appeared and disappeared at Yosemite a lot, and tried to reason that perhaps it was just the way he did things. After all, he'd been gone only about twelve hours. I just hoped he was safe, wherever he was.

Traffic and parking in Harvard Square took more time than I expected, and I was a few minutes late getting to the Harvest Lounge. I looked around the place, then checked with the hostess. Fortunately, Jennie hadn't arrived yet. I sat in a remote private booth and ordered a drink. My mind raced with confused thoughts of Roger, Calvin, Aaron, and Hal; then of Yosemite, Yudi, Wacky-Jacky, and Mr. Leonard; and finally of Branco and Nicole. I was in a mess, and I realized I was counting on Jennifer Doughton's arrival with her important news to set things straight.

Ten minutes later a handsome waiter—not the one who'd taken my order—came to my table. I assumed he was checking my drink (or perhaps some other more personal need), but instead, he said, "Mr. Kraychik?" I nodded, and he handed me a small note that said:

Sorry.
False alarm.
J.D.

False alarm? What about the "unbelievable" facts Jennie had turned up? What about all the enthusiasm she had shown earlier that day? I asked the waiter, "Who gave you this?"

"Someone telephoned. I wrote it down."

"Did they say anything else?"

"Just to give the message to you."

"No other words?"

He shook his head.

"Man or woman?" I asked.

"Woman."

"Thanks." I tipped him, drank up, and left.

I drove to the Choate Group offices, but the place was closed and locked. I went back into town and checked again at my place for a sign from Yudi. He wasn't there, no written message, and nothing on the answering machine. I called Nicole, but she had no word on him either. I got back in the car and drove around the Back Bay searching for him. I knew it would be futile, but I had to do something. How can someone just disappear?

After two hours of aimless driving I gave up and went home. What a nice surprise to find Sugar Baby waiting for me there! Nikki had brought her back and had left a note telling me that she was rooting for me, no matter what I had to do. I poured myself some Pernod and played mousie with Sugar Baby. Then I watched television. Then I poured more Pernod. Then I sulked and brooded. Then I drank more Pernod. I knew I was just marking time, waiting for Yudi to magically materialize the way he did in Yosemite. Finally, around midnight, I collapsed into bed.

That's when I returned to a shady redwood grove in Yosemite. Everything was peaceful and beautiful under one of the gigantic trees. Birds chirped and blossoms swayed. I looked up and saw Yudi sitting on a branch high overhead, holding his suitcase tightly to his chest. I waved, but he didn't see me. Then Lieutenant Branco appeared from behind the tree trunk and walked toward me. He opened his arms to welcome me, and he pulled me close to him. I felt the strength and warmth of his body pressing against mine. Finally, I was safe! He was about to kiss my neck when loud explosions interrupted everything.

Sugar Baby was sprawled heavily on my chest, lapping my neck with her scratchy tongue. Someone was pounding on my apartment door.

"Stan! You in there?"

In my anisette-laden torpor I recognized Branco's voice. The clock near my bed said twenty minutes to seven. I thought, What the hell is *he* doing here at this hour? I wrapped a blanket around my naked body and stumbled to the door. I opened it to see Branco looking tired and sleepy. He wore old jeans and a faded plaid shirt under a black nylon parka. He looked like an ordinary mortal, for a change.

"Sorry to wake you, Stan, but it's serious."

Jesus, I thought. Yudi. My belly tightened in sharp spasms. I felt sick.

"Just tell me, Lieutenant."

"It's Calvin Redding. We found him about an hour ago in the Swan Pond in the Public Garden. He's been strangled with a nylon rope."

"Christ!" The squeezing around my chest stopped. "I thought it was Yudi."

He studied me carefully for a moment, then said, "I'd like to come in."

"Sure. I'll go put some clothes on."

"Don't bother. I won't stay long."

Too bad, I thought.

Sugar Baby appeared in the bedroom doorway and indulged herself with a long stretch. Then she tiptoed gracefully out to evaluate my morning visitor. I asked Branco, "You want some coffee?"

"This is business."

"Don't cops drink coffee on the beat?"

"*Lieutenants* don't have beats!"

Actually, Branco looked as though he needed a real drink, and maybe even a friendly little scuffle on the plush wool carpet in my living room. But that was in the dream, and this was reality. Or was it? Was he really in my apartment at that hour, with me clad togalike in a blanket and nothing else?

"I'll make enough for two," I said, "in case you change your mind." I hiked my blanket up and went to the kitchen to prepare the coffee. Branco followed me, Sugar Baby him.

"Your little friend show up yet?"

"You mean Yudi?"

He nodded.

"No," I said. "I was kind of hoping *you*'d have found him by now."

"We've stepped up our search for him, especially now with Redding dead."

"You don't suspect Yudi?"

"Him . . . you . . ."

The cup I was holding in my hand was suddenly flying through the air toward the kitchen wall across from me. "Damn it to hell!" I screamed as the cup crashed against the wall and broke into three large pieces. Sugar Baby vanished from sight. The blanket almost fell from my shoulders.

"Good thing that cup was empty," Branco said calmly.

"Why me!"

"Because you've been pursuing Calvin Redding with a vengeance since the first killing."

"That's right! And if you'd listened to me, Calvin would be alive now. Damn! We could have wrung the truth out of him. Now we'll never know what happened."

Branco remained calm. "Can you account for your time last night?"

"I was here all night."

"Maybe you had a guest who could verify that?"

I spat the words, "I was here *alone* all night! You can check the bedroom if you dare."

Then the untrusting bastard left the kitchen to look in the bedroom. He came back and said, "Nobody in there. Whose stuff is that in the living room?"

"Yudi's. He was staying here until he disappeared."

Branco went to the two suitcases and rummaged quickly through the clothes inside.

"I hope you've got a search warrant, Lieutenant."

Branco glared at me. "As a matter of fact, I do." He stood up and came back to the kitchen.

I said, "I thought you found your new suspect in Aaron Harvey."

"He wasn't where you said he was."

"He was there yesterday morning. I found him and I talked to him in person, two things *you* seem incapable of doing. But, Lieutenant, you're not still chasing that blackmail angle, are you?"

Branco narrowed his eyes. "If Aaron was blackmailing Redding, why would he kill him?"

"Exactly my point the other night! He wouldn't, unless Calvin put Aaron in his will, or put the condo in his name, or something like that. I don't know. You're the cop! You're the one with the bloody rule book! You go and find out, instead of saying 'no-no-no' to me and then trying to pin a murder on me. All I did was go to sleep last night! Alone!"

On the stove, the little Italian pot gurgled, and the coffee was ready. I poured two cupfuls and pushed one toward Branco. "Here's your fuckin' coffee." I couldn't look him in the face, not after the dream I'd just had, so I sipped quietly for a few minutes. It was good stuff from Celebes. Finally I broke the silence. "It seems all we ever do is argue. Can't we just talk about something neutral for once?"

"Like what?"

"The weather."

"Go ahead."

"It's hot, it's cold, it rains, it snows."

The corner of Branco's lip curled into the tiniest smile, then relaxed. We sipped our coffee without a word. Then I looked at him and saw a weary face. His blue-gray eyes, usually luminous, were veiled with a disappointed glaze. Maybe he really did work hard, even for a cop.

I said, "So, are you still on the case?"

Branco nodded. "But I'm keeping an extra-low profile. I won't go against orders, but I'm going to find that killer."

I wondered how long his renewed commitment would last.

Suddenly Branco banged his cup down like a gavel. "If your friend shows up, tell him to report to me immediately." Then he went to the door.

"Sure thing, Lieutenant. Maybe you could even try to find him yourself, while you're looking for Aaron Harvey." I followed him to the door, and when I opened it for him, I said curtly, "Have a good one."

He turned and looked at me. "Have a good what?"

"Whatever . . ." Then I explained, "That's how they talk out West."

"This is the East," he muttered, and he walked out the door.

What had begun in the world of erotic dreams ended like that.

I opened the shop at nine that morning, did one body wave and a color-cut, then met Nicole coming in as I was on my way out the door at ten-thirty.

She sighed. "*Now* where?"

"Cambridge," I said.

"You were just there yesterday! Has Yudi showed up yet?"

"No, but listen, Nikki, something incredible has happened. Calvin Redding is dead. They found his body early this morning. Strangled."

"Another one!"

"Yeah, and my prime suspect as Roger's killer."

"Well, now who do you suspect?"

"*Whom*, doll. And to be honest, I suspect anyone and everyone, excluding you and me, of course."

"Of course. What's in Cambridge this time?"

"I want to talk with Jennie Doughton at the Choate Group. She didn't show up for our meeting last night."

"So that's what you were up to?"

"Among other things. I want to find out what changed her mind."

"When will you be back?"

"Around one."

Nicole harumphed and shook her head. "Just go!" she ordered.

On the drive to Cambridge the overcast sky turned the variegated trees, which had blazed with color yesterday, murky and dull. I pulled into the Choate Group lot and parked in a place right near the door marked RESERVED in big red letters. The receptionist, my newfound object of torment, was waiting for me at the door, waving his arms in a frenzy.

"You can't park there!"

"Why not."

"It's reserved."

"Is it?" I gave him my best puppy-dog face and I handed the car keys to him. "Then would you mind moving it, Muffin?"

I walked into the building and jogged up the ramp to Jennifer Doughton's office. Through the glass walls I could see she wasn't there. The door was locked, and something else was wrong. Everything but the desks and chairs had been removed from the office she once shared with Calvin Redding. All the drawers were halfway open and empty. I was peering through the thick glass wall when I heard a familiar voice.

"I'm afraid she's gone."

I turned and saw Roy Brickley approaching me. He continued, "It was totally unexpected, but I imagine she's been under a lot of strain and just didn't know what else to do. I wish she'd come to me first."

"What are you talking about?"

"Jennifer Doughton has left the Choate Group."

"How can she have done that? I just spoke with her yesterday."

"I know, and last night she said good night as though she'd be coming in as usual. But when I arrived this morning, I found her office completely emptied. She's just walked out on us, and believe me, I'm shocked. Of course, with this kind of departure it will be difficult to recommend her for employment elsewhere."

"Didn't she leave a resignation letter or something to explain her sudden departure?"

"Nothing," said Brickley.

"It's hard to believe," I said, "especially after ten years with the firm."

Brickley's eyes twitched for an instant. "You seem to know a lot about Ms. Doughton," he said with a beneficent smile. I had the uncomfortable feeling that Jennifer Doughton had been caught snooping and had been fired outright. I felt bad, since I'd put her up to it. Brickley continued, "Is there anything else I can help you with?"

"Have you heard the news about Calvin Redding?"

"What news?"

"Turns out he didn't leave town after all, Mr. Brickley."

"Then you've seen him?"

"The police found him facedown in the Swan Pond this morning. Strangled."

Brickley wavered slightly, then held on to the balcony railing. "Oh dear! My poor boy."

"Hardly a boy."

"Calvin was like a son to me. He was a brilliant talent. Do they know who did it?"

"They're looking for Aaron Harvey."

Brickley shuddered. "I warned Calvin about him. Oh, oh, oh! I must call Vivian. This is horrible, horrible news! She'll be devastated, I'm sure. First Jennifer, and now this!" Roy Brickley hurried up the ramp to the next level, went into his office, and closed the door. His emotion seemed real enough, but I couldn't tell whether it was grief over Calvin's sudden death or some other response.

Then I wondered if Jennifer Doughton's disappearance was connected to Calvin's death. She'd certainly despised Calvin Redding enough to want kill him. And from what I could determine, she had the strength to do it. But would she actually kill him? Had she found some piece of information that had driven her to it? Had she killed him and botched it, so that now *she* was running from the police? Perhaps Jennifer Doughton did have good reason to vanish suddenly. I already knew that neither the police nor I would find a trace of her at her apartment.

I was leaving through the Choate Group lobby when I heard

the receptionist arguing with another associate who wanted the space my car was in. While they bickered, I snatched my keys from his hand, got into my car, and drove off. On the way back to town I suddenly remembered something Yudi had said the first night we were together in Boston. I double-parked outside my place and bounded up the stairs. Perhaps that certain "something" he'd wanted to show me the other night was still in his bags.

18

THE CONCIERGE SYNDROME

It was something I'd never done before, though I'd imagined it often enough. Such behavior was commonplace, even encouraged, among some members of my old-fashioned Czech family. Still, as I began the deed, my stomach churned in disgust, and I actively tried to convince myself that what I was doing had to be done.

I opened the latches on Yudi's suitcase.

The fresh scent of clean clothes rose up from the open case, and I took that as a sign of forgiveness for trespassing on his privacy. I'd finally stooped to the same tactics as my Aunt Letta, a nosy landlady whose specialty was the discreet perusal of her tenants' mail and other belongings. She could teach a French concierge a thing or two.

Everything in the suitcase was packed neatly, almost compulsively so, rolled or folded into packets of related articles. I wasn't sure what I was looking for, but I knew it wasn't clothing. I went through his toilet kit. Nothing unusual there. No hidden compartments, no drugs. When I got to the bottom of the suitcase, I was about to give up. That's when I noticed a small patch of the lining, wrinkled and lightly loose in one corner. As I pushed it back into place, something resisted underneath it, almost like a thin padding. But as I felt around the lining with my clever fingers, I could tell that something had been slipped in between it and the frame of the suitcase. I pulled at the lining fabric carefully until it separated from the bottom of the case. Hidden in there was a large flat mailing envelope of light-weight onionskin paper. I opened it and pulled out photocopies of two letters.

One had been written by Roger Fayerbrock to a California State Assemblyman in Sacramento. In it, Roger was expressing his out-rage over a team of surveyors that was plotting the land around Washington Column in the Yosemite Valley. Apparently, no matter whom Roger had confronted, an air of secrecy prevailed about the work. As a dedicated conservationist, Roger wanted the Assembly-man to find the name of the company that had hired the surveyors.

The second letter was the Assemblyman's reply, and one sentence connected directly to my solar plexus:

> . . .The surveying company in question is under contract by the Choate Group, an architectural consulting firm in Cambridge, Massachusetts, on behalf of their client, Vivian Brickley, who has in-holdings in the Yosemite Valley. . . .

There it was in black and white, the reason Roger had come to Boston. It was clear where my next stop would be. Propriety would have dictated that I call Mrs. Brickley before going to see her, but this was not the time for etiquette. I wanted to catch her off guard. I looked up Roy Brickley in the phone book, but there was no address listing for his name. It was time to ask a favor from a special friend, my personal version of Paul Drake, private agent. I picked up the phone and dialed the operator.

I said, "I need operator two one seven."

The operator brusquely told me to wait. I did, and then I heard a familiar male voice say, "Operator two one seven."

"Darrell, it's me, Stan."

"Stan!" His business attitude vanished for a moment. "How are you?"

"I'd love to chat, doll, but I'm in a bind. I need an address."

He immediately regained his business composure to avoid any suspicion on his end of the line. "Go ahead, please."

"I need the address for a Roy or Vivian Brickley in Cambridge."

"One moment, please." There was a pause, then he said, "Would that be the party at One Eighty Lakeshore Drive?"

"Thanks," I said, and wrote the address down. "I owe you."

"There is no charge for that service, sir."

"Come in anytime, Darrell. Whatever you want, it's on the house."

"Thank you, sir." I detected a quiet kiss over the phone line.

I put the photocopied letters back into their envelope and took them with me. I ran down the stairs two at a time and jogged to the car. Damn! I'd gotten a ticket for double-parking. I figured I'd give it to Branco to fix later. I got it while working for him, after all. Back to Cambridge I went, driving like the autumn wind.

The Brickleys lived on a wide neatly paved avenue that ran directly off Brattle Street. (Brattle Street was called Tory Row before the Revolution, so you can imagine the neighborhood.) Even the way the trees had changed color on their street indicated wealth. The colors seemed cleaner and richer. Their house was a sprawling white three-story colonial, arrayed with numerous gables and dormers and bay windows. It was set back from the street on a vast rise of lush green lawn. For grass to be that green in October in Boston meant the Brickleys had a private gardener and an astronomical water bill.

I parked on the street, even though the signs said PERMIT PARKING ONLY. I walked purposefully to the front door and rang the bell. Soon a young man with smooth olive skin and dark curly hair came to the door. He could have been Branco's baby brother. He wore a white chef's apron over his starched white shirt.

I said, "I'd like to see Mrs. Brickley."

He replied with a heavy accent, "She not home."

"When will she return?"

"Eh?"

"When? Home?" I tapped the face of my watch.

He nodded energetically and smiled with big white teeth. "Ah, *si!* One-oh-clock," he said, proud of his mastery of English.

I looked at my watch. It was half-past twelve.

"Thanks. I'll be back."

"You name?"

I waved my hand and shook my head no. "It's a surprise."

He looked confused.

I repeated, "Surprise," and put my finger up against my lips to signal him not to say anything.

"Ah, *si,*" he said. "Soorpreeze!"

"Right." I went back to the car and turned on the radio while I waited for Mrs. Brickley to return.

Less than half an hour passed when a sleek blue Lincoln sedan glided down the street and turned into the Brickley's driveway. The paint job glistened like a polished sapphire. I recognized Mrs. Brickley by the silhouette of her hair. I jumped out of my car and greeted her in the driveway.

"Hello, Mrs. Brickley!"

She was startled for a moment. "Who's that?"

"It's me, Vannos, from the hair salon."

"Oh," she said with a polite smile. "What are you doing here?"

"I wanted to check on your hair. Your husband said you felt something wasn't quite right with your hairstyle."

"Who said that?" She seemed nervous and confused, and I wondered now if Vivian Brickley's behavior *was* just an act, as Nicole had insisted.

"Your husband told me, Mrs. Brickley. He said you had called the salon about it."

"Did he?" She chuckled nervously. "Young man, I'm *delighted* with your work. If I'd called at all, it would only be to thank you again."

Saying the next words caused a twinge of guilt, but after pawing through Yudi's things, I'd been primed for deceit. (Aunt Letta would be proud.) "Mrs. Brickley, I want to express my sympathy over Calvin's accident. It must have been a horrible blow to you."

She turned her head sharply toward me and spoke with a hardened voice. "Surely it was no accident. I'm certain that dancer friend of his was involved in some way. I hope he's caught and has to pay. Now if you'll excuse me, I'll get Dario to help me with these things."

I stepped right up to the car and reached inside for the bundles. "Let me help you carry them in," I said, grabbing them all up in my arms.

"It's all right," she said brusquely, and tried to pull the bags from me. "Dario will get them."

"It's no problem, Mrs. Brickley. I can do it." I held firmly on to the bags. We were about to engage in a tug-of-war with her groceries.

Her eyes flickered nervously and her lips tightened. "Oh, all right!" she said curtly. "If you insist!" And she let the bags go.

She rang the bell, and Dario opened the door and let us in. He nodded amiably at me as I walked by. He greeted Mrs. Brickley brightly in Italian. "*Ciao, Zia!*"

"*Ciao, caro,*" she sang back.

Then she said to me, "You certainly surprised me there in my driveway."

"I'm sorry if I alarmed you. I was in Cambridge already, talking with your husband. When he mentioned your hair, I thought I'd come by and see you directly, rather than over the phone. I hope I haven't intruded."

"Not at all," she said coolly. "If I seem bothered, it's only because we've had trouble recently with strange men in the neighborhood. Their favorite prey are older women entering or leaving their cars, so I'm afraid you really caught me at the worst moment."

I wondered if I had more criminal blood in me than I realized.

Mrs. Brickley then took a deep breath and let it all out in a big huff, as though trying to relieve her nervous tension. "Now," she said, "I'm about to have my lunch, so if you'll excuse me . . ." She turned to Dario and helped him unpack the bags. Then her face tightened with annoyance again, perhaps with me, perhaps with herself. She turned back to me. "I'm afraid I'm being rude," she said. "Here I am talking about lunch and I didn't think to invite you. I'm sure Dario has made enough." It was a statement of fact, not a heartfelt invitation.

"Thanks, but I'm due back at the salon." Was that a flicker of relief I saw in her eyes? "But could you tell me one thing before I go?"

"What is it?" she asked as she returned to the bags.

"Why were you having your land in Yosemite surveyed?"

"Oh!" shrieked Vivian Brickley, and she dropped a jar of imported capers. It fell to the kitchen floor and bounced off the industrial rubber floor covering.

"*Capperi!*" yelped Dario as he scurried to pick up the jar. He grinned happily at the undamaged jar. "*Non si preoccupi, Zia.*"

Mrs. Brickley took a deep breath and said to me, "Well, young man, I didn't realize how tired I'd become from shopping. I suppose I should have let Dario go out to buy these few things after all. Please forgive me, but I must go lie down now."

"Certainly. Sorry to have intruded like this."

"Not at all." Her words were polite, but her tone was now truly irritated. Her last words sounded as gruff as an order: "*Dario, accompagnarlo alla porta!*"

Dario stood beside me and said, "Please, come." He smiled but firmly pressed me toward the door. I turned back to say good-bye, but Vivian Brickley had already disappeared somewhere within the immense house.

I got into the car and started it. I sat for a moment with the radio turned up loud, deciding what to do next. The question was whether to go confront Roy Brickley about the surveyors or to get Branco to help me. My intuition said to call Branco on the phone and then corner Brickley in person, but instead I went to see Branco at the station. That was another mistake.

I burst into Branco's office exclaiming, "I know why Roger came to Boston!" He was seated with his back to me, looking out the window. He didn't respond, so I asked, "Did you hear me, Lieutenant?"

He answered, "Fine, see you in court tomorrow then."

I gulped. *Now* what was he nailing me for? But when he swiveled in his chair to face me, I saw that he was talking on the telephone. He hung up and said, "What's all the noise about?"

"Read these!" I thrust the envelope containing the photocopied letters across his desk.

He opened the envelope and pulled out the letters. I sat down. Branco read the letter Roger had sent with a kind of weary detachment, but when he read the Assemblyman's response, his mouth actively tightened into a frown. "Where'd you get these?"

"They were in Yudi's luggage."

"They weren't there when I looked."

"You didn't look hard enough."

Branco narrowed his eyes. "Has he shown up yet?"

"No."

I could tell he didn't believe me.

"Stan, if he had these letters with him, it was for a reason. He may have killed Redding in retaliation for Fayerbrock's death."

"Lieutenant, it's not Yudi."

Branco exhaled heavily. He seemed tired of me.

I went on. "I just saw Mrs. Brickley at her place in Cambridge, and when I asked her about the surveyors, she almost collapsed."

"So?"

"So, I think you should confiscate the files at the Choate Group offices."

"What! Stan, you're off on another tangent!" He shook his head. "We can't take their files."

"Why not?"

"We can't go in and seize private property just because their name happens to appear in a letter."

"I'm telling you, the answer to Roger's death—and probably even Calvin's—is at the Choate Group! They hired the surveyors, and Mrs. Brickley owns land out there."

"And I'm telling you, damn it, that you need more evidence than two photocopied letters to take that kind of action. Do you realize the kind of lawsuit that place could throw at us if we're wrong?"

"I don't care. You sat on your butt for lack of evidence, and the main suspect turned up dead."

"He wasn't *our* main suspect," he said angrily. "There's no way I'm going to seize those files."

"Can't you at least look at them?"

"Not without a search warrant."

"Then get a warrant."

His eyes were cold and unyielding. He said nothing.

I asked, "Have you found Aaron Harvey yet?"

"No."

"Cripes, you've had two days! Have you checked out the jazz studios?"

Branco scowled. "Why would we do that?"

"Because Aaron Harvey teaches jazz dance, that's why. And maybe one of the studios has a cozy little room for him to hole up in. That's why!"

Branco picked up the phone, punched some numbers, and said, "Branco here. On the APB for Aaron Harvey. Make sure to check all the jazz dance schools around the city. Right. Apparently the suspect frequents those places." He hung up the phone. "Thanks for that lead, Stan."

"You can return the favor and fix this." I handed him the ticket I'd got for double-parking earlier.

"I don't do that kind of thing."

"C'mon, Lieutenant. I got it working on the case for you. I thought we had an agreement."

"You know there's nothing official between us."

"I know, but I thought it was I help you, you help me."

"I told you, I don't fix tickets!" He was obviously annoyed. Maybe it was the idea of fixing a ticket, or maybe it was his own guilt for not holding to his end of the bargain. I wondered, Which is worse, Mr. Vito Branco? Bending the law? Or breaking a gentleman's agreement?

"What a little pal you are," I said, like Ingrid Bergman to Cary Grant. "If you won't fix the ticket, then will you at least get those files from the Choate Group?"

Branco banged the desk and stood up. "I can see I'm wasting

my breath on you today." He leaned toward me and put his face inches from mine. "The matter is closed!"

"Closed for you, maybe." I stood up and went toward the door, then looked back at him. "You know, Lieutenant, in the beginning I hoped you'd be different. But now I see why we don't get along. You're just another tightassed cop."

"And you're just a goddamn hairdresser! Go back where you belong!"

I left the station stomping my feet and slamming every door I went through. I wanted a drink badly, and I knew a place near the station, a chic club called Denial, right on Berkeley Street. At this hour, it was almost empty. I sat at the bar and ordered a double Beefeater up with a twist. The handsome bartender brought my drink and I quickly took a big gulp.

"Looks like you needed that," he said.

I nodded. "That's not all I need." The bartender winked as though sympathetic to my plight. I wished I smoked. It was another one of those perfect moments for a cigarette.

A few minutes and a few gulps later, the gin was kicking in. That's exactly when a stranger appeared in the doorway to the bar. He peered into the darkness of the room, squinting his eyes and trying to focus. "Hey, Boshton!" he yelled.

The bartender and I looked at each other. He winked knowingly, then said in a low voice just for me, "South End drunk."

The stranger slouched against the door frame and yelled again. "Boshton! That you?" He staggered into the bar and came toward me. Damn luck! "Never geshed you for a daytime boozer, Boshton." His voice was disturbingly familiar, and disturbingly slurred, but I recognized the abbreviated sentence structure. As he approached me, I saw that I'd guessed right: Wacky-Jacky.

"What the hell are you doing here?" I asked.

"Bizznish."

"In Boston?"

"What? Can't do bizznish in Boshton? There a law?"

"No," I said. "But you've got the school back West, and the rocks back West. What kind of business would bring you all the way cross-country to Boston?"

"Lotsa things," he said, and settled himself on the bar stool next to me.

I signaled the bartender and ordered a beer for Jack and another drink for myself. He brought them quickly.

"Thanks," Wacky-Jacky said to me.

"My pleasure, Jack."

He drank almost half the bottle in one long slug, then let out a resonant belch. I said, "I heard you were in town."

"Who toldja?"

"Who do you think?"

"Yaaah, that damn little faggot! I saw him on the plane."

The bartender heard the word and looked toward us, ready for trouble. I waved to him and smiled as if to say, Everything's fine here.

Jack said, "So, he toldja, huh?"

I nodded. "He did, and the police did."

Even in his alcoholic daze, Jack understood what *police* meant, and that I probably knew about his sullied past. "Hey, no problem, Boshton. No trouble. Honesht."

"How'd you find me here?"

"Aaawwww . . . I been hangin' round the station. Knew ya'd talk to the police sooner or later."

"Jack, have you been following me?"

Wacky-Jacky's eyes swirled a bit in their sockets. He wasn't winking at me today. "Jess a li'l, Boshton. No harm, honesht."

"Why?"

"Thought I could help ya."

"Help me with what?"

"Help ya find the killer."

"You help me?" I broke up laughing, but it was my nerves and the liquor, not anything funny.

"Aw, shit!" he said. Then I watched him trying to organize his thoughts, as though he wanted to explain something. Perhaps the beer was sobering him down. After a few false starts, he said, "Got to thinkin' about what ya did," he said, "travelin' three thousand miles, askin' about Roger. And ya hardly knew the guy."

"I told you we went to college together."

Wacky-Jacky weighed my words and shrugged. "Yeah. Well, I come back here to do the same for my old climbin' buddy. Gonna find out who killed him and git the guy."

"You're too late, Jack."

"Huh?"

"The guy who killed Roger is dead. The cops found him this morning."

"Jeezus! Don't say!" Wacky-Jacky took another long slug, then banged the bottle on the counter. "Hell! Now what?"

I drank more gin, and the bartender brought another beer for Wacky-Jacky. He guzzled some, then said, "Wonder if Rog came here for somethin' else, I mean besides climbin' in New Hampshire. Wonder if it's connected with all that trouble with them surveyors."

"You know about the surveyors, Jack?"

His opaque eyes were glazed but still clever. "Oh, sure. Rog told me everything."

"Why didn't you tell me that when I was in Yosemite?"

"Didn't think of it," he said, and belched again, as if to add credence to his words. "Can't think of everything, y'know!"

The gin was dissipating the nervous palpitations Branco had recently caused me. It was also loosening my tongue and my defenses. "Jack," I said quietly, "do you know who hired those surveyors?"

He shook his head dopily no.

"Well, I do."

"Ya do?" He tried to face me directly, but his eyes wandered randomly over my face, and even into the big room behind.

I nodded like a wise judge. "I want to get into their files. I went to the police, but they won't help me."

"Nah, Boshton. Ya don't want the police for that kinda thing. Why not get the stuff yaself?"

"How can I, unless I break into the place?"

Wacky-Jacky blew out a big breath. Perhaps it was to disguise another belch. Then he muffled his voice and said, "Might be able to help ya on this."

"What do you mean?"

"Got a li'l experience in this kinda stuff. You know, climbin' and all." His body teetered on the stool, and his speech was even fuzzier than before, but his brain was still working somewhere in that sloshy, liquor-ridden skull. "I can git into places ordinary folks can't."

I took a mouthful of cold gin, then swallowed it. "What did you have in mind?" I was trying to act cool, but my head was spinning.

Wacky-Jacky grinned slyly. "Go git the stuff ourselves, tonight."

Within five minutes we'd plotted the whole escapade, on a bunch of paper napkins. But escapade is exactly what I figured it was—a caprice, an inebriated exercising of wits, not to be considered seriously. We imagined how we'd climb up the side of the Choate Group building and get in through one of the sky-lights. In our fantastic plan, everything was conveniently uncon-nected to the alarm system. The whole scheme looked good scrawled on paper napkins, but I had no intention of enacting it. Not until Wacky-Jacky put out his big paw of a hand and said, "Is it a deal, partner?"

A long moment passed where we looked into each other's blurry eyes. Was he crazy? Was he serious? Could I trust this man? Of course not! I barely knew him. I'd only climbed once with him, and that was bizarre enough. On the other hand, Branco seemed to be waiting for some deus ex machina to descend and solve the case, incurring nary a split nail. Leave it to me to meet an ethical cop who played by the rules. So what choice did I have?

"Any port in a storm," I muttered under my breath.

"Huh?" said Wacky-Jacky, his hand still stretching toward me and wavering in the air.

So what if the guy had been charged with manslaughter? Most people have some kind of demon in their past. I put out my hand and we shook. "It's a deal!" I said.

We arranged to meet in Harvard Square that night. Then I got up and wobbled proudly out of Denial, feeling like a real man, euphoric that I was finally taking control of my life, even if it was as a criminal.

The world looks brighter, thinking seems clearer, and actions appear braver with gin in the blood.

19

THE END OF THE ROPE

I snapped myself into sobriety for the short drive back to the shop. I didn't want to get hauled in for drunk driving, especially after my last sweet words with Branco.

Nicole pounced on me as soon as I walked in.

"It's after four! Where the bloody hell have you been?"

"Practicing my veronicas with Lieutenant Branco."

"I smell liquor and smoke."

"It was business, honest." (Had I said bizznish?)

"You've been out drinking while everyone around here has been working!" She shook her head impatiently. "At least Ramon was here to help. He covered most of your afternoon appointments, except the ones who walked out because only *you* understand how to do their hair."

"Blessed are they who can feel my fingerprints on their scalp."

Nicole didn't even smile. "You've really scrambled their brains if they believe that."

"*Some* people still have a sense of allegiance."

"Heed your own words, Stanley."

"Nikki, don't be sore. I'm finally on to something. I *know* why Roger Fayerbrock came to Boston." I paused dramatically, but it had no effect on Nicole.

"Stanley, I don't have time for this." She tried to walk away, but I stopped her.

"Nikki, listen, this is it! Roger Fayerbrock was in Boston specifically to see someone at the Choate Group. His meeting Calvin was not the lucky coincidence Calvin made it out to be."

"Stanley," she said, with sparks of annoyance in her bright eyes, "you have customers waiting. We'll discuss this later."

Customers! Here I was on the verge of solving a murder, and about to commit a crime myself just to do it, and Nicole was worried about customers. I knew she wouldn't hear me out now, so I resigned myself to the mundane matter of work. Just to goad her a bit, though, I responded like a flunky. "Yes, M'am!"

I found Ramon working at my station, so I had to use the vacant one at the back of the shop. It's farthest from the windows facing Newbury Street, and it's poorly lit and drab back there. I felt like a schoolboy who'd been sent to stand in the corner for being naughty. Through it all I managed to work on two customers, but my performance was far below its usual excellence. I was so pre-occupied with the adventure awaiting me that night with Wacky-Jacky that I misjudged my chemicals, not to mention the specific London "dry" chemical that was still running through my veins. As a result, the color job was a tad brassy, and the perm came out too soft. I promised both customers that I'd adjust the work within a week, at no charge.

After the shop closed, I joined Nicole in the back room. I couldn't handle any more alcohol, but I was still ready for another session at the Albright Smoking Academy. Tonight Nicole pushed a light blue box of English cigarettes toward me.

"Have you changed brands?" I asked.

"No, Stanley. Those are for you, your very own pack. Consider it a rite of passage."

"Why? I smoke so few?"

"Yes, darling, but you waste so many of mine. It's painful." She drew a rose-colored cigarette from her gold case and lit it. I watched her and envied the pleasure she got from that moment. Smoking was no pedestrian habit with Nicole. In fact, another of her smoker's axioms: Never smoke while standing or walking, indoors or out.

"Now, Stanley," she said, "you may pour us both a drink, and then explain briefly what caused you to be so late this afternoon."

I had the disquieting sensation that I was in the witness box. I poured the drinks, then sat at the table.

Nicole eyed the clear mineral water bubbling in my plastic cup and said, "No gin tonight?"

I shook my head.

"Well, Stanley, I see you have some sense left in you."

Not for long, I thought.

She took a sip of cognac and said, "Now, tell Mother what's been happening."

I began to speak, then realized I was too tired to explain anything. I simply didn't have the energy or the desire to talk about the case anymore. I just shook my head. "Never mind. It's not worth the bother."

Nicole said, "Stanley, please tell me. Something is obviously on your mind. You know it's better to talk about these things than to hold them in."

I knew she was right, but I was tired. The sudden languor was probably an aftereffect of the afternoon cocktail session with Jack, along with the emotional outburst with Branco. I sipped some bubbly water, shrugged, and began.

"It started with some letters Yudi brought with him."

"So he's showed up finally? That's a relief!"

"No he hasn't, Nikki. I went through his luggage and found the letters there." I reddened with shame, but Nicole continued smoking with pleasure and listened for more. What I'd considered a heinous crime didn't seem to phase her at all. "The letters were Roger's, and I read them. They named the Choate Group and Vivian Brickley as the parties who'd hired a group of surveyors out in Yosemite."

"Stanley, what does this have to do with anything?"

"That means the answer is at the Choate Group."

"But you've already been there countless times."

"Yes, but now I know what to look for. Now I have a plan." I lowered my eyes, unsure of how to tell her about the scheme to break into the Choate Group offices. "Except you might not approve."

"You haven't asked my approval for much else recently. Why start now? You can do whatever you like. Perhaps you should even consider changing careers, become a professional investigator."

"Nikki! How could I leave the shop?"

"You've succeeded very well this past week."

I suddenly realized she was serious.

She went on, "You seem to have forgotten, Stanley, that Snips is a full-time business. Perhaps it's time for you to consider a sabbatical."

"Oh, Nicole!" I wailed. "Not you, too! It's hard enough with Branco bucking me, but I can't go through with it tonight if you're against me."

Nicole sighed and tapped her nails on the table. "Stanley, I can't— Oh, never mind! Just tell me what you're planning to do."

"I'm afraid it's drastic." I struggled to light one of the new cigarettes she had given to me. To my surprise, it was easier to smoke then her own brand. "Tonight," I said, surrounding myself with a cloud of uninhaled smoke, "I'm going to break into the offices of the Choate Group."

Nicole said nothing but listened intently, as though I hadn't delivered the punch line yet.

I continued, "I know the answer is somewhere in that place, but Branco won't help me get into their files."

She still didn't respond.

"Nikki, did you understand me?"

She inhaled deeply, then released the smoke from her nostrils in a slow, curling cloud. "I understood perfectly, Stanley, and I realize that you're upset and exhausted. But I also know you can't be serious."

"I am serious."

"Then you've lost your rational mind."

"That's probably true."

She sipped more cognac. "Stanley, you've been somewhat foolish up till now. Passionate, but foolish. But Stanley, *really*, this is criminal!"

"It's the only way, Nikki. Once I've got the evidence I need, I know Branco will cooperate. If I can prove there's something at the Choate Group—*show* it to him—I know he'll go after them."

"No, Stanley."

"There's no choice."

"There *is* a choice. You can get back to your own work and leave the crime business to the police."

"Nicole, two people have been killed and two others have vanished. The police have done next to nothing. They said they suspected me, but they didn't book me. They held Calvin on a pathetic drug charge and released him on bail. He's dead, and now they're after Aaron Harvey and Yudi. Can't you see what's happening? They're just spinning wheels and exercising their rule books while the case fades into oblivion without an answer . . . all because the original victim, Roger Fayerbrock, was gay. If I don't do something about it right now, a killer will get away."

Nicole sat back in her chair. She stared at me for a long time, as though trying to determine my sanity. Then she said, "Stani, for all the time we've been friends, you've known that I love you. Sometimes I think I even understand you. But I think something has changed in you, something I honestly don't understand. And frankly, I'm afraid it's going to pull us apart."

"Nikki, nothing has changed in me. It's just that I finally have a chance to *do* something . . . something I've never done before, never even imagined doing. I can make a difference if I take action. But I'm still the same person inside."

Nicole closed her eyes. Minutes passed so quietly that I could hear the bubbles fizzing happily in my mineral water. When she opened her eyes, they were bright and clear. "All right, Stanley," she said. "Suppose you do go through with this ridiculous secret-agent stunt. How will you do it?"

"I have it all planned." (I was winning her back!)

"I'm sure you do. Alone?"

"No. I have a partner."

"You mean an accomplice. Who is it?"

"Someone I met out in Yosemite, a climber who was very close to Roger."

"Can you trust him?"

"At this point, I have no choice."

"Stanley, you keep saying that. You *do* have a choice."

"No, I don't, Nicole. This is it. *This* is my rite of passage."

Nicole frowned and shook her head. "Or your Waterloo."

"At least give me your blessing."

"You are a foolish, stubborn, ego-ridden man."

"That's it?"

"All right, all right! Go be an idiot with my blessing! When is this media event happening?"

"Midnight," I said, and thought, What relief! If Nikki could be sarcastic, then she still loved me.

She said, "As soon as you're in that place, you call me at home. If I don't hear from you by twelve-thirty, I'm sending the police."

"Nikki, I'm not sure I'll be able to call you. This is a break-in, not an art opening."

"You call me!"

"Okay, okay. And look at the bright side . . . if anything happens to me, the Aubusson carpet is yours."

"Thank you," she said, extinguishing her cigarette with the usual neurosurgeon precision, "but it clashes with my colors."

We embraced for a long moment. Nicole murmured, "Be careful."

It was around eight-thirty when I headed home to prepare for the big night ahead. As I climbed the short masonry staircase leading up to the front door of my building, I sensed something wasn't right. Then I realized that the lamp under the stoop wasn't lit as usual. I got my keys out, and it happened. Someone jumped me from behind and locked my arms. Someone else was in front, pounding strong fists into my gut. I tightened my muscles, but it wasn't enough. I smelled the stench of beer and smoke around me. I kicked violently, but I connected only once to whoever was there. From behind, my arms were yanked back more. Pain sliced through my shoulder as muscle fibers were torn. Through overwhelming dizziness and nausea I heard someone mutter, "Enough." I didn't quite black out, but I wish I had. The last thing I remember was the scent of citrus before I vomited on my Italian leather jacket.

In a distorted dreamlike state, I crawled up the four flights of stairs to my apartment. I felt like a pilgrim at Lourdes: If I made it to the top, I'd be healed. I dragged myself on all fours into my apartment. Sugar Baby was at the door, wrapping herself around my elbows. I closed the door and slumped on the floor. She sniffed at my face, then licked my cheek tenderly. My nurse and lover, a Burmese cat.

After an hour or so I got up. I stumbled into the kitchen and poured myself a drink. Then I filled the bathtub with hot water and soaked in therapeutic bath salts to reduce the swelling and ease the pain that coursed throughout my body. After drying off, I was about to pour another drink, but instead took a couple of painkillers with plain water. I was going to have to be alert in a couple of hours, and my adrenaline would need every break it could get.

I zapped some leftover pizza in the microwave oven, but after a few bites the nausea returned. I gave up with it and went to the bedroom to change. As I put on dark clothing, I reminisced about the night Yudi and I had gone to the slide site at Yosemite. It seemed long ago. That night I was simply anxious. Tonight, I was terrified. I glanced at Yudi's luggage. I meditated quietly for his safety, for now I was sure he was in trouble.

To relax, I played with Sugar Baby. I figured a round of mousie might reduce my growing panic to a manageable nervous tingle. At one point I realized that this could be the last time I'd ever play with my favorite cat. In my heart I knew Branco was right. I was dealing with a killer.

At eleven o'clock I left my apartment and drove to Cambridge. I was grateful the convertible had power steering, because my shoulders hurt a lot. I wondered how I was going to be able to work the next day, assuming nothing dire happened this night.

I picked up Wacky-Jacky in Harvard Square at eleven-thirty as planned. When he got in the car, he slapped my shoulder and said hoarsely, "Hey, fella! Surprised ya showed up! Thought you mighta changed ya mind." He'd been drinking, probably hadn't stopped since our afternoon together at Denial. He whooped loudly. "Gonna have us one hootin' helluva time tonight!" Meanwhile, my shoulder burned from the manly slap he'd just given me.

We got to the Choate Group offices and found the outside wooden gate closed and locked. Consequently, the overture to the main event was to scale an eight-foot fence. Wacky-Jacky crouched, then jumped up and grabbed on to the top. He scooted up the fence like a huge bug. That technique certainly wasn't going to work for me, not with my shoulders moaning in pain under my jacket. Instead, I stepped way back for a good running start. Then I imagined Donald O'Connor dancing up the walls in *Singin' in the Rain*. If he could defy gravity, so could I. I dashed toward the fence and used my strong legs to propel me up in a wide arc onto the planks. At the apex of my mad scramble along vertical fence, I grabbed for the top. The upward thrust of my whole body lessened the strain on my arms and shoulders, but they still hurt like hell. It was only the beginning.

On the other side of the fence was the Choate Group lawn, which thankfully was dense and soft even in early November. I jumped down from the fence and landed on my legs in the plush grass. I got up and stood next to Wacky-Jacky. The air jittered with tension. It must have been the two of us so excited by the main event—Breaking and Entering.

"This climb'll be a piece of cake," he said confidently. Cake, I thought, made with bran flakes and soy oil.

The only light was from the moon and the streetlights on the other side of the fence, but still I could see the three-story building looming high against the dark sky.

"Maybe it's too dark," I said.

"Nah. Full moon's easy to climb on. Not workin' by the rules tonight anyway."

"I'd say not, considering what we're up to."

"Meant good climbin' rules." He unfastened a hank of nylon rope from his belt and attached a large three-pronged metal hook to one end. Then he stepped back from the building and flung the rope high up into the air. The large hook caught on a pipe protruding from the roof. I was impressed that he succeeded on the first try.

Wacky-Jacky said, "Just wanna get up there, get in, and get out, right?"

I nodded. "Right."

"So ain't no time for ethics and honest technique. That's why I brung these." He thrust some metal contraptions at me. "Over your shoes. Clamp on to the rope. Just like climbin' a ladder." He quickly put the clamps over his shoes and climbed up the rope. He was up on the rooftop in less than a minute.

Oh, that it had been that easy for me! Once I finally got the clamps on, I couldn't get them to work right. On one foot, the clamp wouldn't release the rope to let me slide that foot up, while the other clamp was supposed to be holding tight. Eventually I got them to release at the right time, but then they wouldn't grip the rope tightly enough, so when I raised one foot, the other one would slip downward. It was that sensation of moving your legs frantically and getting nowhere—like treading water, or a nightmare.

"Easy, there!" Jack hissed down at me through the darkness. "Wear yaself out."

I ended up hauling myself mostly with my arms. I was soaked in sweat when I got past the first-floor windows, more from the agonizing pain in my shoulders than sheer exertion. Then, mercifully, the clamps decided to cooperate for the rest of the climb. At the top of the rope, Wacky-Jacky pulled me up onto the roof.

"Uhhhnnn." I groaned in pain.

The roof was steeply raked. Wacky-Jacky said, "Now it's just like them rocks we climbed. Keep ya hands and feet flat and follow me." Our goal was one of the skylights. Wacky-Jacky studied them carefully before choosing the one we would crawl toward. When we got there, he began dismantling the metal molding around the skylight. It all seemed so easy that I wondered how many times he'd done this kind of work. Probably I didn't want to know. All I wanted was to see the files in that building and find out what Roger had been trying to do before he was killed.

I helped Wacky-Jacky lift the skylight panel and place it behind the framework that jutted up above the roofing. (We didn't want the glass panel sliding off while we were inside.) I looked down through the opening in the roof into the building. It was a big dark hole. I thought it strange that the place had no night lights. "How are we going to get down?" I asked. Already I was anticipating more pain in my shoulders.

"Watch." Wacky-Jacky produced a rope with numerous loops of nylon webbing attached. "Ya'll like this. S'French."

"What is it?"

"Rope ladder, called a ay-tree-AY. Pretty neat, huh?" He secured one end of the *étrier* to the skylight frame and dropped the other end into the black hole below. "You first."

I shook my head. "It's better if I watch and copy you, like Simon Says."

"Nah. This ain't like climbin'. I gotta hold it for ya. Sometimes they slip, and ya don't wanna be on it when it does."

That's all I needed to hear. I hauled myself through the skylight and gripped the loops of the *étrier* tensely in my hands. Jack grumbled, "Ya feet, stupid! Put ya *feet* in, not ya hands!"

"Hey, pal, I'm using whatever works here." I lowered myself, but the pain searing my shoulders was too much. I just slid down until I reached the end of the rope. Now besides a battered body, I had rope burns on my hands.

I had no idea how far down the floor was. *That* is scary, jumping into total blackness. Before I let go, I reminded myself to breathe deeply and cushion the fall with a dancer's plié: one, two, three, release.

My legs caught the impact, and I rolled softly on the carpeted floor to absorb the rest of the force. Even at that, my aching body wailed, but I didn't care. I was in!

Wacky-Jacky descended the *étrier* quickly and landed softly near me. He spoke loudly into the darkness. "We're here!"

"Sssh! Why are you talking so loud?" I whispered.

"No one here to hear us, is there?" he asked, without lowering his voice.

"I guess not."

"So now what?"

I knew the one and only place I'd find the stuff I wanted. "Give me the flashlight, Jack. I know the way."

The door to Roy Brickley's office was locked, but Jack turned out to be adept at lock picking as well. He got it open easily, too easily.

Inside Brickley's dark office the air held the scent of bergamot from his expensive cologne. I went to his desk and pulled at one of the drawers. It opened, much to my surprise. In fact, all the drawers were unlocked. I quickly rummaged through the contents.

Jack said, "Find what ya need?"

"I don't know." I opened a folder that contained what looked like a formal statement by Roy Brickley. It told of Jennifer Doughton's mental instability and her recent confession to Roy Brickley that people like Calvin Redding didn't deserve to live. The document had been notarized by Roy Brickley's attorney, J. T. Wrorom. It took only a moment's scan of my mental trash can to recall that Calvin's attorney had been the same person. Curious, I thought.

"Whatcha find?" Jack asked.

"I'm not sure." I also thought it peculiar that such a document hadn't been more carefully guarded and locked up, or that it had even been written in the first place. I shined the flashlight around the office and stopped the beam on a huge rosewood breakfront. That's probably where he keeps the important stuff, I thought. When I found every door and drawer on that massive cabinet locked, I knew I'd hit pay dirt. With the flashlight, I got a close look at all the holding latches. If I had the right tool, I could probably jimmy them open. What I needed was a flat, narrow, flexible piece of metal, a piece of metal much like the triple-cut nail file I always carry in my back pocket, even tonight.

I worked the file into the space between one drawer and the cabinet frame. A few minutes of expert jiggling and I was in.

"That's it?" asked Wacky-Jacky nervously.

"I don't know!" God, the guy was insistent! Maybe he was more nervous than I thought. The drawer turned out to be empty, so I tried the other two. The first of those contained flat blueprints. I shined the light onto the top of the pile. The drawing looked like the aerial view of a sprawling resort. The title patch in one lower corner of the blueprint gave me a chill:

YOSEMITE VALLEY
LUXURY CONDOMINIUMS

The remaining blueprints all had the same title but were for different "modules."

Wacky-Jacky said, "Find it?"

"Found somethin'," I answered with a hint of Wacky-Jacky's own inflection. I was going to have a good time telling Branco about those blueprints.

In the third drawer of the breakfront I found piles of correspondence between Roy Brickley and a Leonard Smuckbaum, whose address was a post-office box in Yosemite Village. With a name like that, I thought, it was no wonder he went by Mr. Leonard.

I'd just started reading the first letter when the office lights suddenly came on. I squinted through the glare and made out the unmistakable faces of Roy Brickley and Mr. Leonard.

Wacky-Jacky grinned broadly and said to Brickley, "Got him here just like I promised, didn't I?"

Brickley said, "Yes. You've done well. Now be quiet." He stared at me with contempt. "I shouldn't be surprised to find you here, Mr. Kraychik, yet I am impressed with your endurance."

"I recover pretty fast for a punching bag, Mr. Brickley."

"I regretted having to do that, but I didn't know how else to stop you."

"I can understand that. After all, when the phone call and the letter and the car business didn't work, and breaking into my apartment didn't get you anywhere, you had no choice but to resort to good old-fashioned bullying."

Roy Brickley's face twitched. "Mr. Kraychik, I have never met such a stubborn, persistent person as you. You have caused me great distress, but I'm sure that's all behind us." He leered contentedly. "We can talk openly now, face-to-face."

Wacky-Jacky said, "What about my money? You owe me money!" He started toward Brickley, but Brickley now had a small dark metal object in his hand. Yes, he had a gun. Wacky-Jacky stepped back.

Brickley looked at me and said, "You see the effect you have? People become unreasonable. In the past short week, with all your meanderings over the death of a National Park ranger, you caused more trouble to my partner Leonard here and myself than any obstacle we'd encountered in the past two years. You were, believe me, the last person I thought I'd have to contend with."

"I always do my best. Who killed Roger?" I asked.

"Is that all you can think of at a time like this?"

"You killed him!"

"Nonsense!" snapped Brickley. "Calvin Redding did. Isn't that what you've adamantly believed all along?" He sneered. "Then it must be true, correct? Those young bucks were playing some obscene game and they had an accident. Simple."

"No, Mr. Brickley. Calvin didn't kill Roger. You knew that. You even hired your own Brahmin lawyer to represent him and get the charges dropped. I wonder how much that cost you?"

"That may have been a mistake."

"Not as big a mistake as killing Calvin."

"Nonsense! Aaron Harvey did that. Jealousy." Brickley shook his head and clicked his tongue twice, as if to say naughty-naughty.

"You're lying."

"That's your opinion, Mr. Kraychik. But rather than engage in this idle morbid speculation, I'd like to get down to business."

I glared at him. "I have no business with you." The gun that was pointing my way, however, changed that notion.

Mr. Leonard said, "If I were you, I'd listen to what he has to say."

Brickley said, "Thank you, Leonard." He softened his manner somewhat and continued speaking to me. "I am about to propose an offer that will change your life, and the investment on your part is quite small."

"I have no money."

Brickley laughed. "It's not money we want! At least, not from you. It's much simpler than that." He smiled like a benign schoolmaster, but it was an act. "It's your cooperation," he said. "You must simply stop meddling in this whole matter of the ranger's death."

Those were familiar orders, first from Branco, now from Brickley. How was anything going to get solved if the good guys and the bad guys were telling me the same thing?

"What if I don't agree?" I asked.

Mr. Leonard said, "When you hear his offer, you will. You're just one more in a long line of people who eventually said yes."

"Sounds like an exclusive club," I said.

"You could say that." Brickley and Mr. Leonard smiled familiarly at each other. Brickley said to me, "You see, you are inadvertently upsetting a plan that has taken years to design."

"I don't do anything inadvertently."

Brickley's face twitched again before he went on. "That plan will make every party involved extremely wealthy. I am willing to offer you a percentage share of the proceeds of our project." His voice had an impatient edge to it now. "You will be rich and secure for the rest of your life. I can't imagine what else someone like you could want."

"Where's Jennifer Doughton?" I demanded.

Brickley looked annoyed. "She has intelligently agreed to the same terms I'm now offering you."

"I thought she resigned."

"She left of her own will, after finally listening to reason."

"That's a lie!" screeched Wacky-Jacky, still armed with Dutch courage.

"Shut up!" yelled Brickley, and he turned the gun on him.

In spite of the gun facing him, Wacky-Jacky stepped toward Roy Brickley. "Pay me, I'll shut up!" Then Wacky-Jacky turned to me and said, "Don't believe him."

I said to Brickley, "Is this all related to your wife's land in Yosemite being surveyed? For the condominiums?"

Brickley frowned. "Oh, dear. You know more than I thought. That spoils everything. That's too bad." He looked really sorry about something, and I had the feeling it was me. "How did you find out about that?" he asked.

"Grim determination," I said.

Brickley looked unsure. "I hadn't planned on this."

Just then we all heard a sound from the lobby of the building. Brickley turned his head but kept the gun pointed at me. Suddenly, from within the building's cavernous atrium, we heard someone calling.

"Raymond? Raymond, are you here?" It was Vivian Brickley.

Mr. Leonard said nervously to Roy Brickley, "What is *she* doing here? I thought we were going to finish this business without her."

Brickley nodded and answered quickly, "Quiet! She may not

have heard us. But I'm prepared, Leonard. If she comes up here, I'll take care of it. She'll listen to me." But Roy Brickley looked worried.

Again Vivian Brickley called, this time even louder. "Raymond! I know you're here. I can see the lights in your office and your car is in the lot."

Brickley frowned, then called back to her. "I'm upstairs, Vivian, in my office!" He muttered something angrily to himself, then turned back to me. "It's really too bad you know about the land, Mr. Kraychik. It puts us back to where all this trouble started. You see, you know exactly what Roger Fayerbrock knew when he first came to Boston to try to stop me."

We could hear the hydraulic lift open at the end of the walkway. Vivian Brickley spoke loudly and urgently as she approached the office. "Raymond! The police were just at the house, and I thought you'd want to know they—" She stopped short in the doorway to Brickley's office. She was flushed with excitement. She looked around at the group of us in there. "What is going on here? And what is my *hairdresser* doing here?"

Mr. Leonard gawked at me. "You're a hairdresser?"

I nodded, and noticed that Vivian Brickley's hair still looked damn good. But now she'd switched back to her other, more familiar state—the bewildered matron. I honestly couldn't tell whether she knew what was going on in that office or not.

She said, "Raymond, why are all these people here? You said you'd be finished with work hours ago."

Brickley answered her, "It's all under control, Vivian. You needn't have come."

"But why . . . ? Raymond! Is that a gun?"

Brickley said, "Yes, Vivian. I've had to take this precaution now."

"Raymond, why are the police looking for you?"

"That's enough now, Vivian. I'll explain later. What's more important is that your hairdresser seems to know about your land in Yosemite. You didn't tell him about the land, did you? I've heard that women often tell their hairdressers everything."

Vivian Brickley's eyes burned through me. I suddenly sensed more power in her gaze than the doddering librarian she so expertly portrayed. Her eyes flashed repeatedly between me and her husband. Finally she spoke. "No, Raymond. I've never discussed the land with him."

Praise the gods, I thought. At least the confidence between hairdresser and client was still sacrosanct.

Suddenly Wacky-Jacky blurted, "Ya gonna give me my money or am *I* gonna tell him everythin'?"

"Keep quiet!" Brickley ordered, aiming the gun at him again.

But Wacky-Jacky persisted. "He's lyin'!" He looked at me. "He wanted me to kill the little Filipino!" He pointed a shaking finger at Brickley. "He wanted me to, but I didn't, even though I hate the little faggot."

"He's *Balinese!*" I said.

Brickley screamed, "Shut your mouth!"

"Fat girl's not dead either, the way he wanted. Got her gagged away, too." Then Wacky-Jacky spit on Brickley's calfskin shoes. "Don't wanna hear no more? Pay me now!"

Roy Brickley suddenly broke into raucous laughter that lasted uncomfortably long. "Why should I pay anyone now? Who knows we're here at all, but us?"

Mr. Leonard shuffled his feet nervously. "Now, Roy, keep calm. I'm sure there's a solution that doesn't require any more violence."

Mrs. Brickley stamped her foot on the carpeted floor, but it made only a dull thump. "Raymond? What is he talking about? Are you committing nefarious deeds? Who are these two men?" She indicated Wacky-Jacky and Mr. Leonard.

Brickley tried to speak calmly, but he was all nerves now. "Vivian, I haven't told you about it yet. I wanted to surprise you, but now that we're here . . . Vivian, I've been working on a project that will make you proud of me. It has required the work of many people, most of whom you've never even met."

Mr. Leonard seemed desperate to explain the necessity of his role. "Madam, I've been safeguarding your holdings in the Yosemite Valley. Without me this whole project would have failed."

Jack said, "Hey! I blew up them rocks. Without me, none of you'd be anywhere now."

Mrs. Brickley said, "What is he talking about? Raymond! Explain yourself!"

For an instant, Roy Brickley looked sheepish and weak, and I felt I was witnessing a marriage squabble. I did what I always do in those situations—observe quietly and await the best moment to act or speak. Brickley quickly recovered his bravado. "Now that it's come out, Vivian, I *will* explain everything." Brickley took a step back, as if to address us formally, though he still held the gun on us. "What I have conceived is unmatched in the history of architecture. Even Ayn Rand's *Fountainhead* pales beside my master plan. It will be the ultimate statement of man's control over Nature, and it will make us rich, Vivian."

Mrs. Brickley was now even more agitated. "Rich? Raymond, money has never been a problem."

"Not for you, Vivian, with the founding fathers of Sacramento in your blood and in your bank accounts and your properties. But for me it's different. My family disowned me long ago. I've had to sustain my own income. I've had to work!"

"Raymond, everyone has to work. You're prattling like a spoiled young boy."

"Not anymore, Vivian. Today, I'm a man. This project will prove it."

Vivian Brickley looked at Roy Brickley as a mother would a naughty child who has finally graduated to delinquency. When she spoke again, her voice was controlled and focused, but as usual, she was a few facts behind the rest of the conversation. "Raymond, I hope you're not planning something on the land."

"Of course I am, Vivian! The land is just sitting there doing nothing. It's been waiting for the perfect moment—my plan!"

"That won't do, Raymond. I've told you my intention is to preserve that land. It is to remain natural and unaltered, in perpetuity."

"Vivian, that's too long! We are dying as we speak. I must make my mark on this world!"

Vivian shook her head. "Raymond, this is distressing news."

I saw my moment and spoke. "Wait'll you see what happens now." I directed one superb hitch-kick directly at Brickley's hand, the one holding the gun. The gun flew out the office doorway and over the railing into the atrium. (Just vectors and timing.) Wacky-Jacky immediately jumped on Brickley and knocked him to the floor. While they wrestled around, I lunged for Mr. Leonard, but my shoulder roared in pain, and our man-to-man scuffle resembled a limp-wristed tango.

Then we all heard the shot. Mr. Leonard shrieked, and everyone stopped moving. Vivian Brickley held a small silver gun in her stone-steady hand. "Stop it, everyone! Stop it this instant!"

Roy Brickley was holding his shoulder. It was dark and wet with blood. He sobbed, "I'm shot! You've shot me, Vivian! I'll be scarred! I'll sue you!"

"Raymond, stop whining! It's only a flesh wound. I'm sorry I had to do it, but you've worn me down. I'm tried of your insatiable greed, and I'm weary of your sexual problems. This dirty business is the last straw. I'm through with your boyish antics! I'm calling the police!"

From my clumsy embrace with Mr. Leonard, I said, "May I call, Mrs. Brickley? There's a particular cop I'd like to have witness all this."

But she never had a chance to answer me. Responding to the gunshot, Lieutenant Branco and half the Boston Police Department were already coming in through the front door and running up the ramps to where we were.

"How did you know?" I asked him.

"Your friend Ms. Albright called me."

Damn! I'd forgotten to phone Nicole.

Branco said, "Looks like we showed up just in time, too."

"Saved me the call, anyway," I retorted.

Vivian Brickley said, "Officer, arrest these men!"

Branco said, "M'am, you'll *all* have to come downtown with us."

Vivian looked at me with concern. "Does this mean I'm under arrest, too?"

"Just for questioning," answered Branco. Then, looking at Mrs. Brickley's gun, he said, "I hope you have a license for that weapon."

Mrs. Brickley answered him shortly. "Of course I do! I'm a

markswoman. I've carried a firearm since my days in the foreign service over thirty years ago." Then she remarked to me, "But I've never been arrested before." She giggled quietly.

"Stick with me, Mrs. Brickley," I said. "You'll see a lot you never did."

20

FINISHING TOUCHES

Thursday night, after closing the shop, Nicole and I were in the back room for our customary drink. A thorough massage that morning and strong painkillers had enabled me to work half a day, despite my shoulder injury.

"Was it too much for you today, Stani?"

"Nikki, supervising Ramon this afternoon was a pleasure compared to last night's adventure."

She took out her gold cigarette case and caught me eyeing it. "Where are those cigarettes I gave you last night?"

"I lost them."

"Well, you're not mooching one of mine just to ruin it."

"It's okay, Nikki. I decided to quit smoking anyway."

She laughed. "You never even started!"

"But the desire was there," I said knowingly.

A sudden loud banging on the back door startled us. I went to the door and hollered through, "Who's there?"

"Branco!"

I let him in. He wore a three-piece navy blue suit with the palest blue pinstripes.

Nicole said, "All dressed up and no place to go, Lieutenant?"

Branco said, "I was in court all day."

If I'd been on the jury, I'd have believed whatever Branco said, simply because he looked so damn fine.

Branco said, "Today we heard testimonies from Brickley, Smuckbaum, and Werdegar."

It sounded like a law firm.

"Was I right about Roger's killer?" I asked.

Branco nodded.

"I knew it!" I said triumphantly. "Roy Brickley!"

"Stani!" snapped Nicole. "All along you've been saying it was Calvin."

"I know, doll. But I was wrong."

"Why Brickley?"

Branco was about to explain, but I stopped him. "May I have the honor, Lieutenant? I want to see how right I was."

His mouth tightened, but then he nodded.

"Tell me if I'm off, though, okay?"

Branco said sharply, "Just get on with it."

"See, Nikki, Roger found out about Brickley's plans for a huge condo development in Yosemite. That's why he came to Boston, to put the screws to the Choate Group, since they did the original land survey. Roger threatened to halt the whole project because it would deface a National Park site."

"Then how did it get as far as it did?" she asked.

Branco answered. "Vivian Brickley owns a parcel of land in the Yosemite Valley. Because of vague technicalities in the laws that govern National Parks, the privately held land can still be developed, so long as it doesn't impede on a natural formation."

"Which Washington Column used to be," I added.

Nicole surmised and said, "So with the rock formation gone, work on the condos could proceed?"

"Technically, yes," Branco said in his solemn law-abiding voice.

I added, "But Roger was still trying to halt the project on the grounds of natural preservation. And, since that's what Vivian Brickley had intended for the land all along, Roy Brickley had to stop Roger before Vivian found out."

Nicole asked, "I can't believe she didn't know what her husband was up to."

Branco explained. "Her husband led her to believe that the surveying team was to satisfy *new* laws to further protect any property entrusted to the National Park and Wildlife Service."

I added, "But it was a lie."

Branco nodded and continued. "The surveyors were actually marking the terrain to make sure Brickley's own plans would succeed in slipping through the loopholes in the old laws."

"Goodness!" exclaimed Nicole. "Is the land still in danger?"

"No," said Branco. "In fact, from the start, Vivian Brickley must have doubted her husband's intentions regarding the land, because she'd already filed new trust documents with her attorneys."

Nicole asked, "So, Roy Brickley's master plan was all for nothing?"

Branco nodded soberly. "I'm afraid so."

I added bleakly, "Two deaths and a natural rock formation destroyed, all because of greed." Poor Roger, I thought.

"At least the *woman* was innocent," said Nicole.

"Completely," said Branco. "And the land is safe. This kind of thing can never happen again."

Nicole asked, "But how did Brickley know to find Roger at Calvin's place so he could kill him there?" Then she quickly added, "Oh, they probably arranged the whole thing."

"Right," I said. "Calvin was in on that part of the plan. When Roger arrived, Roy Brickley convinced Calvin to play up to him, offer him a place to stay. That explains why Calvin was so reluctant to invite me for drinks that evening. He wasn't sure how many people would be at his place that night."

Nicole said, "Do you think Calvin knew Roger would be dead?"

I shrugged. "I'm only guessing, Nikki." I asked Branco, "Did their testimonies explain that?"

Branco said, "You're pretty much on target, Stan, except that murder wasn't part of the plan. Brickley went to Redding's place that afternoon to try to buy Roger Fayerbrock off. It didn't go as planned, though. They became violent, and Brickley ended up strangling him. The only thing they didn't foresee was Aaron Harvey, who was supposed to be in New York but who never left town. He was in the apartment when Roger arrived unexpectedly, so he hid in the bedroom closet. When Brickley arrived, Harvey ended up witnessing the killing through the louvers in the door."

"That's why I smelled Aaron's cologne in the room that night! God, Brickley must have almost caught him when he went into the closet for a bow tie."

"It was a close call," said Branco.

I continued, "Who put the ties on Roger? The knots were different, so I suspect two different people."

"We found only one tie, but from what we heard today, there was actually two. Brickley did put on one, and Aaron Harvey admitted to the other."

"Brickley must have done it to incriminate Calvin." I paused. "I guess I believed it, too. But why would Aaron Harvey do it? Just to let Calvin know that he'd been there? Calvin would miss that kind of subtlety." I sighed and shook my head. "What some people do in the name of love."

Nicole asked, "Was Aaron still in the closet when Stani got there?"

Branco answered, "Aaron left the apartment even before Calvin Redding got home, but he watched from outside the building to see what happened once the body was discovered."

"So that's how he knew my face and connected me with Roger! But I'm still curious about one thing, Lieutenant."

"Yes?"

"Who had sex with Roger?" I asked bluntly.

Branco shrugged. "We haven't got an answer on that."

"Didn't Aaron see anything?"

Branco shook his head. "If he did, he's not telling."

Nicole held two bottles up to Branco. "A drink, Lieutenant?"

Branco pointed to the Scotch, then made his thumb and index finger show the space of almost an inch. "Neat," he said to her. I was surprised that he accepted the offer.

"Where did you finally find Aaron?" I asked.

"Just where you said, Stan, holed up in a jazz studio storage room."

I beamed. That admission was as close to a compliment as Branco would give me.

He continued, "And you were right about the blackmail angle, too. Aaron Harvey was blackmailing Brickley for a share in the Yosemite profits. He promised *not* to tell the police that he'd witnessed Brickley killing Roger."

I added, "But that two-timer was also blackmailing Calvin, except he promised Calvin he *would* tell the police everything he knew, if Calvin would sign his penthouse over to him. Calvin naïvely saw it as an easy way to clear himself of any suspicion around Roger's death."

"That's right," said Branco.

Nicole asked, "But if Aaron knew so much, why did he kill Calvin? Shouldn't it have been the other way around?"

Branco and I answered in unison. "Brickley killed Calvin!"

"Brickley!" Nicole looked stunned. "But why?" she said, handing Branco his drink.

I answered, "Once he was released from jail, Calvin was probably double-crossing Brickley for a bigger cut of the Yosemite pie. Brickley answered that ultimatum in his own way."

"Right again," said Branco. Then he raised his glass to me and to Nicole. "To health!" he said.

"To love!" I said.

"To money!" Nicole said.

We all drank.

Nicole asked, "What about Leonard and Jack, the two from Yosemite?"

Branco explained, "Roy Brickley and Leonard Smuckbaum were partners."

I interrupted, "Were they lovers?"

Branco frowned and went on without answering me. "Roy Brickley married his wife for her money and for the land she held in the Yosemite Valley."

"Talk about a smoke-screen marriage," I said.

"Poor deluded woman," said Nicole. "I'll have to talk to her."

Branco continued. "As for Jack Werdegar, Brickley hired him

to cause the rock slide. That's where that Rezon-loaded chock came from. Stan found one that hadn't detonated."

Nicole asked, "But didn't anyone in the valley hear the explosion and suspect foul play right from the start?"

"The Rezon doesn't explode," he explained. "It vibrates things until they reach resonant frequency. Then they just collapse. Werdegar had jammed about a hundred of those things into the rock. Once the rock fractured, the slide appeared completely natural."

"But what was he doing in Boston?" she asked.

Branco said, "Werdegar's been out here a couple of times. First time was last summer, which is when he stole the Rezon from M.I.T. labs. Roy Brickley had learned about the stuff through his alumni contacts at M.I.T. while he was consulting on a special project there. He hired Werdegar to steal enough of it to do the job.

"The second time Jack came to Boston is partly thanks to Stan." Branco raised his glass to me, and I happily accepted the gesture of praise. "When he found Stan asking questions in Yosemite about the killing, he realized he was involved in something more serious than he'd expected. He wanted to pull out, but first he wanted to be paid off. So he returned to Boston to collect, but instead, Brickley forced him to help him again."

"And Leonard?"

"Leonard Smuckbaum flew here to Boston to give Brickley a hand. Brickley hadn't planned on the complications caused by Aaron Harvey and Jennie Doughton and Stan here." Branco took a sip of Scotch and nodded in approval. (He should have—it cost Nicole thirty bucks a bottle.)

I said, "So my meddling kind of helped things reach a climax, eh?"

Branco made the slightest nod.

I said, "And Brickley probably caught Jennie Doughton combing through the Choate Group computer files, as I'd suggested she do."

"That's right," said Branco. "She found out too much, so Brickley ordered Werdegar to kill her."

"I wonder whom he got to call the Harvest and leave that message for me the other night?"

"Probably some unsuspecting staff member," said Nicole.

"I hope he paid her overtime for staying late," I said.

"Huh!" went Nicole. "I want to know who left the threat note? And who broke into Stani's apartment?"

"And tried to run me over? Brickley, of course. He even beat me last night while Jack held my arms. I smelled his citrus cologne."

Nicole lit a cigarette and pulled the smoke deep into herself. "And finally, how does Yudi fit into all this?"

"Ah yes. Yudi," I said. Branco watched me quizzically as I spoke. "He told me everything earlier today, after he gave you his statement, Lieutenant. I had assumed him motive for coming to Boston was to avenge Roger."

"And was it?" asked Branco with a sly look.

Nicole interjected, "He apparently had another personal reason as well, Lieutenant." She rolled her eyes toward me.

I ignored her remark and continued. "The morning he disappeared, he went to the Choate Group. Unfortunately, he flew directly into Brickley's web, and Wacky-Jacky caught him on his way back to town. Brickley's plan backfired, though, because Jack didn't have the nerve to kill him. Or Jennie, for that matter."

"What will happen to the others now?" asked Nicole.

Branco said, "Brickley faces murder-one for killing Roger Fayerbrock and Calvin Redding. Smuckbaum is an accomplice. Aaron Harvey faces two counts of blackmail and one of withholding evidence. Jack Werdegar has destroyed federal property and kidnapped two people. His sentence may be reduced because he took good care of Yudi and Jennie and actually protected them from Brickley."

"Jack needs psychological help more than punishment," I remarked.

Branco's face tightened. "A good measure of both, I'd say." He finished his drink and made for the door. He said good night to Nicole, then turned to me, facing me directly. "And how about you? Where's your little friend now?"

"At my place, resting."

Nicole said, "I hope the nap doesn't spoil his sleep for later."

"I have other plans to spoil his sleep for later," I said.

A small wry smile appeared on the corners of Branco's mouth. "Don't do anything I wouldn't do," he said, then departed quickly through the back door.

Nicole said, "It's nice that you two are on friendly terms. I always said you needed a strong man."

"Nikki, get real! He's a straight cop! The pathway to love for me is a more realistic one, directly home tonight."

She sighed. "Perhaps you're right, Stani. Why pursue an elusive romance when you can have a willing one?"

"Especially since the elusive ones will always be there, eluding me."

Nicole put on her coat. "I still feel sorry for Vivian Brickley, tricked into marriage by her husband."

"She almost couldn't help it. Roy Brickley is a classic example of *puer aeternus*, the eternal boy who avoids the responsibilities of adulthood. People like him prey on others to take care of them. With her strong maternal instinct, Vivian Brickley was an easy mark."

A cab sounded its horn out front. "Good night, darling," Nicole said, and hugged me firmly. "See you in the morning."

"Night, doll." The cab whisked her away. I locked up the shop and headed home, contemplating which delectable method I would use to awaken Yudi.

Up the long flights of stairs I trudged. It had been a strenuous week, filled with more activity than I'd ever had. But one thing was clear from all the running and flying and questioning and arguing and pain—I knew I was alive. Now I looked forward to a night of peace and pleasure with my young guest.

I unlocked the door and opened it, and was surprised that Sugar Baby didn't greet me as usual. Then my nose sensed a strange exotic aroma filling the air. It was a pungent scent from ages past. "Yudi?" I called out. No answer. "Anyone here?" Then I heard soft music coming from the bedroom. As I approached, I saw flickering candlelight from within, and the smell of incense became stronger. I got to the doorway and was dazzled.

My bedroom had become the plush interior of a sultan's tent, with heavy red damask hanging in great billowing waves from a center point of the ceiling. Several small glass oil lamps were arranged throughout the tent, giving off a warm, welcome glow. On the bed lay Yudi, amid tassied pillows and wearing only loose puffy pantaloons of the flimsiest gauze. Sugar Baby purred contentedly by his hip.

I thought, All I want is rest and peace, not bedroom drama. But then I realized that Yudi had created a small dreamy world that offered more interesting recreational possibilities than the traditional bedroom surroundings.

He spoke softly to me, imitating the soothing sounds of Middle Eastern lute music coming from behind the dense fabric. "Welcome, O pasha, to your harem." He lightly brushed together the tiny brass cymbals attached to the thumbs and middle fingers of each hand. Their clear high chime caused a shiver of delight up the center of my back. "Come," he said, "and I will tell you a long, long story."

I flopped onto the bed and nuzzled into his neck. "Start talking, Sharazad. Let's begin at chapter one."